THE HUSTLE

The Other Place Series, Book 1

By Elizabeth Roderick

THE HUSTLE

Copyright © 2016 by Elizabeth Roderick.
All rights reserved.
First Print Edition: May 2016

Limitless Publishing, LLC
Kailua, HI 96734
www.limitlesspublishing.com

Formatting: Limitless Publishing

ISBN-13: 978-1-68058-645-9
ISBN-10: 1-68058-645-9

Dedication

For Les: who has gone where there is too much hot sandwich.

For Bill: who will hopefully be able to read the whole thing now without relapsing.

For Aleah: I'm so glad we made it out.

And for the kid in the park: things would have turned out a lot differently if it weren't for you.

Chapter 1

Liria slumped low in the passenger seat of Lee Harvey's Mazda, watching as he disappeared into a sleeper cab with a middle-aged white guy. He was Lee's third job of the day, and after this they should have enough to get a couple of grams.

At the other end of the parking lot, a woman got out of her car with her little girl. The girl's pigtails swung as she skipped, holding her mother's hand. The woman leaned down to kiss her daughter on the forehead.

Liria's eyelids drooped closed, and her own mother's face bloomed up behind them.

Yellow skin hung over her cheekbones the way it had just before she died. Her mom smiled, her oversized dentures tilting slightly askew. She raised her skeletal arms, holding up a syringe the size of a caulk gun.

Strange patterns, twisted faces, and the shadows of printed words swirled in the brown liquid within. Her mom's eyes glinted with cruel humor. She waggled the needle tip in Liria's face, flinging droplets of oozing dope and flakes of dried blood, and lunged.

Liria's chin jerked up abruptly as Lee Harvey opened the driver's side door. She wiped the drool from her lips, blinking the foul images from her mind.

Lee Harvey grinned. "Have a nice nod?"

Liria wrinkled her nose. "You get enough money yet?"

"Yeah, I got enough. That guy comes through on his route every Friday, and he always wants about three handjobs in a row. I should give him a package deal." He started the car, his hazel eyes glinting with humor.

Liria snorted. "Lee's Discount Handjobs. You could give out punch cards."

He giggled and flicked her on the arm as he pulled out of the parking lot. "So *I'm* done working for the day. You ask your daddy for more money yet?"

Liria glared at him. "No."

"Phht. Why am I the only one making the men spurt money?" He laughed as Liria scowled.

"God, shut up, Lee Harvey."

"I'm just saying. You'd get a much fatter child support check if you gave him what he really wanted."

Liria crossed her arms. "Lay off Cyryl, all right? He gives me money because he's nice and he's a responsible father."

Lee smirked, shooting her annoying little glances. "Even though you're nineteen now? Even though he's super white and you're all Mexican-looking?"

Liria stomped on the floorboards. "*Shut up,* Lee Harvey!"

"All right, all right, I'm sorry, Jet Ski." Jet Ski was his nickname for her—a play on her last name, Czetski. Lee squeezed her shoulder. "You know I'm just messing with you. Cyryl's a nice guy, and you do look a little like him. You have the same forehead."

Liria shot him a burning, sidewise glance, which he returned with an overly straight face. She pressed her lips together to prevent herself from smiling.

They drove to Avery's house. Liria checked her eyeliner in the vanity mirror before she got out, while Lee watched her from the driver's seat, grinning. He ruffled up her dark hair, and she smiled and tried to slap his hand away.

"Bedhead look," he said. "Come on, give me those pouty lips."

Liria pursed her lips at him.

"Perfect." He reached over and grabbed at her boobs as she flinched away, giggling. "You wearing your pushup bra? Avery loves it. He'll give you an extra couple grams for the pushup bra."

"Stop it, you whore." She wrenched herself free and got out of the car.

A French bulldog dashed around the corner as they came through the chain link gate, jumping at their knees and making wet snorting noises.

"Who's a good doggy?" Lee crooned, patting the wiggling creature. "Who is? Who's a good little dog?"

The bulldog ran around in figure eights, flinging

snot everywhere. Liria waded through the commotion to the front door.

Avery answered after the first knock, his face splitting into a grin when he saw Liria. He scratched his low-slung belly. "Hey, Jet Ski."

Liria made herself smile. "Hey, Avery."

Lee Harvey bounded up behind her. "How's it going?"

Avery stood aside to let them in. The dog pushed between their legs and scampered across the living room, his toenails clicking on the white tile. A smell of dog wafted up from the sagging orange couch as Liria sat down.

Avery patted the large pile of curly, reddish hair atop his elongated head, the scant flesh under his arms wobbling. "How much?"

"Two grams," Lee said. His knees splayed as he sunk into a recliner. Avery nodded and went into his bedroom, coming back with a tiny baggy, which he passed to Lee. Lee handed over a messy wad of cash. Avery counted it and shoved it in his pocket, then plopped down next to Liria, draping his arm over the back of the couch behind her.

"How's my girl?" he asked.

"Good." She looked up at him through her eyelashes, fighting her aversion.

"Still staying at Lee and Victor's?"

"Yeah." She bit her bottom lip, letting her leg rest against his. She could feel Lee smirking at her.

"Well, my offer stays open. I have an extra bedroom here, if you want it." His fingers fell onto her shoulder, caressing the curve of her neck, and she let her mind go still so she didn't flinch away.

She smiled. "Thanks, Avery."

***

She and Lee pulled off behind a Taco Bell on the way back to his house so that they could cook up shots.

"Apparently Avery *really* likes being led on," Lee said. He held up the dope for her to see: it was about four grams, instead of two.

"Kickass," she said, trying to smile.

"I wonder how long before he gets wise? Unless you actually plan on putting out at some point." He raised his eyebrows at her over the spoon.

She grimaced. She didn't want to think about it. "I feel sorry for Avery, but fucking him would be like fucking a beanbag chair."

Lee Harvey laughed.

***

They drove on to Lee's house, a fresh wave of dope pulling Liria down into a haze, until Lee Harvey's voice startled her awake. "Wake up, Jet Ski."

Liria pried her eyes open and sat up. She pushed her long hair out of her face and wiped her nose. They were in the driveway of Lee's house.

"Victor won't be home until tomorrow, right?" she asked.

"Right. He has meetings in San Jose."

Relief flooded her as she heaved herself out of

the car. Victor didn't like her much.

She followed Lee down the winding cobblestone path to his little Craftsman-style home. The lawn was jade green and newly cut, and lavender bloomed on either side of the steps leading to the porch. Lee Harvey unlocked the door and turned off the security system.

Liria flipped a switch, illuminating a fabulously neat living room with gleaming wood floors. She flopped on the red leather sofa, sinking into the cushions while Lee Harvey sauntered into the kitchen and came back out carrying cans of 7Up and a handful of molasses cookies.

He handed a can and a cookie to Liria. "Have some sugar, sugar."

She opened the soda and shoved it between her knees, munching the cookie while he turned on Adventure Time.

"Remember when The Mare banned us from watching this cartoon because it was satanic?" he said.

They looked at each other and burst out laughing. The Mare was what they called his mom, Mary.

"Well, she's right," Liria said. "I totally worship Satan now. Peppermint Butler told me to."

Lee snorted, but Liria had to unclench her teeth and bite back all the insults she wished she'd hurled at her former foster-mother. *That sanctimonious bitch, and her creeper husband.* In a way, it was good they'd kicked her and Lee out; they'd been as bad at being biological parents to Lee as they'd been at being her foster parents.

They sat eating their cookies, watching the cartoon. Liria's eyelids fell closed, and Peppermint Butler heaved himself out of the television screen and trotted across the floor.

He wielded his trident like a climber's axe, digging it into the carved wooden legs of the coffee table and heaving himself up, a red cape dangling from his shoulders. He gained the top and speared one of Lee Harvey's cookies. He grinned evilly as he took a bite.

Liria and Lee both jerked awake when the front door opened. Liria's heart floundered and sank as Victor came in, carrying a paper sack of groceries. His nostrils flared when he saw her, and he headed immediately for the kitchen.

"Victor!" Lee said cheerfully. "You're home early, honey."

"They canceled tomorrow's meeting." The bag crinkled as he put away groceries. Liria cringed at the anger in his voice, and she and Lee exchanged a long, frightened look.

Lee's mouth tightened, and he jumped up and bounded into the kitchen. "What'd you bring? I'll make dinner."

"No, that's okay, go watch cartoons with your little friend."

There was a short, charged silence. Liria hugged her knees to her chest and buried her face in them.

"Victor, don't be such an ass," Lee whispered.

There was a bang and a clatter of something slamming against the granite countertop. "I've had enough, Lee Harvey. I work my ass off and you sit here with that fag hag watching cartoons. And you're spending all my money getting high."

"No, I am not," Lee whined. "I just took some Vicodin for my back."

"Don't lie, Lee. You and that bitch are running around doing heroin all day."

Anger and hurt burned through Liria, her warm lethargy evaporating. She got up and slouched into the spare bedroom as Lee and Victor continued to yell at each other.

Her clothes were scattered around on the floor and dresser, and she shoved them in her backpack. She gathered her toothbrush and makeup from the bathroom, then headed for the front door.

She went outside and closed the door behind her, which muffled the sound of fighting. She was halfway down the walk before she heard the door open and footsteps running up behind her. "Jet Ski, wait."

She turned to face Lee. It wasn't until she saw the pity in his face that she realized she was crying. "Oh, Liria, I'm sorry." He pulled her into a hug, and she buried her face in his shoulder, squeezing her eyes shut. "I'll talk some sense into him, and then I'll text you."

"That's okay, Lee Harvey." She pulled out of his embrace and wiped her eyes. "Thank you for letting me stay."

He looked at her searchingly. "Where are you going to go?" She could hear the nervousness in his voice. It was a rhetorical question, because no matter what her answer was, she couldn't stay there.

She looked away. "Maybe I'll go to Avery's."

His face screwed up in disgust. "Oh, don't do

8

that." He shifted on his feet, hesitating, then dug in his jeans pocket. "Here."

He handed her the baggie of dope, and she turned it over on her palm. He was giving her all of it. Amongst junkies, this was an act of almost miraculous generosity. She glanced around to make sure the neighbors weren't watching, then opened the sack and pinched of a small chunk, handing it to him.

"You need this to get you through to tomorrow," she said.

"No, that's okay…"

"Victor won't let you leave again tonight."

His eyes darted uncertainly to the nugget, and he took it with a grimace.

She hugged him again. "Thank you," she said.

"I love you, Jet Ski. Find somewhere to go for a week or so, and then things will smooth out here, okay?"

She nodded. He smiled sadly, then went back in the house, shooting her one last glance before shutting the door.

She cursed as tears welled up again. She wiped them away and walked off down the quiet street, putting one foot in front of the other.

Chapter 2

The sun lowered, casting beams of deep orange across the manicured lawns, her shadow stretching long before her. Liria trudged toward town, her overstuffed backpack jouncing. She had a little under three grams of dope, and about twenty-five dollars. She'd have to figure something out, but she didn't want to think about it yet.

The sun sank lower, and the crickets started up in the hedges. A pickup roared by, and someone hooted out the open window at her. She didn't look up.

Soon the gravel shoulder turned into sidewalks, and shops began to line the streets. Cars drove by with their windows open, music playing, the occupants laughing with each other. She realized it was Friday, and people were starting their weekend.

She went into a gas station and got some gummy worms and butter toffee peanuts, a two-for-one deal, then crossed over into the park.

The sun began to sink below the hills, the light creeping out of the world. She sat on a bench under a gigantic oak, looking up at the sinuous branches silhouetted against the sky as she ate her peanuts.

The oak branches began to writhe. They bent toward her, corkscrewing down to the ground, their leaves rustling. They encased her in a wooden cage, the dying sun gleaming through and casting striped and dappled shadows.

A figure, in expensive slacks and a sport coat, watched her from the outside, his hands in his pockets. He grinned wryly. It was her father, Cyryl Czetski.

Liria's eyes snapped open as she heard the crinkle of cellophane. The oak branches had sprung back to their normal positions, Cyryl was gone, and she realized she'd spilled half her peanuts on the ground.

"Fuck," she muttered, gathering what she could off her lap and putting them back in the package. She briefly considered picking the rest up out of the dirt, but there were wads of gum and ants and who knows what down there. She wasn't that desperate.

Yet. Her money and dope wouldn't last. What the hell was she going to do now?

As she contemplated this, she felt eyes on her and looked up to see someone watching her from over near the gazebo. It was a tall and lanky boy about her age, wearing a white tiger hat, the earflaps hanging down to his shoulders. He stood as still as stone, then seemed to come unstuck. He headed toward her with quick strides.

She watched him approach, tensing up slightly. He stopped in front of her and smiled in a familiar way. He was handsome, his honey blonde hair curling out from under the hat over his broad forehead and high cheekbones.

"You're sad," he said. His spoke very quietly. She had to struggle to hear him over the sound of a motorcycle passing on the street.

Her brow furrowed. His eyes were compassionate, like he knew exactly what she was feeling.

The corners of his lips curled up winsomely as he stood with his thumbs hooked in the pockets of his shorts, one of his feet folded sideways on the ground. "I like this park," he said in that same, soft voice. "It's a good place. And there's an ice cream shop over there where the guy will give me an extra scoop sometimes."

"Yeah, it's a good park," she agreed. She looked him over. "Do you want some peanuts?"

He smiled, showing straight teeth, and she scooted over on the bench to make room for him. She offered him the bag when he sat down, and he dipped his long fingers in, pulling out a handful. His fingernails were clean, and he smelled like fabric softener.

The twilight faded, the orange street lights taking over where the sun left off. He glanced sideways at her. His eyes were blue-grey and curious. He popped peanuts into his mouth one by one.

"I was doing pull-ups on the parallel bars," he said. She could hear him better when he was next to her.

"Oh," Liria said, looking at his wiry arms.

"I did…" his face screwed up thoughtfully, "forty, fifty-seven…fifty-seven pull-ups. Have you seen that internet video with the guy who does the coat rack exercise?"

"No. Coat rack exercise?"

"You pick up your coat and put it on the rack, then take it off, put it on the ground, pick it up." He mimed it with his arms. "Over and over again."

She munched a peanut, raising her eyebrows. "That sounds weird."

"It's good for your whole body. Good for your muscles." He stared at her, silent for a moment. "Where do you live?"

He watched knowingly as Liria's gaze fell to her lap and she tugged at the straps of her backpack.

"I live with my grandma," he said, and pointed across the park. "Over there."

Liria still didn't say anything, a lump rising back up in her throat. She missed the days when it was just her and Lee Harvey. It hurt that he'd let her leave, though she understood why. Victor was his meal ticket, and he loved him, in his way. She wished she had someone to love, someone to love her. She wouldn't treat them like Lee treated Victor.

She wiped her nose. She could feel the kid still looking at her. He wasn't like a normal person, who might glance at her then look away. Finally she looked back at him, because it was more comfortable than him staring. He had a little smile and an unsettling look in his eyes. It wasn't pity exactly, just empathy—too much of it.

"You don't have anywhere to go," he said.

She shook her head, clearing her throat. "No, I got kicked out."

"Your mom kicked you out?"

13

"No. A friend. My mom died two years ago."

He gazed at her sadly. His long fingers came up to fiddle with one of the earflaps of his tiger hat. "My mom kicked me out. She says I'm too much trouble because of the way I am. I came to live with my grandma. I think she'll let me stay. I hope so. This is a good place, with the park here, really close." He stared at her, and Liria stared back. He stood up so suddenly, Liria jumped a little. "Come on," he said.

"Come where?"

He rolled his eyes. "To my house."

Liria hesitated. "Really?"

He smiled teasingly. "Yes. Really. It's just over there." He jerked his head in the same direction he'd pointed earlier, then stood watching her with his eyebrows slightly raised, fidgeting with the hem of his shirt.

"What about your grandma? Won't she get mad you brought me over?"

"My grandma works nights. There's casserole. It has green beans and bacon, and I think potatoes or turnips or something."

The food clinched it for her. He could murder her if he wanted, as long as he fed her first. She stood up and gathered her things while he smiled and bounced on the balls of his feet.

His house was two blocks into the residential neighborhood on the other side of the main street, a little one-story place with dry weeds clogging the flower beds. He took a single key out of his pocket and unlocked the door. Liria realized she didn't know what his name was, and that he hadn't asked for hers.

Inside was a small, tidy living room with a scruffy white carpet and floral patterned sofa. There was a little flat screen TV and a DVD player, but Liria felt guilty for even noticing. She wasn't desperate enough to steal, especially from boys that offered her casserole and a place to sleep.

Yet.

The kid took his red KangaROOS shoes off and placed them on a rack by the door, next to a pair of women's sneakers. Liria kicked off her flip-flops, but when she made as if to put them next to his he stopped her.

"In my bedroom is better," he said.

He turned and led her down a narrow hallway to a small bedroom with a blue carpet. The twin bed was unmade, and the floor was littered with books and sketch pads and charcoal pencils. The walls were bare save for a single framed drawing of a dog asleep in a porch swing. Liria put her backpack and shoes down inside the door.

"You need casserole," he said. "Peanuts aren't enough. I could count your ribs from across the park."

He led her through an arched doorway into the tidy eat-in kitchen, which was painted a cheerful yellow. She sat at the Formica-topped table while he pulled back the foil from a baking dish on the counter and spooned up some casserole.

He brought it over to her and she stared down at it, her stomach growling as she caught smell of bacon and onions. The food was still steaming slightly. "Thank you," she said as he sat down across from her. She felt awkward. "You're not eating?"

"No. I don't eat meat, and it has bacon. I told my grandma, but she either doesn't listen or thinks I won't notice when she sneaks it in, but you can smell it, it's all bacony." He smiled as she took a bite. It was good, and she leaned over her plate, wolfing it down.

"I made myself muffins earlier," he continued as she ate. "You put in bananas, flour, a handful of raw sugar," he held up his cupped palm to demonstrate, "eggs…what else? Vanilla. I bake it on a cookie sheet. It's more like a pancake, really."

She let him talk until her plate was clean and she had scraped the last traces of creamy sauce from it, revealing a pattern of blue roosters around the edges. "Do you want more?" he asked.

Liria was uncomfortably full, and she shook her head. She felt warm, sleepy. He watched her for a moment, then stood up, the chair legs squeaking against the floor. "Come on."

She left the plate on the table and followed him back into his bedroom. He closed the door and stood looking at her. Liria dug her fingernails into her arms, her shoulders tensing.

He sat down cross-legged on the floor and picked up a drawing pad. "You can sleep on the bed," he said.

She opened her mouth to say something, but closed it again as he continued to stare at her. One corner of his mouth twitched up in a lopsided grin. "Don't worry." He curled over his drawing pad, picked up a pencil from the floor, and started sketching.

The kid was weird, but he was cool. Liria crawled onto the mattress and pulled the rumpled quilt up over her legs. The pillow smelled strange but not bad. She supposed it was his smell. She lay watching him draw, the earflaps of his hat tickling his hairy knees. He curled and uncurled his toes as he worked. His toenails were neatly trimmed and his feet were clean.

He glanced up at her. "I'm drawing the Other Place. You can get into it that way, without having to die, which is horrible and uncomfortable." He wielded his pencil with unaffected skill. "It pulls you in. The picture, it's like a portal or something." He grinned boyishly. "Things can happen there that don't happen here in the Physical World. Like, you can fly."

She lay watching him work. He finished with his drawing and set it aside. Liria saw it was a house with two people sitting on the front steps, holding hands. A riot of flowers bloomed in the flower beds, and underneath them was a warren of mole tunnels, with little moles scurrying around, touching noses, and scuffling in the dirt.

The boy turned and rummaged in his bookshelf. He found a bible, then sat back down and started carefully ripping out pages, folding them origami-style into cranes and lotuses and camels. His fingers were gentle and dexterous; she liked watching them as they creased the thin paper.

When he had a huge, toppling pile of the figures, he got out a needle and thread from the drawer of his desk and strung them together. The paper crinkled pleasantly as he worked. He stood on a chair and hung them in a draping arc above Liria's head.

She turned over on her back and looked at them, smiling. They swayed softly in the draft from the air vents and cast weird shadows on the ceiling. "They're pretty," she said.

He grinned and waved his hands like a choir conductor. Liria's heart jumped as the string of figures burst suddenly into orange flames, burning bits of paper raining down around her like shooting stars.

She awoke with a gasp, sitting bolt upright in bed. The boy was still sitting on the floor drawing, and he looked up at her with a knowing expression. "You go to the Other Place too," he said.

He curled over his sketchpad again, and Liria lay back down, her heartbeat gradually slowing. Her brow furrowed as her gaze fixed on a string of origami figurines dangling above her head. It hadn't all been a dream, then.

She drifted back off to sleep.

Chapter 3

She awoke to the sound of a grating female voice.

"Justin, you left the food out, and there's ants all over!"

The doorknob rattled, and Liria sat up in bed, her eyes wide. Pink morning sunlight streamed through the windows. The kid was still sitting on the floor drawing, as if no time had passed at all. They exchanged a look. He didn't appear frightened or nervous.

"Justin, open the damn door," the voice rasped, and the doorknob jiggled again. Liria clutched the blankets. Her stomach clenched and her skin crawled. She needed a shot.

"I'm sleeping, Grandma!" Justin said. It was the first time Liria had heard him speak above a murmur.

"That's bullshit, you never sleep at night."

"I'm sleeping. Go away!"

His grandmother grumbled something and footsteps receded down the hallway. Liria relaxed slightly.

Justin put a finger to his lips. He scooted over to his bookshelf and took something out of a small carved-wood box. He stood and opened the window above the bed.

Liria got up. She gathered her backpack and slipped on her flip-flops, then climbed onto the bed, preparing to hoist herself out the window.

Justin laid a hand on her arm, stopping her. He had a funny look on his face, sort of sentimental, and Liria smiled.

He held out his closed hand, and deposited something in her palm.

Her stomach swooped. It was a rumpled wad of cash. She saw the markings of a hundred dollar bill, and there were more bills underneath it. She clutched them in her sweaty palm. A lot of money. Dope for days, with no hustle.

"I can't…" she managed to choke out, but he rolled his eyes.

"You can. I get Social Security, and Grandma just spends it on roast beef and video poker." He smiled his little smile, sad and knowing. "Go on, out into the world. The Physical World, with the people and their twisted faces. Be careful of those people."

Liria blinked. Impulsively, she bent down and pressed her lips to his forehead, below the hat. He looked startled.

Liria heaved herself up onto the windowsill. The aluminum frame bit into her knees as she eased herself around. The kid grinned boyishly at her one last time before she dropped to the ground and he was out of sight.

She was in a narrow, weed-choked alley between his house and the neighbors'. She snuck out to the street, the tears in her eyes breaking the morning sun into haloes. She wiped them away, but they came back.

A clean house and casserole, and an end to the dope hustle.

She took a deep breath and wiped her eyes again. She opened her hand and unfurled the bills Justin had given her, now damp from her palm.

Two hundreds and a fifty. Holy Jesus. She stuffed them in her pocket, her stomach filling with warmth.

Then it clenched again, and a cold shiver tore through her. She needed to get someplace private to cook up a shot.

She trudged across the park toward the restrooms, the wet grass cold on her feet. It was early on a Saturday morning, and the town was quiet. Woodpeckers squabbled in the high branches of the oaks. There was an old guy digging through the trash, the hems of his sweatpants dragging around his bare feet. She'd seen him before, but she'd never talked to him. He ignored her, muttering to himself as he pulled out cans and bottles, stuffing them in a rumpled paper sack.

There was no one in the women's bathroom. Toilet paper littered the floor, and water dripped from the faucet of the stainless steel sink.

The handicapped stall smelled like pee. She hung her backpack on the door hook and fished out her kit. Her nose ran and her eyes watered as she cooked up a shot while sitting on the floor. The smell of the dope made her want to puke and made her body tremble with anticipation.

Filtered light shone through a dirty frosted window near the ceiling, and a single, bare fluorescent fixture flickered feebly up in the rafters. It was hard to find a vein under those circumstances, but she managed to get one in her forearm on the third try. She pushed the plunger and closed her eyes as warmth and happiness filled her in a rush.

Her sadness disappeared, and she sighed deeply with relief, leaning back against the wall. She had dope, and a little over two hundred and fifty dollars in cash. She could figure something out.

She brushed her teeth and washed her face at the sink. There was a mirror, and she brushed her hair and put on eyeliner. She looked good for not having had a shower.

There was a little coffee shop open on the edge of a park, and she got a mocha and an old-fashioned donut. She sat on a bench by the gazebo, wolfing it down, licking her fingers. The coffee was hot and sweet and made her feel good.

She slouched back on the bench, wrapping her hands around the warm cup.

She needed a place to stay, and she'd run out of options, unless she wanted to go live with Avery. She cringed and quickly dismissed the idea. He'd kick her out in a week because she wouldn't put out, and she'd lose her best connection.

She ran her fingers along the plastic top of her cup. A clean home and casserole. Why couldn't she have family to take her in? She'd even settle for her mother at this point. She had been a frustrating woman, and a real bitch sometimes, but she'd kept most of her looks up until she got really sick, and Liria had to admit she'd been good at finding them places to stay.

Liria hadn't inherited that talent. Men disgusted her, and she was no good at pretending to like them so that they'd let her live with them. Before she'd been staying with Lee Harvey, she'd tried living with a guy named Derek, but he'd kicked her out after a few months. She just hadn't been able to sustain the illusion that she wanted him.

But she did have other family, even if she had to restrain the urge to put air quotes around the word. Would Cyryl take her in?

She felt weird thinking about it. Even if he weren't really her dad, she liked him. He'd always been nice to her. He'd even suggested she come stay with him about a year before, after Lee Harvey's mom kicked her out on her eighteenth birthday. But she'd just been starting to do dope, so she'd talked Cyryl into just sending her money instead.

She frowned at her lap, picking at the split ends in her hair. She regretted it now. If she'd moved in with Cyryl, maybe she'd be in a better place. It had pissed him off when she'd refused. Maybe he didn't want her there anymore.

She pulled her phone out before she had time to get nervous about it.

Lee Harvey had texted her asking if she was okay, but she ignored it.

Her heart pounded as the phone rang. She tucked her hair behind her ear nervously.

Cyryl answered on the third ring. "Hello?"

A shot of adrenaline coursed through her. "Dad?"

"Hello, Liria." His accent colored his words just slightly. So did a tinge of sarcasm. "You run out of money already?"

"No, Dad." Her eyes filled with tears. "I was just…I have some money, but I lost my job, and my boyfriend kicked me out."

"Oh." Most of the dryness left his voice. "Where are you now?"

"I'm in the park here in Paso. I don't have anywhere to go." Her voice cracked, and she wiped the tears out of her eyes again, sniffing. She held her breath. Cyryl was silent.

"You want to come here?" he finally said. His tone was neutral, and she couldn't tell what he was thinking.

"I just want…I just can't get another job when I have no place to stay. I'm all dirty, and my clothes…I don't know what to do."

"You have enough money for the bus?"

She took a breath. "Yeah, yeah I have money. Can I…?"

"You get a bus down here. Text me when you're going to arrive, I'll pick you up."

She heaved a shuddering sigh, squeezing her eyes closed. "Thank you, Dad."

"No problem, sweetheart. You're going to be okay. I'll take care of you. I'll see you when you get here."

She hung up and dabbed at the tears with the corner of her sleeve, then dug her compact out of her pack and checked her eyeliner, wiping away the smudges.

She heaved a sigh of relief, hiding her face in her hands for a moment. Then she texted Avery, telling him she was coming over.

***

Avery offered her a ride to the Greyhound station, so she told him her bus left at ten instead of noon so she could get out of there sooner. After he dropped her off, she bought her ticket and sat down to wait. Two Mexican ladies sat against the far wall, luggage piled around their feet, gossiping in Spanish. A tall black guy sat playing on his phone in the corner. Liria draped her arm over the hard plastic seatback, leaning her cheek against it.

A woman came and sat next to her. She had short burgundy hair, a cute snub nose, and the lithe muscles of a gymnast. It was Rose Lakey, Liria's old counselor. Rose smiled impishly and put a hand on Liria's knee, making Liria's heart beat faster.

"I'm sorry about what happened," Rose said, running her fingers slowly up Liria's leg. "I'm sorry. Come back to me."

The knot of pain in Liria's breast softened. It was what she had wanted to hear, all those months since they had broken up. "I love you, Rose," she said.

"I love you too, Liria."

Liria's head jerked up, and her shoulders slumped. It wasn't Rose sitting next to her; it was some other lady, nowhere near as pretty, her mouth sour and her hair brown instead of burgundy.

Liria grimaced. She missed Rose. When Liria had confessed she liked girls, their counseling sessions had gotten a lot more interesting. But Rose had gotten cold feet after a few months, fearing they'd get caught and she'd lose her license.

They called her bus over the intercom, and Liria got to her feet, along with the Mexican ladies, the black guy, and the not-Rose woman.

The bus was about half-full, and she found an empty pair of seats. She stretched out as much as she could and stared out the window. They started off, taking the winding onramp to the 101.

The two guys in front of her bitched about their ex-wives. Someone behind her talked loudly on a cell phone. "I'm on the bus," she bleated. "Going to see Forrest. Yeah. Yeah. Around five tonight."

Someone sat down next to her. It was the black guy from the station. "You mind if I sit here?" he asked.

"Go ahead," she said.

"Thanks." He shot her a half-smile. "The lady I was next to was really annoying."

She grinned. He stuffed his bag underneath the seat in front of him. He had long legs. His thick knees stuck out from his basketball shorts. "Where you headed?" he asked.

"L.A."

"Me too. I've got a cousin there that opened a restaurant, and I'm going to go help her out. What're you doing there? You an actress?"

She snorted. "Visiting my dad."

"Aw. You look like an actress."

She glanced at him, smirking, but didn't respond.

"Going to see your dad, huh?" he said. "You live with your mom?"

"No, she's dead."

He shifted in his seat. "Oh. I'm sorry."

"It was bound to happen, the way she was."

He broke into a tentative smile. "One of those, huh?"

"And then some."

He laughed. "What's your name?"

"Liria."

"Liria. I like that. Nice to meet you, Liria. I'm Boston." He held out his hand, and she shook it. It was big and warm. "I'm serious, you look like an actress. You got a boyfriend?"

Liria contemplated him a moment, making a calculation. No matter how she answered his question, it could backfire. She was stuck next to him for hours, unless she wanted to make a scene. She decided on the truth. "No. I'm not into men."

His mouth fell open, his eyebrows creeping up slowly in fascination. "Huh," he said. "You got a...you got a girlfriend?"

"No."

"Huh," he said again, running his pointer finger along his upper lip, until she gave him an arch look and he shrugged sheepishly. "No, that's cool, that's cool, just...wow." He laughed. "Shit."

She rolled her eyes and looked out the window while Boston seemed to gather his thoughts. The suburbs of Santa Maria were dwindling into desert, beige hills rising up to take their place against the light blue sky. The hum of the engine was mesmerizing, and she had to force herself to focus.

Boston was watching her. He leaned in closer. "Hey, uh, you ever do coke?" he murmured.

"I don't really like coke."

He grinned knowingly. "No, not your style, right?"

She grinned back.

He was easy to talk to, though she had to decline his requests to give him a detailed account of her sex life. During most of the long drive they talked about shows on TV and parties they'd been to. Boston tried to make it sound like he had lots of friends with money, but she didn't know whether to believe him or not.

Liria texted Cyryl when they passed through Van Nuys, telling him when she'd arrive. As the bus pulled into the station in L.A., Boston scribbled his number on a scrap of paper and handed it to her. "If it doesn't work out living with your dad, give me a call. I can maybe get you a place to live and a job at my sister's restaurant." He lowered his voice. "I also know a guy who can hook you up with the stuff you like, if you need it."

Liria stared at the number, pressing her lips together. She should throw it away. The hustle was so old. She was tired of dopesickness and the horrible things she had to do to fend it off.

She shoved the scrap of paper into the front pocket of her backpack. "Thanks," she said.

Chapter 4

Cyryl was waiting for her inside the bus station. She waved goodbye to Boston and headed toward her father. She hadn't seen him since just before her mom died, but he looked exactly like she remembered, well-dressed and handsome, with a full head of dirty blonde hair and a look on his face like he secretly found everyone amusing and a bit stupid.

He stood with his hands behind his back and examined her with his chin raised, a little half-smile on his lips. "Liria. You look good." His sharp, blue-eyed gaze wandered over her, taking her in. "Too skinny, though. Too pale." He put his arm around her shoulders, and she had to stop herself from flinching away reflexively. "It's good to see you," he said. "It's been too long."

She glanced up at him, trying to see if he were angry with her, but she couldn't read him. She hadn't ever been able to tell what he was thinking.

They walked out to his car. It was a new one, a charcoal grey Mercedes. It looked out of place

29

parked alongside the old Buicks and Kias in the bus station parking lot. He took her backpack from her and stashed it in the trunk while she slid into the passenger seat.

He started the engine and pulled out into traffic. He didn't say anything, and Liria fidgeted, stroking one thumb against the other. She had a moment of panic as the reality of her situation set in. Coming here had been a mistake. She couldn't afford to piss off Cyryl; he was her only source of money. Plus, part of her craved his approval. She didn't want him to find out what a waste of space she was. How was she going to hide the fact that she was a junkie from him?

But she didn't have anywhere else to go.

She looked over and caught him watching her out of the corner of his eye. "So what happened with the boyfriend, eh? What happened with the job?"

Liria picked at her cuticles. She hadn't lied to him exactly. She'd had a job at a coffee shop for about a week, before they fired her for being chronically late. "I got laid off from my job because business was slow. And Derek…" She looked out the window. The sun shone through the yellow haze of smog onto the dull, grey concrete of the sidewalks and streets. "Derek was an ass, it turns out."

He chuckled, and Liria shot him another glance. His teeth were so straight they hardly looked real, but she was pretty sure they were. "Most boys are," he said.

She met his eyes and smiled a little, sitting up in

her seat.

"What about school?" he asked. "You said you were looking into courses at the community college."

"I wanted to, but things have just been so crazy. I got the financial aid application, and they wanted all this information. And then Derek kicked me out."

Cyryl grunted. Liria rubbed her eyes, trying to keep them open. She'd done another shot in the bus' cramped bathroom stall. It had been hell finding a vein as the tires bounced over the road ruts, but she didn't know when she'd have another chance without tipping Cyryl off. Now, she could feel him watching her, and wondered if he knew, anyway.

"I'm tired," she said. "I didn't sleep well last night."

He grunted again, and she cringed inwardly, avoiding his eyes.

They spent the rest of the drive talking about superficial things, movies mostly, but Liria could feel the tension between them, all the important things unsaid. She'd always been comfortable around Cyryl before. He was easy to talk to. The last time she'd seen him she hadn't been doing dope yet, hadn't had to tell lies and pretend to be someone she wasn't. It seemed like part of another life now.

He parked his car in the underground garage of his condo building, and took her up in the elevator, carrying her backpack for her. She shuffled her feet, staring at the floor as he regarded her with a slight smirk. "You hungry?" he asked.

"Starving."

The elevator door opened on a vestibule. A potted palm sat in a shaft of sun from a skylight. He took her down a hallway and unlocked the door to his condo.

Liria's stomach fluttered when she saw it. She'd forgotten how nice it was, with white marble floors and huge windows looking out toward the ocean. He led her through a sitting room and down a corridor to the spare bedroom. The windows were shuttered, the sun bleeding through the slats. A door off to the side led to a private bathroom.

He put her backpack down on the antique dresser. The bag was lumpy and bulging, covered in dog hair from her short ride in Avery's car. Cyryl poked it and glanced at her with dry amusement. "You have any nice clothes?"

She shook her head. "I wasn't able to take much with me when Derek kicked me out."

"Wait here. I have some things."

He went out, and Liria watched after him, wondering what he meant. She opened the shutters and stood clutching her elbows, looking out at the waves breaking on the sandy beach. People played volleyball, and the sun glared bright on the water.

Cyryl came back in with clothes draped over his arm. "Here."

He laid them on the bed. There were dresses and blouses and skirts, still on their hangers, some still with tags on.

She raised an eyebrow. "Why do you have that stuff? It doesn't look like it would fit you."

It made her feel good when he laughed. "I had a girlfriend living here for a little while. When she left she didn't take much. Was in a real damn hurry to never see me again, I guess. I bought her all this shit anyway, so it's right she should leave it."

Liria didn't hear any sadness in his voice about the breakup. She tried to picture him with a girlfriend, but it seemed strange to think of him that way.

He looked her over appraisingly. "She was about your size." He patted the clothes. "Put on one of the dresses. The red one, I think. I'll take you to dinner someplace nice."

He started to go out again, and she made herself reach out and touch his arm. "Dad?"

His biceps twitched slightly, and he stopped. His arm felt solid and muscular, like he spent time at the gym. She removed her hand. "Thanks for letting me stay here, and for everything."

He got a strange, faraway look on his face, and his lips curved in a slight smile. Then he caressed her chin gently. "Don't mention it."

He turned and left, shutting the door behind him. Liria stood staring at the closed door for a minute, her scalp prickling. He was hard to figure out.

She sighed and went into the bathroom.

After a shower, she sorted through the clothes on the bed. Whoever Cyryl's girlfriend had been, she *was* about Liria's size, though her taste had been a lot more feminine. She also hadn't had track marks on her arms; there was nothing with long sleeves.

She stared at the form-fitting blouses and flowy dresses, her chest tightening. What would Cyryl do if he figured out she was using? Would he boot her out onto the streets of Santa Monica with only thirty dollars to her name? Would he hate her?

There was nothing she could do about it. If she put on her own clothes, he'd be suspicious and maybe even offended. So she put on the red dress he'd suggested. It was wrap-style, gathered tight in folds around the waist. The gauzy material tickled the back of her knees.

She examined her arms in the light from the windows, cursing softly. There was no way he wouldn't notice the bruises.

She swallowed her panic. *If he kicks me out, I'll survive. I don't know how, but I will.*

After she put on eyeliner, she realized she only had flip-flops to wear. She shuffled out of the bedroom, crossing her arms to hide them.

Cyryl was standing in the dining room, reading something on his phone, but looked up as she came in.

"I don't have any shoes," she murmured.

He looked at her feet and laughed aloud. "Don't worry about it. You look lovely. You can get some shoes later." He grabbed his keys off of the table. "Margot left a closet full of clothes, but took all her shoes. She fucking loved her goddamn shoes." He scowled. "Let's go, I'm starving."

They went out and got back in the elevator, Liria still hugging herself.

"You like Italian?" he asked.

"Sure." She hadn't eaten anything but a donut all day, and didn't care what she ate. She stared down at her toes, wiggling them, laughing to herself about how ridiculous she looked. He chuckled as the elevator door opened again, and she glanced up at him.

"You'll show these Santa Monica bitches what's what," he said.

Liria found herself smiling.

On the drive to the restaurant, he told her a story about an actress that had suddenly converted to an extreme form of Buddhism halfway through a shoot. She'd insisted that the set be swept of all insects before she entered it, so she didn't risk killing any of them. But then an intern had caught her sneaking a prosciutto sandwich in her trailer.

Liria laughed, remembering why she liked him so much. Maybe she could stay with him in his beautiful house for a long time. He must really think she was his daughter; he'd been supporting her for years. Maybe he actually cared about her.

She crossed her arms tighter over her belly.

The place he took her to was right on the beach, and had valet parking. Her flip-flops snapped against her heels as they walked into the restaurant, and Cyryl shook his head slightly, grinning.

They got a table by the window, and she looked out at the ocean while he ordered a bottle of wine. The beach was crowded with abnormally tan and good-looking people. Some were out surfing, their heads bobbing in the swells. A girl caught a wave as Liria watched, pulling herself upright on her board and gliding along the water, her body graceful and poised. She reminded Liria a little of Rose. The edge of the wave caught the board and flipped it, sending her into the roiling foam.

"So, here you are," Cyryl said. She turned to find him leaned back in his chair, watching her. She shifted in her seat. He considered her a long moment, then sat forward slightly, crossing his legs, pulling at his slacks so they fell straight. "You want to stay with me, eh?"

Blood pounded in Liria's temples. She wiped her hands on her dress. "I'd like to," she said, and was surprised by the true longing that welled up behind the statement. Did she really think she could maintain this ruse?

The waiter showed up and placed wine glasses in front of each of them. Cyryl smirked, then nodded at him.

Cyryl went through the ritual of tasting the wine, then the waiter poured a full glass for each of them before leaving.

Liria stared at hers, chewing on her lip. The sun glinted through it, the alcohol transforming the light into a beautiful deep ruby color.

"I think they're hoping you're at least twenty-one," he said. He took a sip from his own glass. "But it's none of their business, anyway. You don't drink?"

"Not usually, no."

"You're afraid of being like your mother, maybe."

She glanced at him. He'd always read her so well.

"Yes, that's it," Cyryl said, gazing at her. "You don't want to be like that mother of yours." His eyes flashed. "So why do you do smack, eh? Tell me that."

Liria felt the blood drain from her face, and cold sweat dripped down the back of her neck. Her gaze dropped to the table; she saw her menu there, and realized she hadn't even glanced at it yet. She wasn't hungry anymore.

"I'm not stupid, sweetheart," he said. "Don't try to lie to me."

Liria quickly looked back at him, and she held his gaze. There was some warmth in it, she thought, beneath his bitter amusement and hard superiority. There was something she could work with. "I know you're not stupid," she murmured.

"You want to stay with me. You want to take what you can from me and leave again, is what you really want. You want to keep on killing yourself, wasting your life."

"No, that's not what I really want." She picked at her cuticles, fighting back her nausea.

"Then what do you really want?"

"I want a home," she said. "I want a life. I want to get clean."

Was that what she really wanted? The floor seemed to fall out from under her when she thought about the pain of being dopesick, the hopelessness she felt when she wasn't high. But this life was starting to squeeze her in tight jaws, and she didn't know if she could stand it much longer.

It was true: she was turning into her mother.

He sat, looking her over. The waiter came to take their orders, and Cyryl shot her a wry grin and ordered for both of them. She listened, but it was a bunch of words in Italian and she wasn't sure what she was getting. The waiter left, and Cyryl turned back to her, his grin fading slightly. He rested his chin on his hand. "You don't know how to have a home or a life, or how to get clean," he said.

His words were like a sucker punch straight to her gut. He was right. Her eyes filled with tears; she blinked them away, but one still escaped. She wiped it away and dug her fingernails into her thighs, struggling for control.

"Don't cry," he said softly.

That just made it worse. She looked out the window without seeing the view, fighting bitterly against the lump in her throat.

He reached over the table and caught her hand. She looked over at him, frozen. His palm was soft and dry.

"I'll help you," he said. She stared at him, her brow furrowing slightly. He ran his thumb along hers, and she sniffed and wiped her nose with her other hand.

"I'll help you, Liria, don't worry." He squeezed her hand, then relinquished it, leaning back in his chair. He picked up his glass and raised it, nodding toward her own. "Drink your wine. It's good."

She hesitated, then picked up her glass and took a sip. It was tart on her tongue and burned her throat slightly going down. She watched him across the table, trying to figure him out.

Maybe he really could help her, but she didn't know for certain. It was worth a try.

Chapter 5

By the time they left the restaurant her head was fuzzy from her one glass of wine and her chicken sat a little uneasily in her stomach. Cyryl finished off the rest of the bottle, but seemed unaffected, save for a slight uptick in his gregariousness.

He put his arm around her shoulders again as they headed out of the restaurant, and she didn't flinch away, her body full of numb warmth. In the entryway, as they waited for the valet to bring the car, another man spotted Cyryl. They greeted each other familiarly. Cyryl introduced him to her as Josh something-or-other, but didn't tell him she was his daughter. They stopped to talk for a moment. Liria didn't follow the conversation. Josh wore a faded blue button-down shirt, the tips of expensive suede cowboy boots peeking out from under the cuffs of his jeans. He was tan and flippantly handsome, and Liria caught him examining her on the sly.

The men finished their conversation, and Cyryl and Liria went out to the waiting car. "Josh is an

39

actor," Cyryl muttered as he pulled out into traffic. "He's a real piece of shit."

Liria giggled. She felt giddy. Her dose seemed to be wearing off already, and she wondered if Avery had ripped her off with the new stuff.

"This town is full of assholes," Cyryl remarked.

"Every town is full of assholes," she said, and he shot her an amused look.

"Sure, sure, but this is their fucking Mecca. Nowhere do you get more assholes than around L.A. They flock in from all over the world, then strut around having competitions to see who can be the fuckhead messiah. These people, they've turned being an asshole into a religion."

She laughed, and he smiled at her. She liked it when he talked like this to her, like they were on the same team. *He's not kicking me out. He's going to help me.*

Cyryl put the top down on the Mercedes. The balmy breeze caught their hair. The sun was sinking into the ocean, the sky was wide and cloudless, and looking at it made her feel light and floaty. Maybe she really could get clean. She could even go to school, get a good job, and be one of those happy, beautiful people on the Santa Monica beach.

"So this Derek," he said, startling her out of her reverie, "he was an asshole too, eh?"

She looked askance at him, tucking the corner of her mouth back. She didn't really want to talk about Derek. "Yeah, he was a dick."

He was silent for a moment. "He hurt you, I think," he muttered.

Liria glanced at him sharply but didn't respond.

"Yes, he hurt you. He was a real dick."

Liria pressed her lips together, gazing unseeingly out at the horizon. Once, Derek had mixed booze with the meth, dissolving what little mind he had and leaving him with a vacant, bloodshot stare like a riled bull. Liria had hidden in the bathroom. She could still hear the wood of the door splintering under his fists, hear him bellowing. She'd texted Lee Harvey and he'd shown up with one of his bodybuilder friends just in time to pull him off of her.

She tried to smile. "And what about Margot, then? What happened with her?"

Cyryl made a noise of half-amused disgust and ran his fingers through his hair. "Uch, that woman. She had a round little ass and beautiful lips but after a while she was like little needles in my skin." He jabbed his pointer finger repeatedly into his left arm to demonstrate. "Always pissed off about something, but if I asked her what was wrong, she'd just say, 'Nothing,' and sit there with her arms crossed. It was always some silent battle, some sort of cold war in my apartment." He glanced at Liria. "I'll bet you don't do that. I'll bet if you fight, there's some heat in it."

She shifted in her seat and looked away. "I don't like to fight."

"Sure, sure, who does?" He didn't speak for a while, humming a tune under his breath. Lyria kicked off her flip-flops and pulled her knees up on the seat.

"You got your GED, right?" he asked.

"Yeah. Last year." Cyryl had paid for it. It had

been before she'd really started doing dope, and had been tossing around the idea of going to school to study web design.

"You have a criminal history?"

"No." She gave him a quizzical look, which he returned searchingly.

"We need interns in my office. They want college students, but I could maybe get you in there."

"That'd be awesome," she said, smiling.

"You've gotta quit the drugs, though."

Her smile faded. She dug her fingernails into her knees, watching the skin turn white around them.

"What?" he said. "You said you wanted to quit. You going to start fucking me around already?"

"No." She winced. "It's just hard to quit. You don't understand how hard it is. It sucks." It was difficult to even think about, especially when she was already craving a shot. Dopesickness was worse than anything she'd ever experienced.

"You can do it," he said. "You're better than that, than that mother of yours. You can do it."

She looked at him to see if he meant it. It felt good to hear someone say that. His eyes darted between her and the road. He looked earnest enough, but he was hard to figure out.

***

When they got back to the condo Liria headed for her bedroom, but he stopped her. "Where are you going?" he asked.

"To change." It was partially true, but she also

wanted to get high. There was no point trying to quit while she still had dope. She'd wean herself off until it was gone. This would be her last full shot, her last time getting blasted.

He stared at her. She knew she wasn't fooling him.

"Keep the dress on," he said. "It looks good."

He waved her over to the breakfast bar, took a bottle of wine out of the built-in wine rack, and retrieved two glasses. Hesitantly, she went and sat on one of the bar stools as he poured her a glass. Her stomach felt weird, and she was starting to get goosebumps. Avery ripped her off for sure with the new stuff; it had barely been four hours since her last dose.

"Drink it," Cyryl said, nodding at her glass. "It's good stuff. I got it on my last trip to Sonoma."

He sat down on the stool next to her. She took a small sip. It was sweeter than what she'd had at the restaurant.

He spun slightly on his stool, and Liria snorted. He looked goofy, in his slacks with no shoes, spinning on a barstool. "These chairs suck," he said. "Let's sit on the terrace."

He led her out through French doors to the balcony, which overlooked the ocean. The stars were starting to come out, the last green light fading from the horizon. There was an outdoor sectional sofa, and Liria sank into it, pulling her knees up under her, trying not to spill her wine. He sat next to her, close enough that their legs almost touched, and she looked at him uncertainly. He'd brought the wine bottle with him, and set it on the glass and wicker coffee table. He was already halfway through the glass he'd poured himself in the kitchen.

A little breeze was blowing, and it made her nerves tingle. The first part of dopesickness was actually good, in a way, because you felt everything five times as much as usual. But she knew it went downhill quickly. She chewed the inside of her cheek, wondering how she could slip away to get a shot without him knowing.

"It's pretty out here," she said.

"Yes, it's pretty." He gazed at her. He didn't look away, and Liria felt herself tense up, watching him. He was drunk, she could tell, and the way he was looking at her was wrong.

What was in his eyes now, had it always been there? Had she been ignoring it? Had Lee Harvey actually been right about him? Her stomach knotted. This wasn't lost on Cyryl, and he grinned lopsidedly.

"You're not my daughter, Liria," he said.

She was suddenly dizzy. "What?" She clutched the stem of her glass and some of the wine sloshed out on her bare knee.

He grinned wider. "Don't act like you're surprised."

She just stared at him. "Then why…I mean, how do you even know?"

"You look nothing like me."

"That doesn't mean anything. I look like my mom."

"Much prettier," he said.

She clutched her glass harder.

44

"She was fucking some dealer back then, a Mexican guy. He's your father, but he's dead, I heard. Besides, I'm sterile."

Liria was silent for a moment, fighting the urge to vomit. "If that's true, then why did you pay child support?"

He regarded her pensively. "She knew things about me. It was blackmail."

"What things did she know?"

He chuckled darkly and polished off his wine, setting the glass on the table. "I'm not telling you that."

She looked at him searchingly, wondering what it could be. "But then why did you keep giving me money after she died?"

"Because I like you. A girl like you didn't deserve a mother like Iva Guarnera."

Liria was silent, trying to put it all together.

"You don't believe me," he said.

"It doesn't make sense."

He looked out at the darkening horizon, and grinned humorlessly. "No, probably not. It probably doesn't make any sense." He sat up and poured himself another glass of wine, then leaned back again, stretching his arm across the back of the sofa. He picked up a tendril of her dark hair and brushed it behind her shoulder. "I don't like many people," he said. "But you're funny. You're smart."

"The last time you saw me was right before my mom died, right? I was seventeen."

He shrugged, then caught her look and burst out laughing. "You think I'm a crazy creep."

"I also think that you must have too much

money." Her voice was unsteady. Disappointment threatened to crush her, but she pushed it away furiously.

"No one ever has too much money."

She stared out toward the ocean. A bright star had appeared above the waves. When it began to blur, she realized tears were springing to her eyes again. *Fuck this shit, I want to get high.*

"Liria," he murmured, scooting closer. He set his wineglass down, then took hers from her hand and put it down next to his. He put his arm around her, running his thumb along the curve of her waist. His hip was touching hers. "Liria, don't cry." He leaned toward her and pressed his lips to her neck.

She stifled her desire to push him away, to run, and closed her eyes.

"You can stay here with me now. Everything is going to be okay," he said.

He put his hand on her knee, slowly working its way up. He kissed the hollow of her throat, then between her breasts. Liria made herself go still as her mind screamed and her thoughts jostled against each other. She liked Cyryl Czetski, and besides, he was her meal ticket. He was loaded. And she'd never believed he was her father anyway; she'd just hoped.

She'd be an idiot not to let him fuck her. It was possible he'd kick her out the next day, anyway, but probably not; he'd thrown tens of thousands of dollars at her over the past couple years, so he'd likely want more than one piece.

His hand slid under her dress, caressing the curve of her thigh. He pulled her panties aside and slipped

46

a finger into her pussy. Liria tried to pry apart her clenched teeth. She couldn't afford to fuck this up like she had with Derek.

She forced her mind out of the situation, and thought about Rose. She pretended it was Rose's fingers inside her. Her breath quickened, and she gasped as he pushed them deeper, feeling herself getting wet. Cyryl laughed softly and muttered something in Polish in her ear, but she tuned him out and thought about Rose. It was Rose squeezing her tits, pulling her panties off, pushing her dress up her hips. When he put his cock in her, she thought of the time Rose had brought a dildo to one of their counseling sessions. She pressed against him, and felt her pussy tighten around him and get hot, pleasure burning through her as she came. He thrust himself deep inside her, muttering passionately in her ear, moaning her name, and rubbing her nipples with his thumbs as he came too.

When he rolled off of her, she got up, pulling up her underwear.

"Where you going, sweetheart?"

She didn't look back. "To the bathroom."

He didn't stop her.

She went into her room and fished her kit out of her backpack, then shut herself in the bathroom.

She sat on the cold tile floor with her back against the wall, her knees up against her chest. She felt Cyryl's come gush out into the crotch of her panties. She shook so badly it was hard to cook up a shot.

She managed to find a vein on the fourth try, and lights of pleasure went off behind her eyes as she gently pushed the plunger, releasing the dope into her veins. She took a deep breath. She'd quit shaking.

She cleaned her rig and put it away in the little black makeup bag she carried it all in. She stashed it behind a pack of toilet paper under the sink.

She sat for another moment, her chin on her chest. *The man's fucking batshit crazy.*

She wiped the sweat from her forehead and pushed the hair out of her face. *No, he's not. He's just drunk.* If the latter were the case, would he regret this in the morning? Would he blame her, kick her out? She tried to piece together everything she knew about him, to figure out what he'd do next.

Something told her he wouldn't kick her out. And if he really wanted her, if he really liked her, then she had something to work with, if she were careful.

Lee Harvey is going to laugh his ass off.

She took one more deep breath and stood up. She caught sight of herself in the mirror and cursed at her reflection, pulling her fingers through her tangled hair and dabbing at her smeared makeup with a piece of wet toilet paper. Her skin itched and crawled. She looked longingly at the shower, but she wouldn't take one. It had pissed Derek off that she'd always taken a shower after he'd fucked her.

She left the bathroom, only to pace the bedroom a few times. He was out there, waiting. She had to play this game. She had no money and nowhere else to go.

She let out a long breath and went out.

48

He was leaning against the wall outside her door, and she stopped, frozen.

He reached out and grabbed both her hands, then forced them around so he could see her arms. He ran his fingers over the new welts, caressing them as she stood stiffly, watching him warily.

"Liria, why do you do this to yourself?" he murmured.

She didn't answer. He pulled her gently toward him and wrapped her in his arms, rubbing his hand up and down her back, pressing his face into her hair. His arms were solid and strong, and for a moment they felt good around her. She started to tremble again, taking a shuddering breath.

"I want to quit," she said, her voice muffled in his chest. She did. So badly, sometimes. But if she quit, then what? "I don't know what to do."

His hands slid down to her ass and pulled her against him. She could feel his cock getting hard underneath his slacks, and had a moment of panic. She couldn't do this again.

"I'll help you," he said in her ear.

He lifted her chin up and kissed her, his tongue slow and insistent and tasting of wine. She kissed him back, forcing her mind far away into a fantasy.

Chapter 6

Liria curled up on the couch on the terrace with a cup of coffee and her phone, texting with Lee Harvey. Cyryl was at work, and she had the whole condo to herself. She gazed out at the morning sun glinting on the waves, at the people jogging on the sand and walking dogs along the beach. A light breeze blew, bringing the smell of the ocean with it. Her phone buzzed with another text.

Lee Harvey: *You fucked your dad? That's fucking hot. You should write that up and send it in to one of those whack mags.*

She pressed her lips together against a grudging laugh and tucked her wet hair out of her face.

Liria: *You're such a pervert. And he's not my dad, anyway.*

Lee Harvey: *What if he is?*

Liria: Fuck off. He's not. He says he's sterile.

She gulped down some sweet coffee.

Lee Harvey: I won't say I told you so, Jet Ski, but I told you so.

Liria rolled her eyes.

Liria: Fuck off, Lee Harvey.

Lee Harvey: Does he want you to move in?

Liria: That's what he says. Says he'll get me a job where he works, and help me get clean.

Lee Harvey: Aww, that's sweet. You're going to do it, right?

She stared at her phone, running her fingernails up and down her calf.

Liria: I don't know if I can.

Lee Harvey: You can do it, Jet Ski. Just wean yourself off. You're too good for this life, girl.

Liria: So are you, but that's not what I mean. I just don't know if I can keep fucking him without going nuts.

Lee Harvey: Oh, come on. If you could play it straight so you could live in that dung heap with an asshole like Derek, you can do it for an ocean view condo in Santa Monica. Hell, I'd fuck a million old ladies for that situation.

Liria snorted.

Liria: You'd fuck an old lady for half a stale sandwich.

Lee Harvey: No way, it'd at least have to be a whole one. With a bag of chips.

She smiled, but it faded to a frown.

Liria: I just don't get why he's doing this. Why he sent me all the money. Why he's being so nice. He could get a cheaper piece of ass anywhere.

Lee Harvey: But you're a super-hot one. And some old rich dudes are really, really into younger girls. Play your cards right, this could turn out really good for you. And if you get married, you won't even have to change your last name.

Liria cringed.

Liria: Fuck off, Lee Harvey.

Lee Harvey: :p

She chewed her lip.

Liria: I only made it a month with Derek.

Lee Harvey: That's because it wasn't worth it with him. That guy was a real dick. I wanted to beat his ass for what he did to you. Cyryl is nice to you, right? He's not violent?

Liria: Yes. He's always been really nice to me.

Lee Harvey: Stick it out and see where it goes. Sex is just sex, you can do it with anyone. It's the other stuff that matters.

Liria sighed and tossed her phone on the couch, raking her fingers through her hair and staring out at the ocean. She got up and padded inside, heading toward the gleaming kitchen. She opened the fridge and found eggs and bacon and bagels, pulled them out, and started searching for a frying pan.

Lee Harvey was right. It was the other stuff that mattered.

***

Liria was asleep on the living room couch when she was startled awake by a hand sliding up her waist to her breasts. She gasped and scrambled away, kicking out, knocking the cushions everywhere. Then she saw Cyryl's startled face in front of her, and her pounding heart slowly retreated from her throat. She took a deep breath.

A corner of his mouth twitched up in a sheepish half-smile. "Sorry. I'm sorry, sweetheart. I didn't mean to startle you." Gently, tentatively, he put his hand on her knee, slowly sliding it up. Liria made herself relax.

He took off his suit jacket and tossed it on a chair, then lay down next to her on the couch, his hand working its way under her shirt and pulling aside her bra to fondle one of her tits. "I missed you, Liria," he whispered in her ear, kissing her neck.

"How was work?" she asked, hoping to distract him.

He smiled, gently squeezing her nipple, which sent raw shocks through her. "I talked to them today about getting you in as an intern."

She blinked. "Really?" She hadn't thought he would actually follow up on that.

"Yes. They have a position opening in about a month, they're going to start interviews in a couple of weeks. I can get you the job."

She stared at him in disbelief. "What would I be doing?"

"It's a marketing position. Computer stuff, answering phones, mostly." He kissed her, running his fingers down her spine and stroking the dimple above her ass crack. The guy was like a goddamn rutting goat.

She pulled away from him. "Cyryl?" she said. It still felt weird to not call him dad, and she had a moment of nausea.

"What is it, sweetheart?"

"Why are you doing this?"

His hands went still. "What do you mean?"

"Letting me live here and…and the job and

stuff?" Her voice shook slightly.

He smiled. "Because I've always wanted a girl like you, Liria. You're smart and beautiful and good company. And you're an excellent fuck. I knew you would be." His hand slid slowly over her hip, then found her clit and rubbed it gently with one finger. Liria closed her eyes and bit the inside of her lip. The Rose fantasy was growing tired. She'd have to think of a new one.

"Cyryl?" she said weakly.

"Mmm?"

"I'm worried I won't be able to quit dope."

He stopped short, and moved his hand back to her waist. Her heart raced as she met his gaze. She couldn't read his look.

"How long have you been doing it?" he asked. "The heroin?"

"About eight months."

"Not long."

She squirmed at the hard, mocking note in his voice. "Long enough that it frigging *hurts* to quit. It's horrible, Cyryl, you don't understand."

Some of the sharpness left his eyes. "You've tried to quit before?"

"Yes. Once. And I've had to go sick plenty of times because I didn't have money or whatever."

He stroked the curve of her waist with his thumb. "What's it like to be sick that way?"

She considered him for a moment. There was curiosity in his expression; he really wanted to know. "It sucks. You're cold and everything hurts. You puke and have diarrhea. Your muscles get all super tight and you can't sleep, it's like you want to tear your skin off. And you feel like everything is…I mean, you're just really depressed, and you feel like it's never going to get any better."

He brushed the hair from her cheek, tucking it behind her ear. "How long does it last?"

"I don't know. They tell me the worst of it is usually over in three or four days, but I've never made it that long. The longest I've ever gone is a day and a half." Her stomach soured.

"Three days isn't bad, Liria. You can make it. And then you'll feel better and everything will be fine."

She stiffened and glared at him. "You don't know how bad it is."

His eyes glinted as he took in her anger, as if it satisfied him somehow. "Hush, sweetheart. I just want to help you. You're a good girl. You don't need this stuff." He reached around and pulled something from his back pocket, holding it up so that she could see.

It was her kit, and her hands balled into fists as a surge of anger and panic washed through her. "What the fuck, Cyryl? Stay out of my stuff." She grabbed for it, but he tossed it across the room and caught her wrist.

"Don't," he said with a smile of fierce amusement. Liria's teeth clenched. She could feel the power in his arm. He was really strong, especially for a dude in his fifties. "Don't, Liria. You need to quit."

She fought back the urge to kick him. "Not like that, Cyryl. I can't. I need to wean myself off."

"Yes, whatever. What you mean is you need to

keep putting that junk into your body, and make excuses for not quitting."

She tried to jerk her arm away and he gripped it tighter. "*Stay out of it,* Cyryl. You *don't understand.*"

"*Stop,* Liria," he barked, and the tone of his voice and look in his eyes made her go still. "Stop," he repeated, more softly. "I'm trying to help you. You don't need that crap." His expression softened, and he let go of her wrist. She didn't struggle, but lay rigid, breathing quickly. He ran his thumb along the curve of her waist again, but it didn't feel soothing now; it felt like being touched with a live wire.

"I'm not going to quit cold turkey, Cyryl," she said quietly, her voice shaking. "If you try to make me, I'll leave."

His smile vanished, and she felt a surge of triumph.

"You won't leave. Where would you go?"

"I don't care. I'll find somewhere."

"What would you do without my money?"

She got a hollow feeling in her chest, but she smiled dryly. "I'm sure I could find another way to make money." She held his gaze, watched him go pale.

"Liria," he murmured nervously, "you're too good to do those disgusting things."

Deep inside, she laughed. *I'm already fucking for money, Cyryl.* "I'll do what I have to do. My life isn't worth living, anyway."

"Don't say that, sweetheart. I'm trying to make it worth living."

"You're just trying to make me sick and miserable. I won't be able to quit that way. It hurts too bad. I'd go bonkers and go out and get dope somehow."

Liria watched this sink in. He smirked bitterly. "What do you want to do then, eh? Do you really want to quit? Or do you just want to fuck around with me about it? I want to help you, but I'm not going to let you fuck me around."

Her brow furrowed, her anger ebbing. She suddenly felt strange. What *did* she want? Could she really quit dope, get a job, be Cyryl Czetski's girlfriend? She tried to imagine herself in that life, but it was like watching a movie play in her head, watching some smiling actress that looked vaguely like her playing a part. She chewed on the inside of her cheek as she let the other scenario unfurl: she didn't quit, and had to move in with Avery, or sell her ass at the truck stop. In this scene, the part of Liria was played by someone who looked a lot like her mom.

"Tell me how I can help you," he said, and there was tenderness in his voice. He traced the line of her jaw with his fingertips. "You can do this. We'll do it together."

Liria looked into his eyes and saw he was serious, that he really wanted this for her, and felt something inside her begin to give way. Cyryl Czetski wasn't a bad man. He'd taken her in. He was trying to get her a job. He wanted to help her get clean. It was an odd feeling.

"I'd need to wean myself off," she said uncertainly.

"I'll keep your dope for you, and give you a little less each day," he said.

She didn't like it, but she swallowed her misgivings. "If you have any Ativan or whatever, it would help me sleep, and help me not go crazy."

His brow creased. "What's that?"

"It's like Valium." When he looked dubious, she scowled. "It really helps. Do you want me to get clean, or do you just want to torture me?"

"I don't want you to quit heroin just to get addicted to something else."

"I won't." They stared at each other for a moment. Finally, he nodded slightly.

"Okay, Liria. I can get some, don't worry about it, don't worry about it." He put his arm around her, pulling her closer. "It will be okay. It will all be better before you know it. No more dope, no more sickness." His voice was kind, and Liria felt a sudden rush of strange affection for him. She nestled closer, feeling his arms around her. He raised her chin up and kissed her, his fingers creeping back down to her pussy, and she closed her eyes, biting back her bitterness. *It's the other stuff that matters.*

Chapter 7

Liria jogged down the beach, following a strange little man. He was naked, and looked like a small pile of grey flesh atop a pair of stumpy legs. Chills tore through her, sickness taking her over. She knew she had to catch the little man, or she'd never feel better.

She ran faster, but the sand sucked her feet in maddeningly, slowing her steps. Her legs were weak and useless; they wouldn't move the way she wanted. The man stopped and turned around, regarding her with glassy green eyes, and she finally got a chance to catch up. She lunged at him, grabbing for his arm, but her hand closed over thin air as he shrunk down even further, his torso withdrawing into itself, the skin folding up like an accordion. He grinned mockingly, his teeth hanging from his upper jaw like stalactites.

A rattling sound brought Liria out of her haze. She was curled in a tight ball on the sofa, her teeth clenched and her skin sticky with cold sweat.

The rattling repeated, making her jolt with annoyance. Cyryl stood above her, shaking a bottle of pills. "Wake up, Liria. I got you a present."

She looked up at him blearily, wincing and curling up tighter as the full force of her dopesickness hit her. He was holding an ibuprofen bottle. He pried off the cap and shook out a couple of the pills into his hand, dropping them into her sweaty palm. She examined them dully. They were tiny and white and didn't look like ibuprofen.

"Ativan," Cyryl said. "Got them from a guy I know." He sat down next to her and put a hand on her bare leg. His touch made her skin crawl, but she kept herself from flinching away.

"Thank God you're home," she said. "I need my second dose. These fucking pills aren't going to help me right now. The piece you gave me this morning wouldn't have cured a baby's toothache."

He gave her his maddening, superior smile. "You're weaning off. You don't get a second dose today. Take the Ativan instead."

Her stomach clenched. She threw the pills in her hand across the room, and they skidded across the marble floor. "Fuck you, Cyryl. Fuck that. This is only the second day."

He watched her darkly as she backed against the arm of the couch, clutching a pillow over her naked chest. She couldn't stand the feeling of clothes on her skin, and her t-shirt and shorts lay discarded by the coffee table.

"Calm down, sweetheart," he said, still with that smile. "Throwing a fit isn't going to get you your way."

Her fury rose up and made her stomach turn over, a fresh dew of cold sweat dampening her skin. She jumped up and ran for the bathroom.

Darkness closed around her vision as she threw up. She hadn't eaten, so what came up was just acid, and then just excruciating dry heaves. When it stopped, she curled up on the cold tile in a fetal position, shivering, pulling at her hair. *I can't do this. I just want to get high. What the fuck is the point of getting clean for a man like that?*

Her ears rang and the room spun as hatred for Cyryl Czetski overwhelmed her, and she moaned through clenched teeth, writhing on the chilly floor. She had about five grams left, but he was rationing it like she only had two. *And you don't even want him,* the voice in her head reasoned. *This isn't the life you want. You need to quit, but not like this, and not for some creepy old fucker. You can quit later. You can wean yourself off in a way that doesn't hurt.*

Desire for heroin ached inside her, making her mouth water and her nose run.

Then she heard footsteps and looked up to find Cyryl standing over her, his expression touched with pity but still hard. She fought back her anger, though the effort made her nauseous again. She needed him to give her some dope, one way or another.

"This isn't weaning me off, Cyryl. This is misery. *Please.*"

"You knew it wouldn't be easy."

She dug her fingernails into the grout between the tiles. "I can't do this. If this is how it's going to be, I won't fucking do it." She heaved herself up off the floor, her skin searing with cold and her stomach squirming. She hung her head until the vertigo passed, then pushed past Cyryl and stalked into her room on rubbery legs. She pulled a pair of shorts out of her backpack and put them on. It was like running up a hill just to accomplish that much, and she had to lay on the bed to recover.

Cyryl followed her. "What are you doing?" he asked.

"I'm leaving."

"Liria," he said chidingly.

"No, *fuck you,* Cyryl."

"Where do you think you're going to go when you're like this, eh?"

"To get heroin. I know a guy down here. I met him on the bus."

She watched out of the corner of her eye as he went pale. "You're not leaving," he said. "You're not going anywhere."

"You can't stop me." She pushed herself up off the bed, though she felt like her limbs weighed a million pounds. She put on a shirt and grabbed her backpack, but he caught her arm before she could go out the door.

"Liria," he barked.

She glared at him furiously. "I'll call the fucking cops. You can't keep me here."

"Yeah, you'll call the fucking cops, all right. You think the cops are going to believe you?"

"I'll make them believe me."

"Sure you will, sweetheart."

They stared at each other, Cyryl's lips twisting in

a wry grin. She wished she could tear them off his face. She jerked her arm out of his grasp and pushed past him.

He followed close at her heels. "Liria, think about this. Maybe you can get some more dope, but then what? I thought you wanted to get clean. I thought you wanted a better life."

She stopped at the door, leaned her sweaty forehead against it. "I do." Her eyes filled with tears, and she hugged herself, a sob escaping her throat, her backpack dropping to the floor. She was so tired. She just wanted this to end somehow. She had thirty dollars and there was no way she could leave, dopesick as she was. A fresh wave of cold sweat and weakness flooded her, along with self-hatred. She was a worthless junkie with nowhere to go, nothing to live for.

"I don't know what to do," she said. "This is too hard. I fucking hate it...I hate it."

He came over and slid his arms around her, pulling her close and hugging her tight. Her skin burned cold where he touched her. "Liria," he murmured.

She hesitated, but then pressed her face into his chest, breathing in his smell, which brought another dizzying wave of complicated feelings. He was the only person who had ever tried to take care of her. Why couldn't he really be her father? Or why couldn't she just love him in the way he wanted? He stroked her hair as she huddled there, shivering. *If you can just get high, you'll feel better,* the voice in her head told her; part of her wished it would shut up.

"You said you'd help me get clean, but *this isn't working*," she said. "I can't do it this way, Cyryl. *Please.* Wean me off, but wean me off slower. *Please.*" She leaned against him, blood pounding in her temples.

Finally, he puffed out his cheeks and sighed. "I'll give you some more," he said. "Just…just sit down, okay?" With his arm over her shoulders, he guided her to the couch, where she collapsed, pulling her knees to her chest, relief flooding her.

She watched through slitted eyes as he went over to his bag and fished her kit from an outside zip pocket. He'd been taking it to work with him; she'd suspected he was. She hadn't been able to find it anywhere. *The guy's batshit. What if he gets caught?*

He brought it over to her, and when she tried to get up from the couch, he put a restraining hand on her shoulder. "No," he said. "Do it here."

She stared at him in disbelief. "What, you want me to do this in front of you?"

"Yes."

Her hand tightened around her kit so that it wouldn't shake. "Cyryl, I don't want you to see this…"

"What, are you ashamed?" He raised his eyebrows.

Another wave of nausea washed over her. She didn't have the energy to deal with his bullshit. "Fine," she spat. She flipped her kit open roughly. Her hands shook badly and her stomach dropped out from under her when she saw the big, tarry chunk of heroin and smelled its tangy, bitter smell.

She wiped her dripping nose. When she tore off a piece, he put his hand over hers.

"No, that's too much," he said.

She met his unyielding glare and fought back a renewed surge of confused anger and guilt. She couldn't figure out if he was doing this because he cared about her, or just because he was an asshole. "Whatever." She pinched off a tiny bit and put it back with the rest. He looked like he was going to protest again, but she didn't give him time, tossing it in the spoon and adding water.

Cooking up a shot when she was so sick wasn't easy; the smell made her stomach heave and her hands were unsteady. It was even worse with him staring at her. But finally it was done, and she found a vein.

The dope hit her with a burst of raw joy and relief. All her sickness was gone in a split second, along with her anger and sadness. She looked up to find Cyryl watching her with disgusted fascination. "Better?" he asked.

She nodded mutely, feeling a twinge of guilt. Now that she felt better, she wished she'd had the strength to stay sick, to just quit and get it over with. She avoided his gaze as she put her stuff away and put it on the coffee table.

He caught her hand and pulled her closer, wrapping her in his arms. She curled up against him, her head on his chest. "I'm sorry," she murmured.

"No, Liria. I'm the one who should be sorry."

She glanced up at him in surprise, her brow creasing. "Why?"

"Because I fucked up with you, that's why. It's my fault you're like this. I should never have let you go back to that woman, your mother. The first time she sent you to me, I should have kept you. Then you wouldn't be going through this at all."

He gazed at her distantly, his expression odd. "I always knew you weren't my daughter," he continued. "It was always a ruse. She would never let me get a blood test, and we both knew why I was really giving her money. But that doesn't mean I didn't care about you."

She felt a rush of warmth as that sank in, but it got mixed in with the soup of her other feelings. She didn't say anything.

"I was confused as hell when she called me that first time and said she was sending you down to stay for a while," he said. "But she insisted you come, made all sorts of threats. I know now that her life was just crap, that she was going crazy and wanted to get rid of you. I figured that out when I met you and saw how unhappy you were. I shouldn't have let you go back, but I'm a weak man. It would have been a fight, and I didn't feel up to it. I made all sorts of excuses, but the truth is I'm just a coward. Still, even though I abandoned you with that…your mother, you kept coming to see me." He smiled faintly.

"I wanted to come," she said. "I made my mom send me." She gazed at him avidly, hoping he would keep talking.

"I'm glad," he murmured, tucking a tendril of her hair behind her ear. "But you were growing up, and I knew I didn't want to be your father figure anymore. You're so beautiful, and you have a mind of your own. You have spirit."

He kissed her neck just under her ear. Liria closed her eyes and fought back her disgust, thinking about those times she'd visited him when she was younger, how nice he'd been to her. She'd thought it was because he really believed he was her dad, but it was actually because he wanted to fuck her. *So what? He cares about you; does it really matter why?*

"And then," he continued, "there was that nastiness with Iva's boyfriend, and the state took you away." Liria tensed up, remembering. Cyryl examined her face, and she could see his anger and remorse. "I was so furious with myself that I let that happen. But I couldn't get involved in the dependency proceeding, because they'd have wanted a blood test. It would have come out that I wasn't really your father, and then I never would have seen you again." He leaned down and kissed her. "But now you're here," he murmured, his lips against hers. "You're here now, and you're mine. Everything is going to be all right."

Liria let him strip off all her clothes. He ran his lips over every part of her, rubbing her clit with his tongue until she came almost against her will. He fucked her slowly, shoving his cock deep inside of her, muttering passionately in her ear in both English and Polish, sweet things and dirty things she only half understood. When he came he moaned, "Oh, Liria, Liria, I love you."

Afterwards he fell asleep, and she lay in his arms, feeling emptier than she ever had in her life.

Someone finally loved her, but it felt wrong. She couldn't love Cyryl, not in that way. Dully, she contemplated her future. She'd stay with him until he got tired of her, because what he felt for her wouldn't last. He'd figure out sooner or later that she didn't feel the same way he did and it would be over. She'd be worse off than she'd been before.

Blearily, she saw her kit on the coffee table, and her heart thumped. She couldn't believe she'd forgotten; she couldn't believe *he'd* forgotten.

She just wanted one good hit, a *real* hit that made her feel high instead of just normal. She couldn't deal with this. Maybe things would look better with a little more dope in her. Maybe she'd be able to figure out what to do.

Slowly, carefully, she slipped out from under his arm. He stirred, but didn't wake. She took the little bag and snuck into her bedroom, closing the door.

She sat on her bed and cooked up a shot, adding a little extra because this last batch Avery sold her was crap.

As she hit a vein, she listened to the waves breaking on the sand outside, and thought of the surfer girl's graceful, strong body falling into the waves. Liria imagined herself falling with her, their bodies engulfed by the slippery foam.

Chapter 8

Someone was yelling, the sound of it muted and dull, as if it came from the other side of a wall. She opened her eyes, but all she saw were grey and blurry shadows. She had a moment of panic, thinking that a wave had taken her under, and that she was drowning. She couldn't breathe.

Then she gulped air, her lungs burning. Her vision cleared slightly and she saw Cyryl's tear-streaked face in front of hers, his eyes wide with panic. He was yelling her name, and he was naked. Liria was bewildered. She wasn't in the water.

She took another breath, gasping. Her throat hurt and her chest ached. "Liria, oh thank God, oh thank God," Cyryl said. She could hear him better now. He took her in his arms, and she realized she was lying on the floor. She was naked too. Her skin felt thick and numb.

"Cyryl, what…what's going on?" She sounded like a frog, her voice rough.

He clutched her to his bare chest. He was trembling. "You were fucking dead, goddammit,

Lyria," he bellowed, then he broke down sobbing. "I woke up and you were gone and thank God I woke up or you'd be fucking dead."

Her head throbbed as realization worked its way in, and vomit suddenly rose into her throat. She struggled out of his arms and ran for the bathroom, making it to the toilet just in time. She threw up violently, clutching the bowl. Cyryl came in and knelt behind her, holding her hair out of her face until she was through.

She sagged toward the floor and he caught her, picking her up and carrying her to his bed. He tucked her in. It was soft and the sheets smelled clean.

"I'm thirsty," she said. "I need something carbonated, and an ibuprofen." Her head was pounding so badly she could hardly see.

"Okay, okay, I'll get it." He went out, and Liria closed her eyes, sinking into the mattress. She couldn't understand how she could have overdosed. She hadn't done any more than usual.

Cyryl came back in, wearing a bathrobe. He put a can of club soda and a couple pills on the bedside table by her head, then sat next to her helped her to sit up. She swallowed the ibuprofen and carefully sipped some of the soda, trying not to make herself sick again. She leaned back on the pillows.

He put his arm around her, cradling her against his chest. "What the fuck did you do that for, Liria?"

"What happened? I was really dead?"

"You weren't breathing and you were blue. I think the noise of you falling off the bed is what

71

woke me up, thank God." He clutched her tighter.

She couldn't remember being dead. It was just blackness. "How did you bring me back?"

"I gave you CPR." She felt him tense up. "I almost called an ambulance. What the fuck, Liria? You could be dead right now, or in jail! What the fuck were you thinking?"

"I'm sorry," she said. "I didn't mean to, Cyryl. I'm sorry."

"I'm not giving you any more of that crap! You're going to quit for good. I'm taking time off of work and staying here with you so you can't leave. I don't care how fucking miserable you are. You're never going to touch that horrible shit again."

His fingers dug into the flesh of her arms, hurting her. "Okay," she said. "Okay, I'll quit. You can flush the rest down the toilet. I'm done with it." She heard the words as if someone else were saying them. She had to fight back her remorse as soon as they were out of her mouth.

His grip on her loosened a bit. "Good. Good girl. I'm going to do that."

He got up, and she squeezed her eyes closed and lay back against the pillows, clutching herself and breathing steadily. She heard the toilet flush and winced. *I can do it. I have Ativan. Just three days and it'll be over.*

He came back and took her in his arms again. She lay as still as possible, trying not to upset her stomach or aggravate her headache. "It's going to be all right," he said, and it sounded like he was talking to himself.

"Would you really have called an ambulance?" Her ear was on his chest and she could hear his heart beating fast.

"What do you mean? I was going to. You weren't waking up…I thought I was doing it wrong, the CPR. I learned how, but I'd never done the shit before on a real person, just those fucking dummies." His voice was growing rough again. He took a deep breath and blew it out.

"Most people wouldn't have called an ambulance," she said. "They would've just hauled me out and dumped me somewhere, so that they didn't have problems with the cops."

"The cops," he spat. "Fuck the cops. I'm not going to let you die, Liria. I'm not one of those dipshits you used to hang out with. Do you hear me?"

He was almost yelling. It hurt Liria's head and scared her a little. "I know, Cyryl," she said. "I know you're not like them." Vaguely, she wondered what Lee Harvey would have done if she'd gone out at his house. Would he have taken her to the hospital? He sure as hell didn't know CPR.

"I'll take care of you," Cyryl muttered. "You're mine now."

She fought back a fresh wave of nausea. It didn't matter. He'd just saved her life.

"Cyryl?" she said. "Do you really love me?"

His hands were big, strong, and gentle as he caressed her naked body. She still felt numb, her head full of cotton. "Yes, baby," he said. "Yes, I love you." He stretched out next to her, his arms around her as he buried his face in her hair. "I love you, Liria."

She cuddled against him and closed her eyes, letting her fatigue carry her off into a dreamless sleep.

***

The next few days went by in a haze, but it was easier than she'd thought it would be. She took enough Ativan to keep her mostly unconscious. Cyryl didn't go to work. He brought her 7UP and tried to get her to eat, and sat beside her as she dozed and writhed in bed. She got used to him being there. She actually liked it. He was nice to her.

On the morning of the third day after her overdose, she awoke in Cyryl's big, soft bed. He was asleep beside her, snoring softly, his hair falling over his broad forehead. His lips held the ghost of his little, snide grin.

The shutters were open, letting in the grey light of dawn and the sound of the ocean. Liria felt comfortable and calm. She turned over and stretched. Her body felt really good. *I'm clean,* she thought, amazed. *It's over.*

She got up out of bed. Every part of her body tingled. She wandered naked out into the kitchen and drank a can of club soda, which felt nice fizzing down her throat.

She found her phone on the coffee table. She had about ten texts, mostly from Lee Harvey, and she scrolled through them. Victor was apparently still being a dick, so she couldn't go back there. She had

Cyryl. A wave of relief washed over her. She was lucky. He was really good to her. She couldn't afford to fuck this up.

Liria: I overdosed. I'm clean now.

Her thumbs hesitated over the screen, twiddling.

Liria: Cyryl said he loves me.

It was only six forty-five in the morning, so she didn't expect an answer, but her phone buzzed almost immediately, and again, and again.

Lee Harvey: OMG, you overdosed? What happened?

Lee Harvey: Oh, that's so awesome, girl, I knew you could do it.

Lee Harvey: OMFG that's fucking *awesome* ROFLMAO

She told him the whole story as she leaned against the counter eating an apple.

Liria: I don't know what to do about Cyryl, though.

After Lee had stopped being a drama queen about everything, she wrote,

He's going to catch on that I'm not attracted to

him sooner or later, and then I'll be fucked.

Lee Harvey: Then don't let him catch on. You don't have to be attracted to someone to have sex with them. Sex is like a dance. It's performance art. It's entertainment. You rub something just the right way, and you watch the other person lose their mind. Think of it as a sort of game, to see how much power you can have over him. If he says he loves you, I'd say you're already winning.

Liria smirked at the screen for a moment, then put her phone down. Lee was a dickhead and a whore, but he was also right, in a way.

She went back through Cyryl's room and into the master bathroom. It had a huge tile shower with a bench, and a showerhead that poured from the ceiling like drenching rain. She let it run over her for a long time. Her body was awake again.

She had just rinsed the conditioner out of her hair when the shower door opened and Cyryl got in with her.

He looked her over, his eyebrows shooting up in surprise. "You look good." He put his arms around her, and his touch gave her shivers. "You look really good."

"I feel better," she said. She smiled at him, and saw a spark of emotion in his eyes.

"I love to see you smile. It's been so long." He kissed her, backing her up against the cold tile of the shower. Her body burned everywhere his skin touched hers. When his fingers found her clit she came almost immediately, with an almost painful intensity, a moan escaping her throat. She didn't even have to fantasize. Her body just wanted to be touched. Everything felt new.

She looked up at him, his wet hair plastered to his forehead and neck, the water running down his body in rivulets, and thought about what Lee Harvey had said. She pushed him gently onto the bench and leaned down, putting her lips against his ear. "I want to fuck you over and over again," she said. She wrapped her legs around him, slid his cock inside her, and watched his eyes glaze over as he lost his mind.

***

Cyryl took Liria out to lunch to celebrate her being clean. "You need to eat something," he chided, pinching her waist. She was so skinny now that her shorts wouldn't stay up, and she had to wear a sundress Margot had left behind.

He put the top down on the car, and Liria leaned back in the leather seat, feeling the sun on her face. Cyryl talked about Poland, which he had left in his early twenties to come to the United States. He called it a shithole, and told a bunch of exaggerated stories about how horrible it was just to make her laugh. At stoplights he put his hand on her knee or kissed her neck. She was getting used to him touching her, and didn't mind it.

The restaurant was a little bistro downtown with white tablecloths and outdoor seating under an arbor. They sat out in the breezy shade. Liria bowed to his pressure to order a pasta dish involving lobster in cream sauce which was sure to put meat on her bones, in exchange for him telling stories about her mother when she was young.

"Your mother was a horrible actress," he said as they ate their salads. "Fucking horrible. They kept giving her little parts because she was good-looking, and because she slept with everyone." Liria's cheeks got hot, and she wondered why she'd wanted to hear things sure to remind her that she was fucking one of her mom's old lovers.

He gave her an astute look and shrugged. "But then she got too fucked up even for the little parts, and that's that." He sipped his wine.

Liria wanted to ask more questions but couldn't bring herself to. She sat in silence, picking at her salad. He met her glance. "Well, what else can I tell you without making you uncomfortable?" he asked.

She froze, her fork stopped in midair as she regarded him with her lips quirked sideways. "How do you always know everything I'm thinking?"

He reached out and ran his finger along her jawline. "It's written all over that beautiful face of yours." She looked across the table at him, wishing she could read him half as well. A tiny smile flitted across his lips, and he grabbed her knee under the table. His attention was drawn by something over her shoulder, and he scowled and sat up straighter, removing his hand. "Oh shit," he muttered. "It's Pickert." He broke into a wide smile much different from his usual one. "Hey, Norman. How's it going?"

"Cyryl, how are you?" A man came up to the

78

table, slightly younger than Cyryl, wearing jeans and short sleeves. He had dark hair and a nice smile, and freckles were sprinkled across his nose, but it was the girl beside him who drew Liria's attention. She was probably a little younger than Liria, her long blonde hair in a messy braid over her shoulder. Her eyes were a strange, beautiful golden brown. Liria smiled at her and got a shy smile in return.

Norman glanced at Liria and raised his eyebrows at Cyryl. "Is this your family emergency, Czetski?"

"Yes, in fact," Cyryl said. "This is Liria Czetski, my adopted niece. Liria lost her father several years ago, and my sister just passed away recently, so she's come to stay with me for a bit. Liria, this is Norman Pickert and his daughter, Michelle."

"I'm so sorry for your loss," Norman said. He shook her hand, looking startled. Michelle shook her hand as well, an expression of honest pity on her face. Liria felt a little thrill as she touched her, and had to pry her eyes away so she didn't stare. She looked over and caught Cyryl watching her.

"We should get together, us and the girls," Norman said. "We could take the boat out."

Cyryl gave Norman his fake smile again. "Sure, sure. That'd be great. I'm sure Liria would love it. I'll be back in tomorrow. We can discuss it then."

Norman and Michelle said goodbye and went to their table inside the restaurant. Liria couldn't keep herself from watching Michelle walk away. She had perfectly-shaped, muscular legs, and Liria wondered if she played soccer or something. When she looked back up, Cyryl was gazing at her suspiciously. She made herself smirk at him.

"Adopted niece?" she said.

"I had to think of something. If you end up working there, they'll know we have the same last name."

He was uncharacteristically silent throughout the rest of the meal and the ride home. Liria asked him what was wrong a couple of times, and he didn't even answer, just gave her sharp looks. As he unlocked the door to his condo, she steeled herself for what she knew must be coming. When the door shut, she rounded on him, and he stood there with his little smile, clenching and unclenching his hands at his sides.

"Are you going to tell me what your problem is?" she asked.

"I'll tell you what my problem is. The way you looked at Norman Pickert's daughter."

"What do you mean?"

"You like her, is what I mean."

She scowled, her heart beating fast. "I don't even know her, and what do you care if I like her? What, you want me to hate her?"

"Don't play fucking innocent with me, sweetheart. You never look at me like that. You don't want me. You like women. You're a lesbian."

Liria clutched hard at the front of her dress. "Don't you think you're jumping to conclusions, Cyryl? All I did was shake her hand."

His nostrils flared. "I suspected it before, but I was stupid enough to believe it wasn't true."

"Cyryl…"

He grabbed her by the shoulders and slammed her back against the wall, knocking her air out of her lungs.

"Tell me the truth, Liria!" he yelled, his face very close to hers. She cowered but held his gaze. "Tell me the truth!"

"Cyryl, I…" Tears sprang to her eyes and she couldn't finish what she was going to say. She was about to be homeless and alone again, with no one to care about her. She thought she'd played her part better with Cyryl than she had with Derek, but Cyryl was so much smarter than Derek.

"You don't give a shit about me," he said, clutching her shoulders so hard it hurt. "You're just using me, same as always. Just like your mother. Just like all of them."

"No, Cyryl! That's not true!" He yelled something in Polish and slammed her against the wall again. "Stop it!" she screamed. "Cyryl, stop it! I like girls, you're right. But I wasn't using you. I…" She winced.

He went still. "You what?" he said quietly, his eyes filling with tears. "You what, Liria?"

"I wasn't using you. I…I wanted you to love me. I wanted…I wanted you to be my dad."

He let go of her shoulders, the anger leaving his face, his expression odd. She hid her face in her hands, trembling. Her throat closed up. She heard the door open and close. He was gone. She slid down the wall to sit on the floor.

Chapter 9

She didn't stay sitting for long. She didn't want the pain of Cyryl kicking her out once he came back. So she got up and gathered her things, trying to hold back her tears. The voice in her head told her to steal the jewelry in his bathroom or wad of cash she'd seen in the kitchen drawer when she was looking for her hidden kit, but she ignored it furiously. She didn't want to steal from Cyryl. He'd saved her life. And besides, if things worked out, she wouldn't need his money. Though she wanted desperately to get high, she didn't need to. She was clean, thanks to him, and that made her financial situation a lot easier. She squeezed her eyes shut against a fresh wave of grief.

She did take the bottle of Ativan, and a couple of Margot's dresses, shoving them in her overloaded backpack. Then she went out.

Cyryl's car was gone from his parking spot. She put on her sunglasses to cover her red eyes as she left the garage.

She wandered through the streets, trying to put

as much distance between herself and the condo building as possible. She was sure that every car that passed would be him, and she kept her eyes on the ground.

She ducked into a coffee shop a few blocks away and ordered a tall drip, then sat at a small table in the furthest corner and took out her phone.

She stared at the screen dumbly, her heart hammering. She'd missed two calls while she'd been walking, both of them from Cyryl. He'd left her a voicemail message, and she gazed at the alert, wondering what he'd said. For a painful moment, she imagined that maybe he'd called to apologize, to ask her to come back and live with him as his daughter instead of his lover, and she almost listened to the message. But she stopped herself. It was more likely that he'd called to hurl insults and accusations, and she couldn't handle hearing those right now.

Instead, she dug in the front pocket of her backpack and fished out the scrap of paper with Boston's phone number, folding and unfolding it between her fingers, fighting back her nausea. *I'm not going to get any dope. He said he'd help me out with a job, and that's all I'm going to ask him about.* Liria knew from experience that taking up offers from men you met on the bus rarely worked out the way you wanted it to, but her options were limited.

She pressed her lips together and dialed the number.

***

Boston picked her up in front of the coffee shop forty-five minutes later in a white Buick with tinted windows and custom wheels. A friend of his was driving, a young black guy, thin with a kind, babyish face and a cylindrical frizz of hair. He checked her out as she climbed in the backseat, his eyes bright with interest.

Boston grinned and she gave him an awkward hug over the seat back. "Hey, Liria, you look beautiful. It's great to see you."

She settled back in her seat. "Thanks for picking me up, and for letting me stay with you."

"No problem, no problem. Glad to do it. Let me introduce this fine young man to you. This is my friend Nestor."

The driver raised a hand in greeting and she smiled at him in the rearview mirror. "Nice to meet you," she said.

"What did I tell you about her, Nestor? She's like one of those Arabian princesses, right? Long, black hair, and those eyes, they're, like, exotic."

Nestor caught her eye in the mirror and smiled shyly, with a hint of amusement. "Like some sort of princess." His voice was quiet.

Boston leaned against the passenger door and squinted down his nose at her. "What are you, anyway? Are you Arabic?"

She grimaced faintly. "I don't know. My mom said she was Honduran and Cherokee. My...my dad I think was Mexican."

"You think he *was*?" Boston asked. "Weren't you just with him? Did he, like, change races or something? Get some sort of operation to make him

84

a black man?" He and Nestor laughed.

"Man, that'd be stupid, unless you like getting harassed by cops," Nestor said. They laughed again, and Liria tried to smile.

"Cyryl was my…well, I called him my dad, but he's not really. He just kinda raised me. My real dad, I think he's dead."

Boston quit laughing, his smile fading completely as he contemplated her. She stared at her knees, clutching the upholstery, trying to keep her face neutral. "Mmm," he said. "Okay, it's none of my business." He laid his big, warm hand on her shoulder and squeezed it. "You've had a rough life, my princess, but now things are looking up for you. I'm gonna take care of you, you don't have to worry about a thing."

Dread filled the pit of Liria's stomach, making it churn. When people said things like that, there were generally all sorts of things to worry about.

***

They went to the tiny, two-bedroom house Nestor and Boston shared. The carpets were dirty and the kitchen faucet dripped on a sink full of dishes. Boston offered to let her sleep on a futon mattress on the floor alongside his bed. She put her backpack in the room, next to a pile of dirty clothes. A Spongebob sheet hung over the window, darkening the room with a dirty gloom. She pulled it aside and peeked out through the wrought-iron bars into a small patch of dry, overgrown lawn. A broken charcoal barbecue leaned against the chain link fence that separated it from the alley, and a pair of stray cats lounged in the shade of a dead bush. She hugged herself, thinking of the view from Cyryl's condo, the sound of the ocean wafting through the bedroom windows in the morning. *Living with Cyryl wasn't a perfect situation, but at least I was safe. Maybe, if I talked to him...* She took out her phone and gazed at the voicemail box, where Cyryl's message still waited. Her thumb hovered over the play button. She still couldn't bring herself to listen to it. *Wait and see how this turns out,* she told herself.

She went into the living room and sat down on the couch next to Nestor, who was packing the bowl of a bong. He offered her the first hit, raising his eyebrows questioningly.

"No, that's okay," she said. "That stuff just makes me feel weird."

Boston laughed. "You don't like to feel that kind of weird, huh? You just like that heroin." He pronounced it *hair-on*.

Liria picked at her cuticles. "No, I quit, actually. I'm clean now."

Boston raised his eyebrows. "No shit, really?" He laughed, but his eyes were shrewd. "That's great. And you were freakin' *strung out* when I met you on that bus."

Nestor sputtered and blew out a huge mouthful of smoke. It billowed through the stripe of sunlight falling through the gap in the heavy front curtains. "It's hard to quit that stuff, right?" He passed the bong to Boston.

"Yeah, it sucked," she said. "I'm glad it's over."

Her phone buzzed in her back pocket. She froze, and the other two looked at her nervously as she pulled it out.

It was Cyryl again, and her heart pounded. Why did he keep calling? Wasn't it enough that she'd left? She punched the ignore button and shoved the phone back in her pocket.

The two of them still stared at her curiously. She arranged her face into a smile. "So you might be able to get me a job at your cousin's restaurant? Would I waiting tables or something?"

Boston and Nestor exchanged a glance. Nestor buried his face in the mouth of the bong while Boston broke into a wide, sparkling grin. "No, it's much better than that," he said. "If you're into girls like you say, I think you'll be a real asset at my cousin's place."

Liria's guts knotted.

***

Boston's cousin's "restaurant" was one of those places without windows, and had a neon sign depicting winking eyes. It stood on a desolate-looking street corner, next to a graffiti- covered mini mart with iron bars over the windows, the insides of which were plastered with decades of cigarette advertisements. Liria had brought along her backpack in case she needed to make a getaway.

They went through the back door and into a narrow hallway with concrete floors, music thumping through the walls, and into an office where a woman sat behind a cluttered desk. She had a thick waist, a hard face, and curly hair extensions.

"Hey, Cassie," Boston said. "This is the girl I told you about. Liria, this is my cousin Cassie."

Liria didn't say anything while the woman looked her over. Cassie smiled, which made her look a lot friendlier. "Hi, Liria, it's nice to meet you."

Liria smiled back wanly, her hands clenched into fists at her sides.

"Sit down," Cassie said, waving a manicured hand toward a worn, burgundy velvet sofa behind them. All three of them settled into it, Liria clutching her backpack to her belly. Cassie gazed at her, her dark eyes glittering. "So you want a job in my place." Her voice was deep and she had a slow way of speaking that made Liria feel more comfortable.

"Maybe," Liria said. "It depends on what you'd have me doing."

Cassie's eyes flicked to Boston and then came back to rest on her. "Nothing hard," she said. "Nothing difficult. I run a clean and safe establishment, though we may keep it a little under the radar."

Liria gave her a grim smile. "I won't touch any men."

Cassie broke into a knowing smile. "Don't like men, huh? Well I don't blame you." She looked at Boston and Nestor and laughed, an infectious sound that came straight from her belly.

"Humph," Boston said, shifting in his seat.

Nestor shot Liria an intimidated, sideways glance, stroking his budding mustache.

Cassie laughed again. "Don't worry, Liria. You won't be touching any nasty-ass men. Do you dance?"

Liria wrinkled her nose. "No."

Cassie nodded once. "That's okay. That's not where the money is, anyhow, and you look like money to me." She looked back at Boston. "I think you're right about her."

"I'm always right, baby," Boston said.

Cassie looked at Liria again and her expression turned serious. "You'll be working in a back room with a girl named Nadine. Patrons will be watching from behind a two-way mirror, and you won't have to touch them or even see them at all. You get fifty dollars a day plus ten percent of what we bring in from the people watching. That can turn into bank, especially if you do requests, and especially if you're good. Word spreads fast around here."

"Plus you get a place to stay," Boston added. "I know we're *men*, but we're okay. It's a pretty good deal."

Liria held Cassie's gaze, tapping her foot against the floor. If Cassie were telling the truth, it wouldn't be too bad, and if she saved her money she might have enough to get her own apartment soon, and a better job. She nodded. "Okay. I'll try it."

Cassie grinned and leaned back in her chair. "Welcome aboard, Miss Liria."

Chapter 10

Two girls lounged on a sectional sofa in the dressing room, talking, and another sat in front of a mirror, putting on purple lipstick. The girl at the mirror was tiny, with wide eyes and a heart-shaped face, soft lips, and black, frizzy hair pulled into a ponytail on top of her head. She caught Liria's reflection in the mirror and blinked. There was something sad and vulnerable about her. She looked too young to be working in a place like this.

She spun to face them, a question in her brown eyes as she gazed at Boston.

"Nadine, meet Liria," Boston said. "Cassie wants you two to work together, like you'd talked about."

Nadine looked Liria up and down. "It's nice to meet you, Liria."

The other two girls on the couch had quit talking and were smirking at Liria. One of them was blonde, the other redheaded. Boston smiled at them. "And these ladies...I apologize, I forget your names."

"I'm Alice," the redhead said.

90

"Angela," the blonde said, raising two purple-manicured fingers in greeting. Liria gave them a tight smile.

She turned back to Nadine, who was still watching her with deep, dark eyes. Nadine stood up, and when she did, she didn't look so young anymore, even though she probably wasn't even five feet tall. She moved with an inborn, suggestive grace, her round hips swaying over her shapely legs.

"Come on," Nadine said. "I'll help you get ready."

Liria nodded. Nadine's bellybutton showed under her cropped blouse and Liria was mesmerized by it. She had to make herself look away.

The two of them left the room and went out another door, down a dark corridor. Nadine's round ass did subtle and tantalizing things when she walked, and the smooth curves of her butt cheeks peeked below the hems of her shorts.

They entered a room cluttered with boxes and racks of clothing, and Nadine turned to look Liria over. The only light came from a single bare bulb in the ceiling, and her eyes looked almost black. She pulled a couple things from the rack, a short pleated skirt and a cropped white blouse like her own.

"The schoolgirl theme always plays big," she said. "Change into these."

Liria took them, and examined them dubiously.

"They've been washed," Nadine said. "You'll want to bring your own underwear, though. You can bring all your own clothes if you want, but that's a waste of money if you ask me. Cassie doesn't let the clothes get nasty."

Liria hadn't been worried about them being dirty. They still smelled like laundry soap. She just didn't like wearing stuff like this. But Nadine was watching her, and Liria gathered she wanted her to change right then. *I guess this is what I signed up for.*

She stripped off the sundress, shoving it in her backpack, and put on the other stuff. She could feel Nadine's appraising eyes on her. "What size shoe do you wear?"

"Seven."

Nadine handed her a pair of strappy heels. When Liria was all dressed, Nadine looked her over again. "You look good," she said.

Liria couldn't see herself, but she felt stupid. She tugged at the hem of her skirt and tottered on her heels.

Nadine gently took Liria's wrist and ran her fingers over the track marks on her forearms and inner elbows. Liria shivered at her light touch, which was so different from Cyryl's, different even than Rose's, which had been rough and athletic.

Nadine raised an eyebrow. "Heroin?"

"I quit."

"Not long ago."

"No, just a couple days."

Nadine didn't let go of her wrist, and continued to look at her. The top of her head only came up to Liria's chin. "You like girls for real?"

Liria couldn't read those dark eyes. She nodded.

Nadine's soft lips curled up at the edges. Then, slowly, she stepped closer to her, stood on her tiptoes, and kissed her.

Her tongue was gentle and caressing, and tasted sweet, like she'd been eating candy. Liria's breath caught in her throat, and heat spread from her lips, tingling through every nerve in her body.

Much too soon, Nadine drew back. "That should make this easier, if you like girls." She smiled and looked up at Liria through her lashes. "Come on, let's get some makeup on you."

She took her back out into the room they'd been in before. Alice, Angela, and the men were gone. It was just the two of them. Nadine took her backpack from her and put it in a locker, handing her the key. "Be careful of your stuff around here. Some of the girls aren't trustworthy." She gestured to the seat in front of the mirror, and Liria sat down, barely glancing at her reflection. She didn't want to see herself dressed like this. There was a counter littered with makeup under the mirror, and Nadine picked through it and found some eyeliner. "I'll do you up," she said. "Close your eyes."

Liria did, and Nadine painted her eyes with gentle, deft strokes. Liria could still taste her tongue, and her heart beat faster.

"Why did you quit heroin?" Nadine asked.

Liria smiled humorlessly. "Because it sucked."

Nadine laughed. "Yeah, it does, but that doesn't stop most people."

Liria was quiet for a minute. Nadine put away the eyeliner and began brushing her lids with shadow. "I was staying with a friend," Liria finally said. "The deal was I had to quit if I stayed there, but then it didn't work out anyway."

"Ah."

"But I don't want to start again," Liria said, digging her fingernails into her palms. "That shit controls your life."

Nadine finished with the eye shadow. "Look at me." Liria opened her eyes. Nadine gazed at her, one corner of her amazing lips curling up. "You look good," she said. "You're beautiful, too beautiful to be shooting smack."

"You're too beautiful to be working in a place like this," Liria said, and Nadine laughed.

"The money's good, better than I'd get anywhere else, and there are fringe benefits." She straightened up, and reached into the pockets of her miniscule shorts, bringing out a tiny baggie of white powder. Liria's heart sank and her stomach writhed.

Nadine tapped some of the coke out onto a little mirror on the counter and chopped it into four lines with a supermarket club card. Liria watched mutely. Nadine rolled up a dollar bill and held it out to her. When Liria made no move to take it, Nadine smiled. "It makes it easier. It makes it feel better."

Liria stared at the coke, feeling slightly ill.

"It doesn't get you hooked like the other stuff. It's just like strong coffee," Nadine insisted.

Liria wasn't sure why she took the dollar bill from her hand. *It makes it feel better,* the voice in her head repeated. *It makes it easier.* She leaned over the mirror, plugging one nostril with her finger and snorting a line with the other. She tilted her head back and closed her eyes, sniffing as the coke dripped bitter down the back of her throat. A few seconds later, her ears rang, and a rush of adrenaline tore through her, her heart thundering. She opened her eyes again and smiled, and Nadine smiled back. Nadine jerked her chin toward the mirror. "There's another one for you," she said.

Liria shook her head and handed the dollar bill to her. "No. One's enough."

Nadine shrugged and bent over the mirror, and Liria stood up to give her room. When Nadine straightened, all three lines were gone.

"Feels good, right?" she said, and Liria nodded, a feeling of exhilaration crawling up from her feet to her scalp. Nadine's pupils were dilated, her lips curled into a beguiling smile. She was breathing fast, her breasts rising and falling under her scanty top, and Liria couldn't take her eyes off of them. Liria tugged her closer by one of her belt loops and kissed her, running her fingers down Nadine's bare waist and along those perfectly round hips, her skin smooth and brown and perfect. Nadine pressed those hips against her, making Liria ache, then pried herself away, grinning. "Save it for the show," she said. She took her by the hand and pulled her back down the hallway.

The music got louder, and Liria's senses pulsed along with the beat. Everything looked bright and beautiful, even the dirty concrete floor and smudged walls. She smiled to herself as she watched Nadine's round ass wiggle ahead of her. She was about to get paid to fuck a hot girl. Her life had never been better.

Nestor was sitting on a stool outside a closed door, his feet propped up on one of the rungs. The door had a one-way mirror, and Liria could see Alice on the floor of the room inside, naked except for tall heels. She was lying on her back with her hips in the air, playing with a dildo. Nestor's eyes crawled over Liria's body as they walked up. He pursed his lips and gave Nadine a wry grin. "I love my job," he said. "You guys ready?"

"Yep," Nadine said, straightening her bra. "Alice almost done?"

"She's got about another minute," Nestor said.

Liria watched Alice through the window as she rolled on the floor, sliding the dildo in and out. It was tiresome to look at. Liria had met a lot of girls like Alice in her life: spoiled, good-looking straight girls. They used sex to get what they wanted, but she didn't think they actually liked it.

Nestor rapped on the window with his knuckles. Liria noticed he wasn't watching the show. Alice stood up and put her clothes back on, then sauntered toward the door. Nestor opened it to let her out. She gave them all a fake smile as she strode off down the hallway.

Nadine looked up at Liria with a sly little grin, then pulled her through the door. Nestor shut them in.

There were one-way mirrors all around the room. It was furnished with a straight-backed chair and a futon mattress. There was a box full of sex toys, a yoga ball, and a pole.

Nadine reached out and pulled Liria closer by the fabric of her blouse, and Liria put her arms around Nadine's tiny, bare waist, breathing fast. For a moment, she could feel all those hidden eyes on her, but she could feel Nadine's soft, warm tits nestled under hers, and her dark eyes were shining up at her. Liria soon forgot about the spectators. A wave of desire rushed through her. She smiled and cocked an eyebrow, then leaned down close to Nadine's ear. "I'm going to make you come for real."

Nadine laughed. "I'd like that."

Liria pushed her down gently onto the mattress, spread her knees apart and knelt between them. She unbuttoned Nadine's top, undid the front hooks on her lacy push-up bra. Her breasts sprang free, round with big, dark areolas, the nipples pointing up slightly. Liria cupped her hands around them. They were warm and heavy and silky, and she caressed them as she ran her tongue around and around each of her nipples until they got hard.

"That's good, baby," Nadine said. She reached up and pulled apart the snaps on Liria's top. "Show me your titties, honey. I want to see them."

Liria undid her own bra, showing her big breasts, her nipples smaller than Nadine's and dusky pink. Nadine smiled. "Those are nice. Those are real nice." Nadine pulled her down and kissed her, squeezing her nipples gently between her fingers, pressing her hips up against hers. Liria ached deep inside, her breath coming quicker. She kissed Nadine's jaw, her neck, bit each of her nipples softly, making her moan. She slid her lips across her flat, brown belly to her bellybutton. She hadn't been able to take her eyes off of that bellybutton, peeking out between the hem of her shorts and shirt, and now she finally had her tongue in it. She slowly unbuttoned Nadine's shorts and shimmied them down her shapely legs.

She didn't have panties on, and her pussy was

waxed smooth, her little brown clit showing at the top. Liria pressed little nibbling kisses from her bellybutton down to her pussy, then found her clit with her tongue, rubbing it round and round slowly while she tickled the creases of her thighs with her fingers. Nadine arched her hips up, moaning. "Oh, that's good. Don't stop that." Liria didn't stop. She pressed harder with her tongue, and slid two fingers up into Nadine's wet pussy. Nadine moaned, and Liria pushed her fingers deeper, thrusting them in harder, rubbing harder with her tongue, until Nadine cried out, her pussy tightening around Liria's fingers and getting wetter, her hips shuddering. "Ah, yeah," she said. "Oooh, baby you fuck me good." Liria's own clit throbbed hot as she sat up and sucked her fingers.

Nadine smiled. She reached up and pulled Liria down and kissed her. She laughed softly in her ear. "You're a beautiful bitch. You're a hot, beautiful bitch."

Nadine turned over and flipped Liria onto her back, her soft lips curling up impishly. Her hair was coming out of the ponytail and droplets of sweat glistened on her nose. She pulled Liria's skirt off, and Liria gasped as Nadine's little firm tongue found her clit. She ached with disappointment as the tongue slid up, all the way up her body until her lips met hers again. Nadine kissed her, her tits warm and soft against her own. She pressed her hips into Liria's, moving them in circles, her wet pussy sliding over hers. Liria arched against her, wanting more, needing more. She grabbed Nadine's round ass and pulled it harder against her. She'd forgotten all about the people watching, about the hard world outside these walls, about anything but Nadine's lithe body, her wet and slippery pussy. The world went white as she came, pleasure burning through her, and she moaned and said Nadine's name.

She opened her eyes, gasping, and saw Nadine smiling down at her. "I think our fifteen minutes were up about fifteen minutes ago," she said, kissing her quickly, and the world clunked back into place.

They put their clothes back on. Liria was a little dizzy, the coke starting to wear off. She could feel the eyes on her again, and her skin crawled.

The door opened as they approached it. Nestor was still there, and Boston was with him. Both of them had a glazed-over look. "Why didn't you call time?" Nadine chided.

"Ain't no one gonna call time on that," Nestor muttered, blinking, and Nadine laughed.

"Come on, baby," she said, smiling up at Liria. "Let's go sit down."

They went back in the other room. No one else was there. Nadine got out her purse and started chopping up more coke on the little mirror. Liria felt awkward and empty, and sat on the arm of the couch, staring at nothing, her pulse pounding in her ears.

Nadine glanced over at her. "Come do some more of this blow, you'll feel better." Her expression was neutral, with no hint that she was looking at the woman who had just fucked her silly in front of a bunch of people. Liria's heart suddenly ached with loneliness, and she hugged herself, wondering what her problem was. Nadine smiled and came over, kissing her forehead. "Come on, baby, this stuff is always hard at first. You just need another line." Liria was consumed with longing as she looked at Nadine. She took the rolled up dollar bill from her manicured hand, and went over and snorted another line.

She got another rush as it dripped down her throat, and she closed her eyes while it flowed through her. Her emptiness dissipated, filled by the warm hum of the drug. She smiled, and Nadine smiled back. "Better?" Nadine asked.

Liria nodded, taking a deep breath, her soul seeming to settle back into place. *Everything is okay. I can do this*. Nadine leaned down and snorted two lines, then stashed her stuff back in her purse.

Boston came in, his eyebrows raised. "Nice show, ladies." He grinned, his eyes wandering over their bodies. He handed Liria and Nadine each an envelope, and continued to stand close to Liria, looking her over. His hand moved as if to touch her, and she strode quickly over to stand by Nadine.

Nadine opened her envelope and flipped through the cash inside, then laughed. Her eyes shone at Liria. "We did good."

Liria opened her own envelope. It was two hundred twenty dollars. If that was ten percent of what the house had made, that was pretty amazing for half an hour. She exchanged a surprised smile with Nadine, who was jumping up and down, giggling.

"Cassie wants three shows a day out of you two," Boston said. "Can you do that?"

"Oh, you bet I can," Nadine said. "How about you, Liria?"

Liria's guts knotted up again as she looked at the other woman, her dark and deep eyes, her cute, hot little body. She didn't really want to fuck her in front of people for money. She wondered what it would be like to be alone with her, to fuck her in a quiet bedroom somewhere. She wanted to hold her afterwards, fall asleep in her arms.

But if you can get paid for it, are you really going to turn that down?

The coke pushed out her doubts and filled her with wellbeing. *When you get enough money, you can get a better job, and maybe Nadine will quit too, and come with you.* She smiled tentatively. "Yeah, I can do that."

Nadine broke into a grin, then skipped up to her and gave her a quick kiss. "We're a good team," she said.

"All right, all right," Boston said, grinning, his stare skimming hungrily over Liria's body. "I'll go tell Cassie."

Liria watched Nadine walk back over to the mirror to fix her hair, then went over and unlocked her locker, taking out her backpack and stashing the cash in the front pocket. Her phone was in there, and she felt it buzzing.

She took it out, her heart thumping. It was Cyryl again.

Her scalp prickled. *Just get it over with and talk to him. Let him tell you off, and then he'll quit calling and you can forget about it.* She took a deep breath, pressing the answer button as she walked out into the hallway.

"Hello?"

"Liria! Thank God. Where are you?"

She took a couple of breaths. "I'm—I'm with friends," she said.

He cursed. "You're not doing fucking smack again, are you?"

Guilt and surprise bubbled up inside her. "No, Cyryl."

"You'd better not be doing that shit again, or I'll fucking kill whoever you're with."

"I'm not doing heroin, Cyryl." She stared at her feet, clutching the phone with a sweaty hand. She heard him take a deep breath and let it out.

"Liria, please, come home," he said, his voice quieter, pleading. "I'm sorry I got angry with you. I'm sorry I hurt you. I just…I just love you so much. Please, baby…"

"You want me to come back?" she asked incredulously.

"Yes," he said vehemently. "Yes, Liria. I love you. I need you, sweetheart. You say you like women, but you like fucking me too. I know you like it. I made you come, Liria. I could feel it."

Liria trembled, angry and sad and guilty all at once. She squeezed her eyes shut, remembering the feeling of Nadine's body pressed against hers. That had been so much sweeter, so much more right than with Cyryl, even though it had just been a show with all those people watching.

But she did like Cyryl. He was nice to her, he cared about her; he said he *loved* her. He'd saved her life, and he was easy to talk to. Not to mention he had a nice house, and money. She glanced around at the dirty walls and littered floor. Cyryl was *safe.* She tugged at one of the pleats in her skirt. "Yeah," she said. "Yeah, you did, Cyryl. You made me come." She winced.

"This…this thing with the women, it's just a phase. I can make you happy, Liria. I've wanted you for so long. You belong with me. Think of all I've done for you, and you abandon me like this."

A jolt of anger made her stiffen. "It's not a phase, Cyryl."

"Then why did you like it when I fucked you, eh? You like pussy so much, why did you want my cock so bad? Over and over, like you said. Over and over."

She squeezed her eyes shut, letting her anger dissipate. The coke was making her feel too good, making her think that everything was okay, that she had a good job now, that she didn't need Cyryl. But her more rational mind told her to step carefully, and her heart told her not to push him away. *You can't burn this bridge. Cyryl might be the only true friend you've ever had. And you might need him again someday.* "Cyryl, I…" She bit her lip. "I do love you." She fought back a wave of dizziness and nausea. It was true, in a way.

"Liria, my love, my baby, please come home. I'll come get you, wherever you are."

She gritted her teeth. "I can't. Not yet."

"What? Why?"

"I'm just…I'm just confused right now. You don't understand…"

"Come be with me. I'll make it better for you,

sweetheart."

"I need time." She fought back very real tears, and wiped her runny nose. "I need to get used to this, Cyryl. A few days ago, I thought you were my dad."

He went silent, and she waited, her heart pounding. She didn't know if she'd fucked up, if she'd pissed him off or hurt his feelings too badly. When he spoke his voice was flat, and she still couldn't tell for sure if she'd done permanent damage. "Okay, Liria. Okay. You need time, that's fine. You take some time. But where are you staying? What are you going to do? I'm not going to give you money so you can run around doing smack again. You say you love me and you need time, whatever, but I'm not going to let you fuck me around."

"No, I don't need your money." Her tone was harsher than she'd intended, and she tried to soften it. "I have a place to stay at my friend's house, and he got me a job."

He cursed in Polish. "What kind of friend is this? What kind of fucking job, Liria?"

She fought back her anger again. "He's a nice guy, his name is Boston. And it's a job at a restaurant."

She could hear him breathing. "A restaurant?"

"Yes."

"This friend, this *Boston…*"

"He's just a friend, Cyryl. Nothing else."

"If he fucking touches you, if you have something going on with him, I'll fucking kill him, do you understand me, Liria?"

"*Stop it,* Cyryl!" She closed her eyes and took a deep breath. She thought about what Lee Harvey had said, that sex is like performance art. *Not just sex, but the whole relationship. It's all a show.* "Stop it, Cyryl," she said in a softer tone. "I don't love any man but you. I don't want to fuck any other man." It was technically true.

She heard him sigh. "Liria, baby," he murmured, "I want you back. I want you next to me tonight."

"I just need some time, that's all. Okay?"

There was a short silence. "Okay," he said. "Okay. But I'm going to call you tomorrow."

"That's fine."

"You answer the phone when I call, Liria."

"I will."

"I love you."

She swallowed. "I love you too."

He hung up, and she shoved her phone in her backpack. She leaned back against the wall, wiping her eyes and nose and letting the tension drain from her body. Slowly, her bad feelings ebbed, replaced by the pleasant optimism of the cocaine.

Nadine peeked out into the hallway. "There you are," she said. She came out and put her arms around Liria, slowly working her hands up her back. "What're you doing out here?"

"I had a phone call to make."

Nadine smiled, and kissed her. Liria was starting to get a feel for how she kissed, and how she moved her body, how her curves and her lips fit against her own. She wondered if Nadine actually liked her, or if all of it was fake, just part of the show, sort of like what she had going with Cyryl.

Nadine kept her arms around her, looking up at her pensively. "What are you so upset about?"

Liria forced herself to smile. "Nothing."

Nadine raised an eyebrow. "Yeah? Was that call from the man it didn't work out with?"

Liria's smile faded. "What makes you think that?"

"Just a hunch." Those brown eyes examined her face. "Come sit down and forget about it. Cassie wants us to do another show in an hour."

Liria nodded dully. Nadine's brow furrowed as she watched her, but she didn't say anything. She took her by the hand and led her back into the sitting room.

Boston and Nestor were there on the couch, and they scooted over to make room for them. Liria made sure Nadine sat between her and Boston.

"Hey, ladies," Boston said, smiling. "You've already got people waiting for the next show, you know."

Nadine laughed, but Liria just crossed her arms over her chest and didn't respond. The coke was already starting to wear off. She felt Nadine glancing at her and avoided her gaze, leaning back against the cushions and closing her eyes. She was starting to get a headache, and wondered how she'd handle doing another show. She didn't feel like doing more coke. Her stomach hurt and her enthusiasm was drained.

The others made idle chitchat, but Liria didn't make any attempt to follow it. She felt jittery and tense, and her confused feelings about Cyryl and Nadine pooled in her stomach like a bad meal.

The conversation stopped abruptly, and Liria opened her eyes. Everyone seemed on edge. She followed their gazes to see a man standing in the doorway, filling up the whole doorframe and grinning cruelly, his thick arms crossed over his chest. His head was shaved, the skin of his short neck gathered in fleshy folds like love handles.

"What are you doing here, Robert?" Nadine said, her voice tinged with panic. "I already paid you this week."

Robert grinned wider. "I just came by to check on you. I heard you got something new going on. Making a bit of money."

"That's none of your business," Nadine said.

"I'd say it's exactly my business, Nadine. You'd be dead if it weren't for me. I took care of you when no one else would. If I hadn't, you wouldn't be here making any money at all."

"The deal was a hundred a week, and that's just 'cause you're a bully. I don't owe you shit. I'm not your slave and never was."

Robert's tiny, deep-set eyes flicked over to Liria. "This the other girl I'm hearing about?"

"She ain't got shit to do with you," Nadine said, sitting forward on the couch, her eyes flashing.

"She wouldn't be making any money, either, if it weren't for me. She'd just be one more slut waving her ass around for the perverts that come in here."

"Now, let's be reasonable," Boston cut in. "I think we've been generous with you, Robert. Don't stretch it."

Robert uncrossed his arms, swinging them at his sides. "I think we've been generous with *you*, letting this place operate in this neighborhood. If you're going to be a pain in the ass, maybe it's not worth it to let this business continue." His little piggy-eyed gaze sought Nadine and Liria, and he smiled. "Or maybe I'll just take these two with me if they're such cash cows."

A burst of adrenaline shot through Liria's veins.

"The fuck you will," Nadine said, her hands balled into fists.

Robert snickered. "Yeah, I think that's what I'll do, in fact." He made a move toward them, but he didn't get far, because Nestor was up in a flash. A gun had appeared in his hand out of nowhere, and he had it pointed steadily at Robert's broad belly. Robert froze, his expression tense and furious.

"You just move on out of here," Nestor said in his quiet voice. "Go on."

Robert's gaze darted to the gun barrel, then back to Nestor's face. "You just fucked up, Nestor. You just fucked up bigtime."

"Gabriel will disown your stupid motherfucking ass before he backs bullshit like this," Nestor said. "We've got pull too. Now get the fuck out of here, before I just shoot you in your ugly, no-neck face and tell Gabe you never made it here."

Robert scowled, trying to look tough, but Liria could see the fear in his eyes, the sweat stains forming under his muscled arms. "Fuck you, Nestor. Fuck all of you." He turned and stormed out, his heavy footsteps receding down the hallway.

Nestor stood for a few moments longer, then shoved his pistol back in his waistband, tucking his shirt over it.

Boston blew out air between puffed cheeks. "Holy Moses," he said. "Oh no."

"That fucking asshole," Nadine said. Liria saw she was crying, and Liria herself was shaking. She tentatively took one of Nadine's clenched hands in her own. Nadine looked over at her, and they exchanged a frightened glance.

"This is gonna be trouble," Boston said, standing up. "I'll go tell Cassie." He went out. Nestor sat down at the other end of the sofa, shaking his head, looking worried.

"What was that about?" Liria said.

"That fucking asshole thinks he owns me," Nadine said, pounding the couch cushions with her fist. "I used to work for him, but when this place opened Cassie offered me a job, and I took it because it was a lot better than what Robert had me doing. But Robert said he wouldn't let me work here if I didn't pay him part of the money I made, to compensate him for room and board or who knows what. He thinks he's hot shit because he works for Gabriel, but he isn't."

"Gabriel isn't going to involve himself in this," Nestor said. "You never should have paid that cocksucker anything."

Nadine pressed her lips together. "Thanks for standing up for me, Nestor."

"No problem. It was bullshit."

Liria felt sick to her stomach. Part of her longed to be safe in Cyryl's rich condo, and thought about calling him. Then Nadine turned her beautiful eyes on her and smiled, and Liria forgot all about it.

"I'm sorry you had to see that shit, honey,"

Nadine said.

Cassie came in with Boston, her jaw tight. Her rage seemed to make her bigger, snapping off of her like electricity, her hips swaying with it. Her burning glare fell on Nestor. "What's this bullshit I hear about you pulling a fucking gun on Robert?"

Nestor raised his eyebrows. "He was trying to shake down your ladies and take them out of here. What did you expect me to do?"

"What, he was just going to haul them out into the street, kicking and screaming?" Cassie said. "Out in broad daylight? He wouldn't try that, even in this neighborhood."

"You don't know what he'd try, Cassie," Nadine said. "That motherfucker is crazy. You should have seen some of the shit he did to me."

Cassie gazed at Nadine, her nostrils flaring, but some of the steam went out of her. "Gabriel is going to be up in my business now."

Nestor waved that idea away. "Gabriel doesn't give a shit about some schoolyard squabble, and he's small-town when it comes down to it, anyway."

"Well, we'll see, I guess." She looked at the three of them thoughtfully, standing with her hands on her wide hips, tapping her long, painted nails against her sides. "I'm not saying Robert isn't full of shit, because he is. But I just don't need no trouble. I want you three to scoot out of here for a week or so until this calms down."

"What, Liria too?" Boston said. "What did she do?" Liria had had the same thought, but didn't want to say anything; she wanted to be where

110

Nadine was.

"Yes, Liria too," Cassie said. "Sounds like Robert got some idea about her."

Liria chewed her lip. Nestor blew out a long breath, and Nadine glared at Cassie through slitted eyes. "Where do you expect us to go?" Nadine asked.

"Now, calm down, Nadine. I've got a brother over in Vegas. He's a businessman, owns an auto shop and some other stuff. Has a few rentals, and he has one you can stay in."

Liria chewed her lip harder, wondering what the catch was.

"You guys need to go now, though," Cassie said. "If Gabriel decides to get involved, he'll have someone over here in a minute."

"Jesus, Cassie," Nestor said. "You're gonna run us out of here like the police are coming?"

"Don't mouth off to me, gunslinger," Cassie said. "Think you're some sort of thug, pulling guns in my place? I should throw you out, see how you'd do trying to get a real job instead of staring at pussy all day."

"Whatever," Nestor said, getting to his feet. "We're going."

"That's right, Mr. Badass," Cassie said.

"I'm taking them to Perry's, then?"

"Mmmhmm. He'll give you directions to the rental."

Nestor looked at Liria and Nadine, sighing through pursed lips and patting his tower of hair nervously. Nadine got up, muttering under her breath, and started gathering her things. Liria stood up as well, shouldering her pack. She wanted to change out of the stupid clothes she was in, but with Cassie glaring at them all, she didn't want to delay them leaving.

Boston came over and put his hand on Liria's shoulder. She flinched slightly. "Sorry about the drama," he said. "That fucker's just on steroids or something. I don't think he would've actually tried to take you out of here. He's just bluster. We'll get this worked out."

Cassie's expression softened a little. "I'm sorry too, Liria. This was none of your business, and that dumbass Robert shouldn't have dragged you into it. We'll have you back here and raking in the tips before you know it." She shook her head sadly, smirking. "Don't know what I'm gonna tell those people waiting out there to see you two."

"Tell them to go shove a dildo up Robert's ass for entertainment," Nadine said. She'd shoved all of her belongings into a big purse and raised her eyebrows at Nestor expectantly.

"You all take care, and I'll be in touch," Cassie said.

They all left, Nadine still huffing. Liria didn't know how to feel. This job was uncomfortable for her, but things might get even worse.

Chapter 11

Liria stretched out in the backseat of the Buick as Nestor cursed at traffic. Her shoulders were knotted up, her head hurt, and she wanted a shot badly. *Just one. Not enough to get strung out again. Just enough to make me feel better.* She thought longingly of all the dope Cyryl flushed down the toilet. *What the fuck was I thinking? Why did I let him do that?*

It just made her feel worse, thinking about Cyryl. She couldn't believe she'd fucked him. What if he were lying about being sterile? What if he really was her dad? Worse yet, what if she were pregnant? She pulled her knees tight to her chest.

In the front seat, Nadine stared distantly out the windshield, her arms crossed, paying no attention to her. *How could I have ever thought she really likes me? Now that we don't have to put on a show, she doesn't even know I exist.*

Liria took a deep breath, trying to relax. *It's just the coke hangover making you feel this way. You shouldn't do that crap.*

113

Being conscious was painful, her nerves twanging like rubber bands. She wiped the cold sweat from the back of her neck and fished in her backpack for the Ativan. She swallowed two of them dry, spread her sundress over her as a blanket, and curled up as the pills carried her off into the warm womb of sleep.

She awoke hours later, when the hum of the car's engine ceased. Her cheek was stuck to the vinyl seat, and she was clammy and sore. She sat up, blinking.

It was dark outside. Orange streetlights illuminated a quiet cul-de-sac populated with modest adobe houses, their edged lawns ringed with solar lanterns and shrubbery. Nestor gazed back at her with tired eyes, running his hand over his frizz of hair. Nadine was asleep against the passenger door, her head propped on a wad of clothing.

"Are we here?" Liria asked.

"Yeah. This is Perry's house. Doubt he's still awake, but we'll see."

"What time is it?"

"Two thirty."

Liria stretched, rubbing her eyes. She felt a lot better than she had before going to sleep, but her head was fuzzy from the Ativan.

"Wake up, shorty," Nestor said, nudging Nadine with his knee. "We're here."

Nadine stirred, then sat up, wrinkling her nose. She blinked, a dull look in her eyes, and gathered her things from the floorboards.

They all climbed out into the cool desert night. Crickets chirped in the bushes. Above, a few stars bled through the orange stain from the city lights.

Nestor knocked on the front door while Nadine scowled sleepily at her feet and Liria hugged herself against the chill.

The door opened, and a man's deep voice spoke from the darkness of the entry. "Hey, come on in."

"Hey, Perry," Nestor said, as they filed into the house. "Sorry to bug you so late, but Cassie drove us out of there with a pitchfork."

Perry chuckled darkly as he shook Nestor's hand. "Yeah she was all riled up when she called me." He gave Nadine a one-armed hug and then turned to Liria, examining her curiously. He was a big man, tall and thick, his hair in short cornrows, wearing a black t-shirt and sweatpants. "You must be Liria." He shook her hand, grinning lopsidedly. "Cassie tells me you and Nadine are quite a hit at her place."

Liria glanced at Nadine, but she stared blankly at the floor, not looking at her. Liria smiled at Perry. "Yeah, I guess we put on a good show."

He patted her on the shoulder. "Well, welcome to my humble abode. You should just stay the night here, and go to the rental in the morning. I'll show you all where you can sleep."

Liria was hoping she'd have to share a bedroom with Nadine, but Perry's house was huge, and she got a room to herself. It was small, with a thick beige carpet and built-in bookshelves loaded down with CDs. The closet and corners were jammed with guitar cases, amplifiers, and other musical equipment. It had a twin bed neatly made with a Star Wars comforter, which smelled dusty.

Liria changed out of her stripper clothes, into her soft, baggy pajamas, then curled up under the blankets. The big house creaked as it settled. Liria wished she had someone to put her arms around.

Her mind wouldn't settle down. She lay there, wondering how Nadine felt about her and what she should do about Cyryl, and couldn't get back to sleep. She got up and opened the window, letting in the sound of crickets and the faint breeze, then dug in her backpack for her phone.

She had a text from Lee Harvey, which had arrived a little after midnight.

Lee Harvey: Victor kicked me out.

"Oh, Lee Harvey, what did you do?" Liria moaned aloud, flopping down on the bed.

Liria: WTF happened?

The answer came immediately, as she figured it would, even though it wasn't quite four in the morning.

Lee Harvey: Well, I kinda took an advance on his credit card.

Liria sighed, biting her lip.

Liria: Lee Harvey, you dick. Why did you do that?

Lee Harvey: He wouldn't give me any more

money, and I had a slow day at the truck stop. It pissed me off. He was ruining my life. First he kicked you out, and then he was all on my case about the drugs and getting a job.

Liria smirked. Lee Harvey was a hot mess in the worst way, but she missed him. He was a true friend, and his ability to create drama was mesmerizing.

Liria: Where are you staying?

Lee Harvey: Right now I'm at Mother Marey's, but she says I can only stay a couple days unless I follow her "rules". She wants me to get a job, go to church, and spend two weeks at Christian camp to make me straight.

Liria snorted.

Liria: They want to pray the gay out of you? Good luck. If there were a God, not even He would be able to make you straight.

Lee Harvey: I know. If Jesus appeared in person right now in a blaze of light and trumpets, and was all, "Repent, Lee Harvey," I'd be all, "No way, honey."

Liria stifled a giggle behind her fist.

Liria: I can picture it. Jesus appears right now in your bedroom to try to straighten you out, but when The Mare comes in to wake you up in the morning, she finds you and the Lord totally naked and doing it in your bed.

Lee Harvey: I miss you, Jet Ski.

Liria: I miss you too, Lee Harvey. Are you going to go to straight camp?

Lee Harvey: I don't know, it could be fun being cooped up with a bunch of repressed boys. Those guys are crazy easy.

Liria snorted.

Liria: Tell me about it, you whore.

Lee Harvey: Oh, hush. How's it going with your daddy?

Liria's smile faded. She texted him the whole story, amidst his gasping responses.

Liria: And now I'm in Vegas at some guy's house.

Lee Harvey: What is the guy going to have you doing in exchange for a place to stay?

Liria: I don't know. I'd wondered the same thing.

Lee Harvey: Fuck that shit. Get out of there, go

back to Cyryl's. At least you know what to expect from him, and it's harmless enough.

She hesitated, pulling at her bottom lip.

Liria: I might go back there, but I'll stick it out here for a bit, see how it goes.

Lee Harvey: Ahh, I see. You're into this Nadine chick, right?

When she didn't respond, he sent another text.

Lee Harvey: You have too much of a heart, Liria. You need to forget about love and look out for your best interests.

Liria scowled.

Liria: There's nothing wrong with having a heart.

Lee Harvey: Okay, sure, but don't waste it on a fucking stripper coke whore who has problems with the mob, Liria. Because I guarantee you that this chick is looking out for her own best interests.

Liria had to fight down a lump in her throat.

Liria: I'm just so tired of being alone.

Lee Harvey: You'll always have me, Jet Ski.

You and I will never fuck each other around like that. You're my sister, and I love you.

Liria: I love you too, Lee Harvey.

Lee Harvey: If you get tired of hanging out with those goobers let me know. I'll come down there, and we'll do Vegas together.

Liria smiled.

Liria: Really? I don't have much money, though.

Lee Harvey: Don't worry about it. I have my ways. But be sure about it before I come, so you don't run off on me to be with your little stripper.

Liria threw her phone down and put the pillow over her head.

She wished she had a shot to help her sleep, but she eventually dozed off, and woke up when a beam of sunlight hit her in the face.

As her dreams faded, she blinked, watching the drifting dust motes and listening to the silence of the strange house settled around her. The spare room felt desolate and lonely, and Liria had a heavy feeling in her middle. She didn't belong anywhere. She had no home of her own.

She sat up and held her head in her hands until she was able to make herself feel a little better. *At least I'm not dopesick.*

Her phone said it was four minutes after seven. No one was going to be up for a long time, but she was starving. She stared out the window at the suburban roofs and lawns under the hazy, hot Nevada dawn. She doubted there was a restaurant anywhere nearby—it looked like housing developments as far as she could see—but she probably had time to raid the fridge before Perry woke up.

She snuck out of her room, her footsteps silent on the thick shag carpets. As she passed Perry's room at the top of the stairs, she heard something and paused. It was Nadine's voice, moaning, "Ah, that's right, baby, that's how I like it," and Perry's voice, muttering something back.

Liria's stomach curdled, and she slipped quietly back into her room, her appetite gone.

She lay face-down on the bed, breathing steadily through the musty blankets, fighting back the lonely ache in her breast. Lee Harvey was right: Perry seemed like he had a lot of money, and Nadine was just looking out for her best interests. Liria wished she were as cold and calculating. Life would be much easier if she didn't have a heart. She could just stay with Cyryl and pretend to love him in the same way he loved her, without feeling guilty, without wanting something more.

She turned over and lay staring at the sunbeam crawling lazily across the floor, feeling dull and helpless. She thought about texting Lee Harvey to come to Vegas, but she knew he'd probably be asleep now. *And what's the point? If he comes here, what do I do after he goes home again? Go back to*

Cyryl? No matter what she did, she'd just end up homeless and unwanted somewhere else, or else using her body to buy comfort. Sorrow pressed her into the mattress, and she longed desperately for the relief of dope. *I'm never going to have a good life. I'm never going to find a nice woman to love me, so why shouldn't I just be high? Why should I be miserable and sad?*

She could call Lee Harvey, and he'd bring her some. There was no point being sober for a life like this.

Warm, rosy thoughts of being high with her best friend spread over her like a fuzzy blanket. All those good times they'd had together beckoned to her, a stark contrast to her current situation, stuck in a stranger's spare bedroom, hundreds of miles from anyone she knew. But then she thought about the horrible hustles she'd been reduced to when she was sick and had no money. She'd stolen and begged, done disgusting and uncomfortable things.

She clutched her pillow and slowly tried to put herself back together again. *It's better to be clean,* she told herself, over and over again. *No matter how unhappy you are now, it can always get worse.*

After a while, she heard someone moving around. The thought of facing Nadine and Perry made her cringe, but her stomach was growling again, and she'd have to leave the room sometime. She got dressed, then slipped out and went into the kitchen.

She was relieved to find Nestor. He had the fridge open, and he was gazing at the contents with pursed lips. He smiled at her when she came in.

"Nothing in here but hot dogs and pudding cups." He shut the fridge. "Let's go get some breakfast."

Liria twisted the hem of her t-shirt. "What about Nadine and Perry?"

Nestor gave her a dark and knowing look. "Those two won't be up for hours. Come on, let's go."

The morning was already warming up as they got into the car, a shimmering heat haze forming over the distant, dry hills. They wove through residential streets lined with nearly identical, beige stucco houses, and onto the highway. "This looks like a normal town," Liria said. "I always thought Vegas was some weird place."

"You've never been here before? Yeah, it's only the Strip that's all fucked up and epic. The rest of it is just normal. It's a good place to live and work, actually. Lots of money here if you know how to grab it."

He pulled off on an exit and into the parking lot of a diner. The smell of cooking bacon went straight to Liria's stomach when they walked in. "I'm fucking starving," she said, rubbing her belly.

Nestor grinned. "That's what I like to hear."

A waitress seated them in a booth and brought them coffee. Her face was worn and worried, but her smile was kind. Her hair was dyed black, her eyebrows tattooed on. As Liria poured sugar in her coffee, Nestor leaned his elbows on the table. "I wanted to talk to you about something."

Liria got a cold prickle at the back of her neck. "Yeah?"

"I just…You're not, you know, really one of

Cassie's girls. I mean, you don't want to fuck men for money."

"No, I don't," she said, clutching the sugar dispenser.

"Well, I wanted to warn you." He lowered his voice. "Perry and Cassie have a little escort business here, and I'm pretty sure they're going to try to rent you and Nadine out as a team. I heard Cassie talking about how she could make more money off you here than at the club."

Liria's guts writhed and she set the sugar down a little too hard. "What? So was that whole thing with Robert a setup or something?"

"No, no, no. I'm not saying that. I have this feeling they're just going to take advantage of this situation."

Liria stomped her foot. "Fuck that. I knew there would be some sort of catch, but I didn't think it would be that bad."

He smiled grimly, his eyes darting around the restaurant. "Yeah, I didn't figure you'd like it. Nadine doesn't really, either. She's trying to talk Perry out of it." He leaned back in his seat with his hands behind his head, looking out the window. The sound of Nadine fucking Perry shouted through Liria's skull, and she winced, curling in around herself. If Nadine were doing it to try to gain some leverage with him, she didn't see how that would work.

The waitress came to take their orders. When she was gone, Nestor turned back to Liria. "You're not strung out or anything, right? Nadine said you just quit heroin."

"Yeah."

He looked at her thoughtfully. "You're too good for this life. You've gotta find your way out of it."

Liria's gaze dropped to the Formica-topped table. She spun her cup of coffee around and around. "I don't know if that's true."

"Don't say that. Don't let life smack you around and kill your spirit, Liria. You're a nice girl, and tough, and smart, I can tell."

Liria looked up at him, cocking an eyebrow. "Why are you telling me this stuff?"

He broke into a grin. "Man, you are jaded." She just stared at him, and he shrugged. "I just like you, I really do. And I've been wanting to get out from under Cassie for a while. I have a friend here who runs a nightclub, and I was thinking about defecting over there. I hoped you and Nadine would come with me."

"What kind of nightclub?"

"Just a regular one, with DJs and dancing and drunk Vegas tourists. Real jobs, clean ones, pretty much above-ground, and you wouldn't have to do any sex stuff other than harmless flirting."

Liria squinted at him, tapping her coffee cup. "What's the catch?"

He held his hands up in a gesture of innocence. "No catch. I swear, no catch, Liria. I just like you. I like Nadine. You guys deserve better. For my part, I'm tired of being dodgy and carrying a pistol like a thug, and watching all that gyrating, humpety fake sex just gets old, frankly." He looked at her a moment, a tiny smile on his lips. "Though that show you put on with Nadine was something different, I won't lie." He looked like he was about to ask her something, but then just shook his head, and she was glad. She didn't want any more questions from men about her sex life. "Anyway what do you think? Will you do it?"

"Aren't Perry and Cassie going to get pissed if we all leave? And how deep do you go in their operation, anyway? Are they even going to let you go?"

He leaned back in his seat and grinned. "We'll just tell Perry we're going down to the Strip since you've never seen it, and we won't come back. And this is too petty for them to worry about going after us. It's no problem." He sat staring at her, squeezing his spongy hair in his fingers. "So, you in?"

Liria stared at him over her coffee cup, chewing the inside of her cheek. It sounded better than selling her ass for Perry. "Okay, I'll try it."

Nestor grinned widely. "Awesome."

Chapter 12

When they got back to Perry's house, they found Nadine huddled at the breakfast table clutching a mug of instant coffee. Her hair was out of its ponytail and wild, sticking out in all directions. She gave Nestor a loaded look, her pretty mouth twisted up in an angry and desperate frown.

"What's up with you, girl?" Nestor said. He and Liria sat down at the table with her, and her gaze flicked to Liria. Liria held it steadily until some of the wariness went out of it. Nadine searched her face for a moment before turning back to Nestor.

"Perry wants us involved in some bullshit, just like you thought." She scowled. "If I wanted to be a whore, I'd have stayed working for Robert. He says the money will be better than anything we were getting in L.A., but I doubt that. Boston opened his big mouth about Liria just kicking heroin, and I get the feeling he wants to pay us mostly in drugs."

Liria clutched her elbows and stared off at nothing.

"Perry still asleep?" Nestor asked.

127

"Yeah, he'll be sleeping it off a while."

"Well, let's go," Nestor said.

Liria and Nadine looked at him. "What, now?" Nadine said.

Nestor shrugged elaborately. "What, you want to stick around and give Perry a goodbye hug?"

Nadine bolted her coffee and stood up. "Let me get my bag."

As she stretched out in the backseat of Nestor's car, Liria's phone buzzed.

Lee Harvey: I'm coming down there. The Mare just took me to a prayer group, and they all sat in a circle around me, put their veiny old lady hands all over me, and prayed for Satan to get sucked out. I can't deal.

Liria smiled, but then it melted away. She chewed hard on the inside of her cheek, tasting blood. Her fingers hovered over her phone screen, wanting to ask him to bring her dope. She squeezed her eyes shut and clenched her teeth.

Liria: When are you going to be here?

Lee Harvey: Tomorrow morning.

Liria's stomach fizzed. He'd have dope, one way or another. Did he have a connection down here? Her body ached with fear and longing, and she felt a ghost of the dopesickness she'd so recently left behind. She rubbed her eyes with the pads of her fingers until it passed.

Liria: I'm going to try to get a job in some nightclub now. I'll text you when I know what's up.

Lee Harvey: Bailing on your new boss already, eh?

Liria: Yeah, it was some bullshit. They wanted me to be a whore.

Lee Harvey: I thought so. I'm glad you're getting out.

Liria smiled.

Liria: I can't wait to see you.

Lee Harvey: Me too. I'll see you tomorrow.

Liria leaned back in her seat, trying to clear her head.

***

Nestor's friend's nightclub was in one of the hotels on the Strip. When they came down off the highway and into the clamoring jungle of tangled architecture along Las Vegas Boulevard, Liria couldn't keep herself from laughing. "This place is messed up," she said, her nose all but pressed against the window.

Nestor shot her an amused look. "Totally. I love it here."

Nadine frowned distantly as she looked out the windshield, her foot tapping against the floorboards. Liria wondered what her problem was. Maybe she just needed a line or something. Her energy made Liria's teeth clench.

They parked in a cavernous garage behind the casino and walked in through the back door. It was already oppressively hot outside, and it was a relief when the automatic doors opened and the cool blast of air conditioning engulfed them.

The casino floor bubbled with lights and noise. They wove through the aisles between the slot machines and blackjack tables. Nadine kept rubbing her lips together and squeezing the skin of her elbows between her fingers.

Nestor looked askance at her. "You okay, boo?"

"Yeah, I'm okay. Just hope this doesn't turn out to be a shit show."

"It won't," he said.

They took the escalators up to the mezzanine. The nightclub was in the back, closed, a red velvet rope blocking the entrance. Nestor scooted around it, and the other two followed him, ignoring the stares of the people passing by.

They strode across the silent dance floor, a disco ball gleaming dully in the low light. "Cameron!" Nestor yelled. His voice cut rudely through the stillness, and Nadine flinched.

"Who's that?" a voice replied from the back. A young man emerged from a hallway, smiling when he saw Nestor. "It's you already!"

He took stock of Liria and Nadine as he patted Nestor on the back. He was dark-haired, green-eyed, and slick, his checkered button-down shirt tucked into belted white jeans.

"Hey, it's so nice to see you," Cameron said. "I was starting to wonder if you'd been swallowed by a whale or something. The last time I saw you was, what, around Easter?" His eyes kept darting to the women.

"Yeah, in April, that party where the guy got tangled up in the fairy lights." They both snorted with laughter. "Cameron, this is Nadine and Liria, the girls I told you about. This is my friend, Cameron, but you can call him Shrimp."

Cameron grimaced good-naturedly. "No, you can't." He shook their hands. "It's very nice to meet you guys. We should sit down in my office."

Nadine shuffled sullenly as they went into the back, her arms crossed tightly, while Cameron bounced on his feet, swinging his arms and chatting animatedly with Nestor. They went into a small office, which was mostly taken up by a cluttered desk. A tinted window looked out onto the parking garage, and a glass cabinet filled with framed photographs sat in the corner. One of them was of Cameron standing with his arm around Britney Spears, and there were others of him with Hulk Hulgan, Jerry Seinfeld, and Miley Cyrus.

Cameron sat behind the desk, his knees splayed, and the rest of them took chairs on the other side. Liria tapped on the armrests and examined the man in front of her as he flashed them all a white-toothed smile.

"So, you've come crawling to me for jobs, huh?" He laughed.

"Psssh," Nestor said, smiling. "Who's the one that's been begging?"

"I'm just messing with you. I'm glad you're here. Business is good and I need help." He turned his gaze on Liria and Nadine. "Are you guys twenty-one?"

"Yeah," Nadine said.

"No," Liria said, her shoulders tensing as soon as she said it. Should she have lied? But Cameron just smiled.

"No big deal. You mind working under a fake identity?"

Liria pushed her lips into a smile. "No, I don't mind. What would I be doing, exactly?"

He shrugged nonchalantly, but his eyes darted to the corners of the room. "Just waiting tables, mostly. I've been looking for some good servers, and they're harder to find than you'd think, especially ones that look like you guys." Liria felt a dullness spread through her guts. "You could start tonight. Are you in?"

"Sure," Liria said. *It's nothing. Just a job.*

"Whatever," Nadine replied.

***

Cameron spent an hour training them in drink service and running the till. Nadine stared off at the walls like it wasn't worth her time. Liria sent her quizzical glances, but got no response.

He also was able set them up with a room in the hotel at a discounted rate. "It will come straight out of your paycheck," he explained. "You'll have enough for a deposit on an apartment in no time, working for me." He smiled his flawless smile again, and squeezed Liria's shoulder; she stood rigid so she wouldn't jerk away.

They got the key and went to their room for a break. Work started at eight. Their suite was on the second floor and had a view of the hotel behind where they were staying, but the carpets had fresh vacuum tracks and the walls weren't scuffed. It had two queen beds, piled high with pillows and modern, monotone quilts. Liria pressed her chin to her chest and Nestor looked at her with his lips quirked. He offered to take the couch. He sprawled out on it, sighing, his feet sticking over the armrest, and she eyed him sheepishly.

"Thanks, Nestor. What does Cameron have you doing, anyway?"

"Security."

She pursed her lips at him, eyeing his skinny arms, but was distracted by her phone buzzing in her back pocket.

It was Cyryl. Liria sighed and ducked into the bathroom to answer it. Nadine finally looked at her with some semblance of interest as she shut the door.

"Hello?"

"Liria, I miss you." His voice sounded subdued, and she pictured him at work, hiding in his office with the door shut. She gripped the phone tightly. She didn't have it in her right now to sustain the lie that she wanted him. She felt drained and flat.

"Cyryl, I…" She slumped against the wall, staring blankly at herself in the mirror, and turned on the fan so they couldn't hear the conversation outside. "I'm so tired," she found herself saying. "I feel so alone here."

"Come back to me," he said. "I'm lonely without you too."

Liria closed her eyes. She wished she were talking to someone she had an actual emotional connection with, someone who would hear what she was actually saying instead of what they wanted to hear. "I'm not ready to come back yet. I wish I could make you understand."

"Then make me understand, eh? Make me understand why you say you love me, but you won't come back."

Liria's throat tightened. "Because I…I…" She gripped the edge of the granite countertop. *Maybe someday he could love you for who you really are. Besides, you need him…* She took a deep breath. "Cyryl, I've never really loved anyone. I don't know how to do it. I'm afraid you'll fuck me over like everyone else has."

"Liria, you know I wouldn't do that. You know I'm not like those stupid assholes you hang out with. Look at all I've done for you."

"I know. But it's hard. Give me time to trust you. Just don't abandon me." Her voice shook. No matter how she felt about him, and she wasn't even sure she knew how that was, he was all she had, besides Lee Harvey.

"I won't," he said. "I'll never leave you, sweetheart. You need any money? Are you okay?"

"I don't need money. I'm okay." *Look at how good I am. I don't need your money.*

"Are you sure?"

"I'm sure."

He sighed. "Good, good. I love you, baby."

"I love you too, Cyryl."

She hung up the phone, staring blankly at her reflection. How long before she started believing her own lies? Would it be so bad if she did?

***

Working in the nightclub was like a strange dream. She was the scaffolding that held up other people's drunken shitheadedness. She went around cleaning tables and taking orders, dodging the increasingly glassy-eyed, loudmouthed, grabby clientele on the dance floor. She forgot a couple of drinks, and a woman yelled at her for bringing her an old fashioned instead of a scotch on the rocks, but overall it wasn't so bad. She took pride in being one of the few sober and useful people in the room.

The crowd started to thin out at around three in the morning. Liria cleared some empty glasses from a table in the corner, where a woman sat staring at her phone. The woman looked up, and as their eyes met, Liria's heart stuttered. The dim light of the bar fell over her, making her look like a Renaissance painting done by candlelight. Her pupils were large and ringed by clear irises, which were a light color. Liria couldn't tell which. She had a thick, strawberry blonde braid falling over her left shoulder. She smiled; she had a lot of lip to smile with, and Liria watched them in fascination.

"Hard night?" the woman asked.

Liria smiled back and shrugged. "I've had worse. Can I get you anything?"

The woman paused a moment before responding, with an uncertain half-smile. Liria felt warmth spread all the way down to her toes. All of a sudden, it was like they were the only two people in the room. "A diet Coke?" the woman said.

Liria rushed to the kitchen with her tray full of empty glasses, then to the bar, filling up a glass with diet soda. Cameron was counting money at the till, and looked Liria up and down out of the corner of his eye, smirking. "Good job tonight," he said. "You can call it quits after you take that out."

"Thanks, Cameron."

Liria brought out the drink to the red-haired woman, who watched her walk up.

"Thanks," the woman said. She opened her mouth again and closed it, biting her amazing bottom lip. What she wanted to say was laid out there between them.

Liria let those unsaid words soak into her body. "Is there…something else you want?" She felt her cheeks go hot.

The woman laughed. She had a giggly laugh, like a kid. She stirred her Coke with the straw. "When do you get off work?"

"He just let me off." The words poured out of her mouth too quickly, and she shifted on her feet, wincing.

"Can I buy you a drink?"

Liria smiled, not quite able to believe her luck. "Yes…I mean, you don't have to buy it. I get them free." She hoped the light was low enough to cover

136

her flaming cheeks. "I'll be right back."

She went back behind the bar and got herself a Coke, feeling Cameron's eyes on her as he tallied receipts. "Hanging out for a bit?" he asked.

She glanced in his direction, wrinkling her nose.

"She's cute," he said. "Good luck. And, oh, Liria?" She stopped as she was going back out to the floor. He came up to her and put a hand on her shoulder as he spoke close to her ear. "If you're going to leave with that woman, come have a quick chat with me first."

Her brow furrowed. "About what?"

He patted her shoulder. "Nothing important. Just want to get something straight about our policy regarding customers." He grinned at her raised eyebrows. "Don't worry about it, screw whoever you want, send me pictures, I don't mind. Just talk to me first."

"Um, okay."

He squeezed her shoulder and walked off. Liria watched after him a moment, then went out to sit with the woman.

The redhead scooted over on the bench seat, and Liria sat down next to her, clutching her glass. She wore a skirt and tall boots and a grey v-neck t-shirt. Liria couldn't keep herself from looking at her bare expanses of smooth, freckled skin. Liria wondered if she had those freckles everywhere.

"I'm Arty," the woman said, and smiled at Liria's look. "Short for Artemis. My mom…well, you can imagine. One of those hippie types."

Liria laughed. "I'm Liria. My mom was just crazy."

"And Hispanic, maybe. *Lirio* means lily in Spanish, right?"

Liria sipped her Coke and nodded. "I don't speak it, and neither did my mom, but she still named me that for some reason. You speak Spanish?"

"Just a little." Arty studied her closely. "Your mom…she's dead?"

The bench seat creaked as Liria shifted, not sure where to look. "Yeah, years ago. But we weren't close."

"Still, I'm sorry."

Liria chewed her straw. The woman was looking at her like she needed a sympathy hug, and that wasn't the look she wanted from her. "Enough about our crazy hippie moms," she said. "What brings you to Vegas?"

Arty laughed again. There was something unconstrained about the sound that made Liria think she'd be really good in bed. "I'm here on business," she said. "My boss is here for a conference and he brought me along."

Liria pictured the freckles on her thighs. Or would they be eggshell pale? "What do you do?"

"I'm a personal assistant." Arty smiled wanly. "It's boring work. I make a lot of phone calls, pick up dry cleaning."

Arty sipped her drink, her lips puckering around the straw, soft like a glazed donut. Liria looked around the bar, uncrossing and crossing her legs, the bench squeaking again. Nadine was still waiting tables, confronting the customers with a face like they'd just offered to fuck her mom with a crowbar. Nestor was behind the bar with Cameron, probably talking business.

She looked back at Arty, who watched her with a faint smile. Liria had no idea how to do small talk. Most of her relationships got pretty quickly to the sex or the yelling or the drug deal. She wondered what this woman would do if she just scooted over and pressed her lips to the little, pert crack between her tits, but figured that wouldn't go over well. She was a personal assistant, whatever that was, in tall boots she probably got at Nordstrom.

Arty's grin bloomed again, lopsided and sly. "How long have you lived in Vegas?"

"Just got here today, actually."

Her eyebrows shot up. "Oh, really? Where did you live before?"

"Central Coast of California. Paso Robles."

"You came here for this job?"

Liria shook her head, her brow furrowing slightly. "I just came. With a friend. I just sort of ended up here, but luckily my friend knew the guy who runs the place." She sipped her Coke, watching the fizz bubbles find their way around the ice cubes. She could feel Arty giving her that you-need-a-hug look again. This is why she couldn't make conversation with normal people. Even the simplest of inquiries into her personal life led to her involuntarily hocking an emotional loogie onto the table. When she looked back over, Arty broke into a grin again. Her back teeth were a little mismatched and cute.

"Vegas is a pretty great place to just end up. I love it here."

Liria felt a shy smile creeping up into her face

from some place where it had hidden, forgotten in the darkness, for years. "Why do you love it here?"

Arty shrugged, ducking her head. "I love watching people being ridiculous."

Liria laughed. "Is that why you're talking to me?"

Arty snorted, and stretched one of her crossed legs out to nudge her, the soft leather of her boot brushing Liria's bare ankle. Liria's breath caught in her throat. "No," Arty said.

Their eyes met, and Liria felt her body lean toward her. *Why are you talking to me, then?* she wanted to ask. But that was too bold. It would be the conversational equivalent of snapping her bra or giving her a gentle titty-twister. "Well, I'm glad you're talking to me," she said instead. "I'm sure I'll do something ridiculous soon enough, to keep you entertained."

Arty laughed.

They talked. Arty made it easy for her by not asking personal questions. She told a story about how she'd gone to Europe with a couple friends after college, how they'd tried to buy weed in Frankfurt and ended up in this weird, cramped flat with some guy's sister trying to do sex things to them for money. Then she told another about being at a party in San Diego, and some Mexican guy had offered her thirty thousand dollars to marry him for immigration reasons.

Arty lived in New York, but came to Vegas a lot. "Just about once a month," she said. *She made a point of mentioning it.*

It was almost four in the morning by the time

Arty checked her phone and said she needed to leave. "You going to be here tomorrow?" she asked.

Liria nodded, curling her fingers in her lap so she didn't reach out and hook her by the shirt collar, sliding her finger between her breasts, pulling her closer.

"I'll be here," Arty said. "I promise."

Liria sighed as she walked out. She didn't want her to leave, but it wasn't so bad watching her go. She had an ass like she did a lot of yoga.

Liria took their glasses back to the kitchen, the melting ice cubes swimming in brown water. Cameron shook his head at her, grinning, as she walked past the bar. "That's tough, girl," he said. "Better luck next time."

She stuck out her tongue. "Oh, shut up. She says she's coming back tomorrow."

He gave her an odd look. "That's sweet of her."

Nadine had just ended her shift, so they wandered together through sparse crowds out of the club. Some people were fall-down drunk after a long night, others were just waking up and settling into their slot machine routine. Liria's eyeballs throbbed with fatigue and she felt like her feet had been put through the wringer. Nadine strode along beside her through the glittering casino floor to the elevators, her tight lips holding back a snarl. Liria finally couldn't stand it any longer. "What's your problem?" she asked.

"This is bullshit, is what," Nadine burst out as the elevator doors slid closed. "I want to go back to L.A."

Nadine's eyes filled with tears as she stared at

the mirrored elevator walls, clutching at the short skirt of her uniform. The doors opened again, and the two of them were silent as they walked down the hall to their room, Liria staring at the hypnotic geometric carpet pattern rather than at the other girl.

"What is there for you in L.A.?" Liria asked when they were shut in their room. "Why do you want to go back there?"

"My people are there. My sister and my nephew. They're not much, but they're all I have. And my sister said she was going to help me get a job at the nursing home she works at when a spot opens. A real job for once." She flung herself down on the couch. "But that fucking Robert went and fucked up my life again."

Liria stood picking at her cuticles, hoping she wasn't the one giving Nadine the you-need-a-hug look now. "This is a real job, right? Better than what we were doing in L.A., at least, or what Perry would've had us doing."

Nadine rolled her eyes. "This ain't no real job. Seems like it for now, maybe, but just wait. This world only wants one thing out of girls like us. There's only one thing we're good at." Nadine looked up at her, her eyes hopeless and furious, and Liria's shoulders slumped. She sat down next to her. Tentatively, she put her arm around her and pulled her head onto her shoulder. Nadine let her, tears streaming down her face.

"We're good at other things," Liria said. "It doesn't have to be like that."

Nadine sat silently, nestled in the crook of Liria's arm. After a while, she got up and washed her face and got into bed. Liria did the same, feeling hollow.

She dreamt she was back at Cyryl's place. He had a swimming pool in the middle of his condo floor. The sun shone through the crystal blue water, casting graceful patterns of light all across the ceiling. Liria swam and dove, twisting through the water like a seal.

Cyryl stood on the side, tossing glittering trinkets into the water, golden starfish and little charm bracelets with dangling ships and fish set with jewels. Liria retrieved them, tossing them back up into the air for him to catch.

"That's good, baby," he said. He pulled a hoop from behind the couch, and held it above the water. He snapped his fingers and it burst into blue flames, which shimmered like the water, graceful and translucent in the sunlight. The fire licked around the hoop's edges and his fingers, not seeming to burn either. "Now jump up, sweetheart. Show me what you can do."

Liria retreated to the other end of the pool, then dove into the water, kicking her legs to gather speed. The water sparkled around her like liquid diamonds as she shot through it. She concentrated hard as she approached the hoop, flinging herself out of the water at just the right moment. She glided through the ring of flames, flying through the air, her body twisting sinuously, then descended in a graceful arc and plunged back into the water, which embraced her body like smooth silk. She floated back up toward the surface and emerged, beaming happily at Cyryl.

"Good job, Liria," he said. "We're almost ready for the show."

***

Liria woke in the soft hotel bed. The sun shone mutedly through the thick curtains and the air conditioning hummed. The unfamiliar walls of the hotel jarred her for a moment; she couldn't remember where she was, but then it all came back to her. She turned over. The clock on the bedside table said it was 11:49.

Nadine's bed was empty, the blankets rumpled, but Nestor was still curled up on the couch, wrapped in a quilt and snoring softly.

A note of tension lingered in the air. Liria sat up and looked around.

Nadine's purse and shoes were gone, and Liria's backpack lay in the corner, open, her clothes pulled out of it and scattered across the floor.

Liria jumped out of bed, cursing. The front pocket where she'd stashed her money was empty. She checked the pocket again, and then dug through the rest of the backpack, hoping the money would suddenly appear there, that it was a joke or a mistake.

"That fucking cunt!" Liria yelled. "That stupid bitch!" She cursed herself for being stupid enough to trust Nadine.

Nestor sat up, snorting, his eyes wide and bewildered. "Whatsgoinon?"

Liria began to cry, tears coating her cheeks.

"Fucking Nadine is gone, and she took my money."

His eyes gained focus, and he grimaced. "Shit." He jumped up, his long, skinny legs bare under his boxers, and went over to his own bag. "Fuck me," he moaned. It was also open, the contents flung all over the floor. He dug through it, muttering to himself. "Fuck that. Fuck that."

Liria felt a bit better. At least they were both stupid together. But the world was a cruel place when you had no money, full of dirty hustles that slurped you up and spat you out slimy at the end, your full belly slowly emptying, the next hustle already lurking.

He looked up at her, the anger in his eyes fading to pity when he saw her crying. He came over and took her in his arms.

"Don't cry," he said.

"That bitch," she muttered, pressing her cheek against his t-shirt. *I comforted her. I thought she liked me.* She squeezed her eyes shut.

"It's okay, Liria," Nestor said, stroking her hair. "Don't worry about it. We counted the money last night, and you made about two hundred in tips. Cameron will give us Nadine's tips too when we tell him what happened, and she made almost as much as you did."

Liria took a deep and shuddering breath, her stomach unknotting a little. She'd forgotten about their tips. Why had Nadine even left? She could have made more money sticking around than stealing from them.

"Don't worry about it," Nestor said again. "We're better off than she is, wherever she is. She'll get hers."

Liria leaned against him, taking another deep breath. He was right. Everyone got theirs in the end.

Chapter 13

They went to the buffet and charged it to their room. Liria piled her plate up high with fried chicken and mashed potatoes, and Nestor laughed at her when she sat down. "You can go back, you know. You don't have to, like, break the plate with all that food at once."

"I'm hungry," Liria said, her mouth full.

"Good," he said, munching a mozzarella stick. "You could use some meat on you."

Liria scowled. She felt her phone buzz and took it out, her expression brightening. "Lee Harvey's here," she said.

"Who?"

"My friend, from back home." She typed out a reply. "He's on his way to the hotel."

Nestor grunted, his sharp eyes on her, and Liria hid her face behind her hair. *Just because he's here doesn't mean I'll have to get high.* "Lee Harvey's a good guy," she said. "And he's getting his own hotel room so you don't have to worry about it. He's not a mooch." When Nestor kept looking at

147

her, she threw down her chicken breast. "Hey, you're the one that thought Nadine was trustworthy, so don't look all like that about *my* friends."

He winced and poked at his food. "I thought she was trustworthy, but I think she just couldn't live without the coke." He looked back up at Liria, his lips curling into a faint grin. "And what kind of name is Lee Harvey, anyway?"

Liria broke into a reluctant smile and picked her chicken back up. "His mom is a fucking hot mess. She hates the Catholics and thinks J.F.K. getting shot was part of Jesus' plan."

Nestor laughed. "Holy shit."

Liria rolled her eyes. "Yeah, I know."

***

Lee knocked on the door of their hotel room when they were lounging off their unnatural buffet fullness, watching a reality show about teenage gypsies.

Liria jumped up to answer it. Lee Harvey stood there in his rolled-up skinny jeans and neon sneakers, his arms open. She fell into them.

"Jet Ski, oh I missed you." He hugged her tight. Then he held her out in front of him, his hands on her shoulders. "Let me look at you. You're so pretty! Your eyes are so bright! You look so good! I'm so proud of you for getting off the bug juice."

Liria felt sick heat rise to her face. *I won't ask him for dope.* "Thanks, Lee Harvey."

"And I have a surprise for you," he said, grinning. "You inspired me. I quit too."

She looked him over appraisingly. He stood still, withstanding her inspection, the corners of his mouth twitching. It was hard to tell. His pupils weren't contracted and he wasn't as pale as usual. She gave him another hug. "Wow, Lee Harvey. That's great. I'm proud of you too." If he were lying, it was to make sure she *didn't* ask him for dope, so that she could stay clean…and so he could keep it for himself, in a place where he had no connection.

She stood aside and he came into the room. Nestor lay back on his pillows, watching him with a hint of amusement. "Lee, this is Nestor," Liria said.

Nestor held out his hand, and Lee came over to shake it. "Pleasure to meet you," Nestor said.

"Nice to meet you too," Lee said, in the sort of hesitating voice he used for straight guys he thought were good-looking. Liria hid her grin behind her fist. Lee was such a slut.

Nestor gazed at Lee pensively. "You're staying here in the hotel?"

"Yeah," Lee said. "I just checked in for a week." Liria wondered how he'd paid for it, and decided she didn't want to know.

"You know," Nestor said, "if you wanted a job…the place where we work just had an unexpected opening, and I think you're the kind of person the owner is looking for."

Lee's glittering hazel eyes darted from Nestor to Liria. "A…a *job*?" He smirked slightly. "Is that this nightclub thingy you were talking about, Jet Ski?"

Liria nodded, her eyes fixed on Nestor.

"It's a good job," Nestor said, "pays really well

and you get a discount on a hotel room."

Lee had a sort of frozen look, his mouth partly open. He glanced questioningly at Liria, who shrugged slightly. It could be fun working with Lee Harvey, though she had to repress a shudder of foreboding. *It's nothing. Just a job. You're being paranoid.*

Lee grinned sparklingly at Nestor. "All right. I'll try out for the job, if you want."

***

Nestor explained to Cameron what had happened with Nadine, and he agreed to split her tips between them and advance them in cash. "Sorry that happened, you guys," he said as he counted the bills out on the bar, which was clean and shiny, smeared only with their distorted reflections. "Some people just don't know how to live right."

They introduced Lee Harvey. Cameron took one look at him and hired him on the spot. He spent some time training him while Liria and Nestor did laundry and took a nap. When all three of them reported for duty a little before eight, Cameron took Liria and Lee aside.

"It's Friday night," he said, "so be ready to get slammed. Tips can be really good if you're friendly and give good service."

Liria caught his look and the tone of his voice, and her scalp prickled. Lee Harvey apparently noticed it too, because they exchanged a glance.

***

The club filled up fast that night, as Cameron had predicted. Even though there were five other servers on duty and four bartenders, Liria was so busy she didn't have time to breathe. Even so, she kept scanning the crowd for Arty, getting little thrills of adrenaline every time she saw a girl with red hair, or a round ass swaying on the dance floor. But none of them were her. She wasn't anywhere. *She didn't like me. She'd never like someone like me. She was just being nice. If she'd really wanted me, she'd have taken me back to her room last night.*

The dance floor was crowded, and quite a few men tried to pull her onto it as she skirted past, trying to get to the tables. Cameron kicked one of the drunks out when he grabbed her, making her spill a tray of drinks. He was some guy in a faded 49ers t-shirt with a strip-mall haircut who stumbled and slurred his curses as a security guy dragged him out by the arm.

Later, when she bent over to pick up a cleaning rag, Liria felt fingers slide up the crack of her ass. She turned, fuming and sick, to find a man in expensive jeans grinning at her, his friends laughing into their drinks. Cameron came over and patted the guy's shoulder and made him apologize to her as she stood twisting the rag in her hands

He took her aside afterwards. "That guy's the CEO of a Silicon Valley tech company. Just for your information, in case that sort of thing makes you like him more."

She glanced back at the guy with his douchey bedhead hairdo, a thick gold wedding ring on his stubby finger. "It doesn't," she said, and Cameron nodded.

"Fair enough." He looked down his nose at her before slipping back through the crowd to the bar.

At about midnight, when she and Lee Harvey were both filling up their trays with drinks, Lee leaned over and spoke in her ear. "I think I've found the man of my dreams." He wiggled his eyebrows, grinning. Her shoulders tensed as she watched him walk off toward the back, his hips swaying in his tight shorts.

Liria didn't get a chance to see Lee's supposed soulmate until much later, when the place started to clear out. Most of the customers were too drunk to do much else besides flop on back to their rooms and await their crushing hangovers. She was clearing away glasses and wiping tables when she saw Lee in a dark corner with a man. He was older but good-looking, his brown hair cut slick and parted on the side, his jaw strong and even. He had on jeans and a button-down shirt, but he wore both uncomfortably. It reminded Liria of the time she'd seen her high school principal at the grocery store on a weekend. He'd looked weird in his street clothes, like he still should have been in a suit, and this guy looked the same way. He was too clean-cut to be hanging out with someone like Lee Harvey, jeans or no.

Lee Harvey was practically sitting in his lap. The man smiled, showing abnormally sharp incisors like a vampire, and she snorted to herself. Lee would probably be turned on if the guy really were a vampire.

When she turned to go back to the bar, she noticed a woman sitting in the far corner, watching her. She smiled when she saw Liria looking, and Liria felt a pang of sweetness. It was Arty.

Liria walked over, trying not to rush. "Hey," she said. "I thought you weren't going to come."

"I've been here awhile, but I was hiding behind the morons."

Liria scrunched her lips up against a giggle. "Can I get you anything? Diet Coke?"

"Please."

Liria floated over to the bar as Cameron watched her with raised eyebrows. "She did come back. Well, I'll be damned."

"Told you," Liria said, smirking as she poured the diet Coke.

"I've got more good news for you," Cameron said. "You're off for the night."

She looked up at him. She glanced over at Lee Harvey, who was still in close conversation with Vampire Man, and Cameron grinned wryly.

"Your friend was officially off-duty an hour ago, but he's still working it. He might be here awhile." He winked. "Just remember what I told you last night, about seeing me before you leave with her."

Liria nodded, frowning, as he turned to take an order. Curiosity gripped her as to what his "policy regarding customers" was. Something made her not want to ask.

Arty watched her as she brought up her drink. "Are you off soon?"

"He just let me off."

Arty scooted over on the bench to let her sit down.

Liria picked at her cuticles. "I really didn't think you were coming."

Arty broke into a slow grin. She reached out and took Liria's hand. "Of course I did. I said I would, right?"

Liria's breath caught in her throat. They gazed at each other a moment, then Arty leaned forward and their lips met.

Those lips felt every bit as good as Liria had imagined they would, soft and gentle but full of need. Arty's kiss made Liria want to lay her out on the bench seat.

The other woman pulled back slowly and smiled. Liria's fingers crept up her knee, sneaking under the hem of her skirt.

Arty's smile vanished. Liria followed her gaze and saw Lee Harvey leaving with his mystery man.

She abruptly gathered up her purse. "I'm sorry, I'd better go." She looked at Liria, who sat stricken, her mouth falling open. "I really am sorry. Will you be here tomorrow?"

"Yeah," Liria said in a small voice.

"I'll try to make it back." Arty stood there, clutching her purse. For a breathless moment, Liria thought she might change her mind, or at least give her a phone number. But then her mouth hardened and she went out after the two men.

Liria watched her go, her chest aching. Arty must work for the man Lee Harvey was hanging on. But personal assistants weren't expected to take

154

notes during their bosses' dirty sex, were they?

Maybe she just hadn't liked her, and was looking for an excuse to leave. Maybe she thought she kissed like a slobbery puppy or something. Was her breath bad? She checked it, breathing against her cupped hand, but couldn't smell anything.

Liria took the glasses back to the kitchen, her lips still tingling, which just made it worse. Cameron caught her eye, looking startled for some reason. "Tough luck," he said.

Liria shrugged.

She limped back to her room on sore feet, took a shower, and fell asleep watching a reality show about a religious family with an overabundance of very hot daughters.

Chapter 14

Liria woke to a violent pounding at the door. The digital clock next to the bed said it was one in the afternoon. "Housekeeping!" a voice announced in a shrill, ascending shriek more appropriate to warning guests of an approaching tornado.

Liria hauled herself out of bed, told the maid to come back later, and took another shower.

She let the water run over her head, thinking about Arty. *Don't let it get to you. She's just some girl.* By the time she got out, Nestor was awake, and they headed down to the buffet together.

Lee Harvey didn't answer their knock when they went by to see if he wanted to come. The **'Do Not Disturb'** sign was on the door.

"He was probably out late with his man," Nestor said. "Don't bug him."

She sent Lee a text when they were eating, hoping it would wake him up.

Liria: Your friend convince you to vote Republican?

She didn't get a response. Cyryl called when they were at the table, but she didn't have the heart to answer it. She'd call him later.

Later that afternoon, when she and Nestor were lounging on their beds watching Simpsons reruns, she texted Lee again.

Liria: Must have been a long night, big boy.

She tapped her phone against her knee, her eyes darting to the screen every few seconds, but no response came. "I hope they didn't run off together," she said.

"Maybe they took Cameron with them, built some sort of dick pyramid," Nestor said, and Liria snorted. "I've been trying to get a hold of him to ask if we should come in early tonight, and he's not answering. It's not like him."

Liria stood and stared out the window, rolling her phone over and over in her hands. "I'm going to go for a walk."

Nestor gazed at her with slightly pursed lips. "Okay."

She took the elevator down and wandered around the crowded casino, scanning the aisles and chairs for Arty. Did she gamble? She didn't seem like a slots girl. Maybe poker, or blackjack on an off day. But it was just dull-eyed, wispy-haired gamblers at the slot machines and tables, tourists crowding the aisles, and she forced herself to quit looking. *Stop being a dork. She ran out on you like you farted in her face. She doesn't like you.*

Depressed, she slouched into the hallway by the

bathrooms and called Cyryl. "Hey, beautiful, how's the waitressing going?" he asked.

"It's all right, really." She flicked the ends of her hair between her fingers.

"Hah. You shouldn't be doing that crap. Come home and I'll get you a job with me."

Liria grinned wryly to herself. "I might do that. But then you'll get fired when you get caught fucking me on your desk."

Cyryl made a low noise in his throat, and Liria stared at the carpet, daydreaming about pushing Arty back onto a desk, pushing her tweed skirt up over her hips, and searching her thighs for freckles.

"Baby, I want to do that to you right now," Cyryl said huskily.

"You want me to fuck you?" Liria said, closing her eyes. "You want me to crawl on top of you on your desk and fuck you?"

"Mmm, oh yes, baby, I want that. I want you to ride my dick with your little wet pussy."

"I want you deep inside. I want you to make me come." She wanted Arty's long fingers inside her as Liria sucked on her nipples, stray paperclips digging into her bare knees.

"I'll make you come, Liria. I'll fuck you deep. I'll pound my cock in you deep and make you come hard—ohhh."

After she hung up, she opened her eyes to find a short Hispanic guy watching her as he wheeled a garbage can down the hall. She ducked into the bathrooms and rubbed one off, thinking about Arty as two ladies at the sinks talked about Keno.

Lee Harvey still hadn't texted her as she left the

bathroom. She decided to go out on the Strip. It took her a while to find the front doors, the aisles around the slot machines winding in circles, but eventually she spotted them.

The heat pounded against her skin like a hammer. The sidewalks were crowded with sweaty tourists. She went to the drugstore and bought some new lipstick and body butter, still checking her phone.

Finally, she went back into the cool hotel, took the elevator back to Lee's room on the eighth floor, and knocked again. "Lee Harvey, wake up," she said, pounding harder. He didn't answer. The **'Do Not Disturb'** sign was still hanging on the knob. Maybe he'd gone back to the other guy's room and had been there all day, but he would have wanted to gossip about it with her by now. Surely the Clean Cut Vampire would have given him at least five minutes respite to send a text.

"That your friend in there?"

Liria turned. It was a round-faced maid, wheeling a cart laden with towels and soaps down the hall.

"Yeah, it's my friend's room," Liria said. "I'm worried about him. I haven't heard from him all day."

The maid smiled. "Hungover, maybe."

"No, he doesn't drink. We work together at the nightclub here. He should be up by now."

"Aaaah. You work at the nightclub? Is it a good place?"

Liria smiled. "Yeah, it's crazy, but I like working there. Just started a couple days ago."

The maid squinted at her in silence for a moment. She shrugged. "I'll go in, see if your friend's there sleeping. Maybe he needs some towels anyway."

Liria stood back from the door as the woman knocked on it again. "Housekeeping," she said, but she only waited a few seconds before sliding her master key and opening the door.

Liria peered inside, shifting her weight from foot to foot. It was dim in the room, the curtains closed. The maid wandered in with a duck-footed waddle. "Anyone home?" She stopped dead. A second later, she rushed toward the bed, saying, "Ohmygod, ohmygod, are you okay?"

Liria's blood ran cold. She dashed into the room. The maid was bent over the gap between the bed and the wall. A sneakered foot protruded past the end of the bed, and Liria felt a sickening jolt: it was Lee Harvey's neon sneaker. She pushed past the maid, who was wailing in Spanish, and saw Lee Harvey sprawled out on the carpet. His limbs were at weird angles, his neck propped up against the base of the armchair. His eyes were partially closed, one more than the other, the vacant pupils showing under the lids. Liria's breath stopped. *It can't be.* She blinked.

The maid turned toward her, her face screwed up with anguish. "He's dead!" she screeched.

Liria fell to her knees by Lee's side, a sob escaping her throat. She grabbed his hand, but quickly jerked away. His flesh had been cold and stiff under her fingers.

"Lee Harvey," she choked out. She couldn't

believe it; it wouldn't register. She kept expecting him to sit up and smile and tell her it was a stupid joke. She kept thinking she saw his chest move as he took a breath.

The maid fumbled with the walkie-talkie in her belt and started speaking rapidly into it in Spanish, her tone frantic. She went back out in the hallway, crying. There was a hiss of static as someone responded over the radio, sounding incredulous.

Liria knelt there by her friend with her heart pounding in her ears. For a few moments it didn't occur to her to do anything different.

Her gaze fell on something on the bedside table. It was a little nugget of dope, a syringe, a spoon with a brown wad of cotton, and the residue of his last shot.

Liria's junkie instincts took over and she grabbed it, all of it, and shoved it in the pocket of her shorts as she stood up.

The maid continued to wail into her walkie-talkie. Liria looked down at Lee Harvey. He didn't look like her friend anymore. His body looked weird, like a mannequin. She gulped air, her vision clouding. *He overdosed.* Slowly, she turned away. She didn't want to be here. She wanted a shot, wanted to get back to her room, wanted to wake up and be somewhere else, someone else. Wanted it to go away.

She headed for the door, but just before she got there a figure blocked it.

Liria felt like she'd been hit by lightning. It was Arty. "Everything okay in here?" she said. Then she got an odd look on her face. "Liria?"

Liria clutched her elbows, her chest tight.

"What's wrong?" Arty asked. Arty hesitated slightly, then put her arms around her. Liria stood stiffly, not sure whether to collapse into her arms or run away.

Arty examined her face, then pushed past her and went into the room. She looked down at Lee Harvey. She didn't scream, or gasp, or even flinch. She just went pale, her lips forming a hard line. She came back over and put her arm around Liria's shoulders, guiding her out of the room. "Come on," she muttered. "You don't want to be here when the police come, right?"

Liria shook her head. They went down the hall, and Arty unlocked another door at the end, holding it open so Liria could go in.

It was a suite with a separate sitting room. It had floor-to-ceiling windows and a balcony overlooking the Strip.

Arty turned to her, her brow furrowing. In daylight she looked older than she had at the bar, with slight wrinkles around her eyes. Liria clutched herself around her middle so she didn't fall apart. She had a hard time breathing. Her chest wasn't big enough for her lungs.

"He was a friend of yours?" Arty asked.

Liria choked on a sob, making a horrible noise. Arty pulled her into her arms. "Hush. It's okay, it's okay." Liria huddled there, trembling. It felt good in Arty's arms. It felt good, if she didn't think about anything else.

Eventually, Arty led her into the bedroom. There was a king-sized bed, neatly made, and Arty pulled back the covers. She helped Liria take her shoes off. Liria winced as she sat down, the needle in her pocket poking her. It was sticking out, along with the handle of the spoon, and Arty saw it, her eyes going wide. Arty slapped Liria's hand away as she reached for it, and pulled the stuff out herself with careful jerks, dropping it on the bedspread: the syringe, the spoon, the dope.

Liria's hand made an involuntary grabbing motion to take it back, but she stopped short when Arty's eyes flew wide. "Don't touch it!" Her look softened somewhat. "Is that stuff from your friend's room?"

Liria's brow furrowed slightly. She nodded.

Arty grimaced. "Are you crazy?" She examined Liria closely. "Stay here, okay? I'll be right back. Will you stay here?"

Liria nodded mutely. Arty went into the bathroom and came back with a washcloth, then used it to carefully pick up the paraphernalia from the bedspread. Liria watched her do it, opening her mouth twice to protest, but shutting it again both times. She desperately wanted a shot, but she let her take it away.

Arty left. Liria heard the door close, and she wrapped her arms around herself. She sat, looking out the window. The city was spread out below, filled with little people crawling along the sidewalks, the Strip jammed with cars. Far away, past the city, a line of dry, empty ridges rose up. All that world out there, still somehow functioning, existing, even though Lee Harvey was gone.

Liria shivered. Lee Harvey was gone. He had

blinked out of the world. He'd been wrapped up in his life, living it like it would never end, but now it was over.

She squeezed her eyes shut, tears leaking from beneath her lids. A powerful wave of agitation hit her, and she stood up. She should leave. She should run as far away from here as possible, to a place where the pain couldn't touch her. Back to Paso. She could go to Avery's. If she could just get high, then she would be able to think straight. She'd know what to do. She clenched her fists thinking of the dope Arty had just taken away. Why had she let the bitch do that? Why hadn't she stopped her?

She heard the door open again, and Arty came back in. Her hands were empty, the dope gone. Liria looked at her, and her fists unclenched. Her red hair was loose, falling in smooth waves over one shoulder. Liria remembered the feeling of her lips, the taste of her tongue.

Arty came over and took her in her arms again, and Liria let her, clenching her teeth against her grief and indecision. "It's okay," Arty whispered. Liria took a shuddering breath, her desire to run away faltering in the warmth of the other woman's embrace.

"He's dead," Liria said, and her grief clutched her and dragged her down. "Lee Harvey's dead."

"I'm sorry, Liria."

Liria huddled against Arty again. After a while, the other woman helped her out of her shorts, then gently pushed her back on the pillows, where she lay as rigid as a log. Arty went into the bathroom and came back with a bottle of pills and a glass of water. She helped her sit up again, and shook some pills out onto her palm.

"Here, take these," she said.

Liria stared at the little white pills. She looked up into Arty's eyes. In the daylight, she could see they were light green tinged with blue, a beautiful color.

"It's okay, they'll just help you sleep," Arty said.

Liria's eyes unfocused as she thought about sinking down below the pain. She took the pills between her fingertips, dropped them on her tongue where they started to dissolve into bitterness. Quickly, she gulped some water, wincing.

"Those will help," Arty said. "Lie down, you'll feel better in a bit."

Liria laid back. Above her, a fire alarm blinked in the popcorn ceiling, and she stared at it blankly. Arty sat next to her, stroking her hand. Warmth began to ooze into her, her brain filling with white noise.

Arty's voice rippled through the liquid cocoon that surrounded her. "You knew your friend before you started working there at that nightclub?"

Liria's voice seemed to come out of some detached corner of her body. "I've known him for a long time. I was a foster kid in his house." Her voice broke. Lee Harvey was gone. All those nights they'd stayed up together, gossiping, slugging back cough syrup and giggling at nothing; all those times they'd skipped school and laid in the park, staring at the sky. They were over forever. Dulled pain thumped through her, and she clutched the blankets, tears washing her cheeks. Arty stretched out next to her, gathering her in her arms.

The bed rocked on gentle waves. The streaks of sunlight on the ceiling rippled, reflections off of choppy water. Arty's voice came from a great distance as Liria floated away from her. "You're living in this hotel? You and your friend?"

"We're staying here. Wanted to earn enough money to get a real place."

"Who were you living with before?"

Liria clutched at the blankets, which seemed insubstantial under her fingers, melting away into another reality. "Nowhere. I didn't have anywhere." She squirmed, and Arty's arms tightened around her.

"Did you live in New York before you came here?"

"No, I lived in Paso Robles." No, that wasn't right. She had been with Cyryl...had she? It seemed unreal now. "I mean, I was in L.A., right before I came here."

"What's your relation to Peter Czetski?"

Liria tried to navigate the twists and turns of her thoughts in order to make sense of that. "Who?"

"Peter Czetski, in New York. How are you related to him?"

Liria shook her head trying to clear it. "I don't know...I'm not really a Czetski. Cyryl...Cyryl's not really my dad." She hugged herself. She felt like she was tangled up in a net like a dolphin, and thrashed around trying to throw it off.

"It's okay, Liria," Arty said. "It's okay. Shhh." Arty's arms were wrapped around her, strong and warm. They felt like a net. Arty stroked her hair. It felt good, and Liria quit struggling.

166

"How long had you known the owner of that nightclub?" Arty asked.

It took a lot of effort to answer. She had to search around in the thick mud of her thoughts for words, and she barely remembered how to move her tongue. "Just met him."

"Was it a good job?"

"I liked it." Liria looked around the room, squinting through the halo that covered her vision. Was she supposed to be at work? She tried to sit up, but hands pulled her down again. Those hands were soft and gentle, but Liria's body was vacant, her cold, stiff flesh collapsed on the floor between the bed and the wall. An animal fear gripped her, the dark void of unknowing threatening. Cyryl had saved her from overdosing, from that void. Lee Harvey had gone into it, and it would take her too. She twitched and whined, and Arty's arms tightened around her, holding her there, keeping her from drifting into nothingness.

"Just relax, Liria. You're safe here. I've got you." She stroked her hair again, her touch like a soft breeze. "You say you liked your job. Why did you like it?"

"I liked having a normal job. Just serving drinks."

"Aaah. No funny stuff? The manager didn't ask you to do anything else?"

"No. I kept waiting for him to, but he didn't."

"Why were you waiting for him to?"

"I just had a feeling. He acted weird sometimes." Liria could hear the waves breaking on the beach. It was soothing. She wanted Arty to stop talking so she could hear it.

"What about your friend? Did he ask him to do anything besides serve drinks?"

"Not that I know of. It was his first day. His first day there."

"That's good, Liria." Arty kissed her on the forehead. "Go to sleep now."

The sound of the ocean filled Liria's ears as her raft was slowly carried toward shore. The sky was covered in popcorn, and the surf was littered with hotel furniture. Lee Harvey sat on a floating table, his ankles dipped in the foam. He was wearing a conical green party hat, and he smiled, blowing a noisemaker, the paper tube unfurling in her direction like a butterfly tongue. "Welcome to the party, Jet Ski!" he said.

Liria smiled and crawled off the mattress into the water, which closed around her in a rush of warmth. It wasn't wet. It was like blankets. She swam toward Lee Harvey, but he blew the noisemaker again and his table spun further out to sea. Liria saw a shore in the distance, lined with tall buildings wreathed in flashing lights. A neon sign advertised "Hot Sandwich" in huge, blinking letters.

"Lee Harvey! Come back!" Liria kicked out toward him desperately, but she felt someone grab her arm.

She whirled, gasping. There in the water with her was Justin, the odd boy she'd met in the park. He smiled sadly at her, treading water effortlessly. He looked out over the water, toward Lee Harvey.

Her friend was fifty yards away now.

Justin frowned. "You don't want to go there. It's not your place. Too much hot sandwich."

Liria gazed at the far-away form of Lee Harvey, floating on his table. He was almost to the other side. She'd never reach him now. The invisible hands of the current tugged at her legs, and her heart ached as her head slipped below the water into confused darkness.

Chapter 15

Liria awoke in the night, silver shadows solidifying around her. She felt disoriented and dizzy for a moment. The room was laid out in unfamiliar lines. Her stomach felt dry and sick, and heaved when she sat up too quickly.

A shadow loomed up beside her on the bed and Liria gasped and scooted away.

"It's okay, it's just me," Arty said.

Sickness overwhelmed her as she remembered Lee Harvey's waxy, blank face. She stumbled out of bed. The room lurched as she fell to her knees. She got up again, her mouth filling with vomit as she searched for the bathroom, the walls jutting out at odd angles to block her path.

She made it to the toilet, but just barely. The tile was cool under her knees. She threw up and threw up and threw up. Her head throbbed, her skin bathed in cold sweat.

Her stomach settled down, but her head still hurt. She heard footsteps behind her. Arty's gentle hands helped her up, led her back into bed. Liria curled up on the pillow top mattress, and Arty tucked the clean sheets around her, climbed in next to her.

"How did I get here?" Liria asked. There was Lee Harvey's face, then there was a stew of images viewed through a veil. Lapping waves. Little white pills. Had this woman given her pills? Her stomach churned.

"I found you in your friend's room. The maid was screaming out in the hallway."

"Why did you bring me here?"

"Because I like you." Her cool fingers brushed her forehead. "Because you need a friend." Arty slid her arm around her waist. Liria tensed up, but then relaxed. She smelled good, like strawberries and coconut. Arty stroked her back, and Liria remembered the freckles. She remembered her lips, her kiss. Liria nestled closer, felt her breasts pressed up against her. She lay for a long while, breathing in her scent, letting her hand explore the curves of Arty's round ass, feeling her shiver.

But the pills must have been real. She was sick, and she couldn't remember. "You gave me pills," she said.

"Yes, to calm you down and help you sleep. I didn't know they'd make you so sick."

"What were they?"

"Midazolam. It's just a sleeping pill."

"Well, they work like a fucking charm. You must have a hell of a time sleeping."

Liria felt the muscles of Arty's back tense, then relax again. "I have bad insomnia sometimes."

Liria's head throbbed, and she lay still for a moment, waiting for it to subside. "Well, if you have shit like that, I'd imagine you have some ibuprofen. Could I have some? My head is crazy hurting."

"Wait here."

Arty got up out of bed, and Liria watched her, her long legs and polka-dot hipster panties, the weird undulating light from the Strip washing over her. She went out of the bedroom and came back with a pill bottle and a half-size can of 7UP. Honor bar soda in a Vegas suite. Not cheap.

Liria winced as she sat up. Arty sat beside her and handed her the pills, stretching her long legs out on the rumpled sheets. She popped the soda and handed her that too, and Liria glanced at her bare thighs as she gulped down four ibuprofen, letting the soda fizz fill her aching head. The freckles thinned out above Arty's knees, and her thighs looked smooth and creamy-pale. It was dark, though, so she'd have to get a better look to be sure. She drank down the rest of the can, letting it hiss around her teeth and down her throat, settling nicely in her stomach.

Liria closed her eyes and rested her head against the headboard. She felt comfortable, except for her headache. She knew she was hurting, she knew the reality of Lee Harvey's death was waiting to gnash her up again, but that was far away. The pills hadn't completely worn off yet.

Sleeping pills. Liria wished she had this woman's doctor, if that's what she got for insomnia.

She sat there for a while. The clock on the bedside table said it was one forty-two in the morning. "I didn't go to work, or call or anything,"

Liria said. "I probably lost my job."

"I don't think you'll have to worry about that." There was a subtle note of tension in Arty's voice that made Liria watch her closely. She sat with her back against the pillows, her little handful breasts propped up on her crossed arms. She was wearing a tank top, and Liria wanted to strip it off her, if this headache ever went away.

"I don't have any money or anyplace to go," Liria said. "No one is paying for my suite in Vegas. I needed that job."

One corner of Arty's mouth curled upward. She brushed the hair from Liria's forehead. "You're staying here with me for a while." Arty didn't quite look at her as she leaned forward and pressed her lips to her neck below her ear. "How's your head?"

"Getting better," Liria breathed.

"Good." Arty dragged her fingertips along Liria's belly, up under her shirt, and squeezed each nipple, sending little jolts through her body. She straddled her and kissed her, a hand on each breast, and Liria arched up toward her, grabbing her ass.

Arty kissed her just below her bellybutton as she slid her panties off. Liria gasped and moaned as she slid her tongue over her clit, inside her, moving it slowly in and out, then back up to her clit, rubbing and sucking gently as she pushed two fingers deep inside. Liria pressed her hips up, and Arty pushed her fingers deeper, rubbing them against just the right spot, where it felt so good, slowly but gathering intensity. Liria came in an overpowering wave.

Liria lay back on the pillows, sweating, and the

other woman lay down next to her. She reached down inside her own panties and rubbed her clit. Liria pushed the crotch of Arty's panties aside and slid her fingers into her wet pussy. Arty kissed her, rubbing herself harder, then gasped and shuddered as she came.

The older woman pulled the blankets back over them, putting her arm around Liria, kissing her gently. "Go back to sleep," she said.

Liria was warm and comfortable. Her headache was gone, and her grief for Lee Harvey was just a dull ache in the background of her mind. Something was going on here that she couldn't see, but she'd worry about it in the morning. If she'd lost her job, she'd likely lost her hotel room too, so there's no way she'd turn down a night in a Vegas suite with a sexy woman. She curled up against Arty's warm body and drifted off.

***

She woke up to the sound of her phone buzzing. Sunlight streamed across the bed. Arty was tangled up in the rumpled covers with her red hair draped across her pillow.

The room swam slightly as Liria got up; the sunlight was too bright, but her headache was gone and her stomach was fine. Liria found her shorts crumpled on the floor and pulled her phone out of the pocket.

It was Nestor. Liria answered it, her heart thumping.

"Hello?"

Arty stirred, turning over.

"Liria, where the hell are you?" Nestor's voice was tense and panicky.

"It's a long story," Liria said. "Nestor..." Her voice caught. "Nestor, I found Lee Harvey dead."

"Fuck. No fucking way." She heard him blow out a huge puff of air. "Dude, Cameron's dead too."

Liria froze, her ears ringing. She turned to walk out of the room, and heard Arty get up out of the bed. "What? How could that...how could he be dead too?"

"This is fucked up. Where the hell are you? I'm waiting for you at a restaurant here north of town."

"You're waiting for me?"

Arty snatched the phone from her hand before Liria even knew she was there.

"Liria's staying here with me," Arty said into the mouthpiece. Liria could hear the murmur of Nestor's confused protest. She tried to grab her phone back, but Arty caught her wrist, giving her a hard look. "Don't worry about who I am. Anybody asks you about her, she got homesick and left Vegas on Friday night after work. Right? Got it?" Liria heard Nestor yelling as she tried to wrench her wrist away. She tried to grab her phone with her other hand, but Arty forced her against the wall with her elbow in her sternum, meeting her eyes and mouthing, "Stop it." She was stronger than she looked.

"Because," Arty said into the phone, "I know what you're up to, and I will make sure certain other people know, if you fuck with me." There was silence on the other end of the line; all Liria could hear was her own breathing, her pulse pounding in her ears. "You should get the fuck out of here," Arty said. "Your friends tried to scam the wrong people."

She cut the call and tossed the phone across the room, where it slid across the carpet and clicked against the wall. Liria struggled out of her grasp and stood panting, staring at her. "What the fuck…"

Arty's mouth drew tight. "You need to not talk to those people anymore."

"What? Why? Nestor's my friend. What the fuck is going on?"

"That place you were working at wasn't just a nightclub. You're in danger now."

Liria stared at her, her scalp prickling. "What do you mean?" *Lee Harvey is dead. Cameron is dead.*

Arty's eyes searched hers, then she gestured back toward the bedroom. "Come sit down."

She went through the doorway. Liria hesitated, picking at her cuticles, but eventually followed her.

The older woman leaned back against the pillows, her bare ankles crossed. She dialed the hotel phone. Liria sat down next to her as she ordered a pot of coffee and a plate of bacon, eggs, sausage, hash browns, pancakes, and fresh fruit from room service. Liria stared at her, her mouth dry.

Arty hung up and returned Liria's stare.

"That's like a hundred and fifty bucks of room service," Liria said. "This suite can't be cheap either. Who do you work for? And what do you mean I'm in danger?"

Arty looked at her a long moment, crossing her

arms, her foot jittering. She blew out a breath, deflating her puffed cheeks. "I work for a dipshit named Melvin Capella. He's Senator for the state of New York. That was the man your friend left the club with the other night."

This information sank in like a fist to the gut. Liria swallowed hard against the bile rising in her throat. "That was a senator?"

"Yes, that fucking asswipe is a senator."

Liria pounded the mattress with her fists. "He didn't overdose, right? Lee Harvey? It wasn't a coincidence. Someone killed him and Cameron. Your boss did it. He didn't want anyone to figure out he'd fucked him, so he killed him somehow." Liria's throat closed up. He'd killed Lee Harvey. She wanted to crush his windpipe, grab him by the expensive tie she was sure he usually wore, and pull it tight until his face turned purple.

Arty looked at her and covered one of her clenched fists with her hand. "The senator doesn't have the brains to kill anyone."

Tears welled up in Liria's eyes. "Then what happened? Why is Lee Harvey dead?" She snatched her hand away. "And how are you involved in it?"

Arty pinched the narrow, freckled bridge of her nose for a moment. "I'm not involved," she said, looking over at Liria earnestly. "I would never…this is a huge fucking hot mess."

Liria hugged herself, trembling, her instincts screaming at her to run, but held there by her need to know what happened to Lee Harvey, and the memory of Arty's arms around her. "Then tell me."

Arty sighed and frowned at her knees. "You

didn't have a chance to figure it out yet, but the place you worked is an open secret on the Strip, notorious for employing people who go to bed with customers. The wait staff go back to people's rooms, and then those people get a surcharge on their hotel bill. If they contest it, the manager threatens to call their wives. Most people who go in there know about it and play along, but even with the unwary it works enough of the time to make them good money."

Liria's eyebrows drew together. "But that doesn't make sense. Cameron never asked me..." She trailed off. *Just want to get something straight about our policy regarding customers.* Her stomach cramped.

"He would have asked you eventually, I'm sure," Arty said. "And, even without asking you, if you'd gone back to my room with me, I'd have been charged. I think his plan with you must have been to eventually arrange threesomes, because women who pay for sex are definitely a niche market, but I'm sure he'd have tried to charge me all the same."

Rage tore through Liria. Had Nestor known? "So you thought I was a prostitute."

Arty grimaced. "At first, maybe. But no...you were too shy...it was cute. When you said you'd just started working there, I figured out that you probably had no idea what was going on there yet. I felt a little sorry for you." Her lips twitched into a faint grin. "Besides, if you had been a prostitute, I'd have considered paying for it."

Liria squirmed, looking away. Nadine had been right. People only wanted one thing out of girls like them, and guys like Lee Harvey. *But Lee Harvey liked being a whore. It was a game to him.*

And he'd died for it.

Tears spilled from her eyes and Liria wiped them away with tight fists. "But I don't get why my friend is dead. Everyone knew that he was supposedly a whore so why would someone kill him for it?"

Arty frowned, tapping her knee with her fingers. "I didn't know this until afterwards, but apparently the manager had a second scam running, at least in the case of some of his more high-profile clients. From what I gather, your friend stole some information from the senator, from his cell phone, at Cameron's request. Cameron tried to blackmail Melvin with it. But he got in over his head this time. Apparently Senator Shit For Brains is involved with some shady characters himself, and those guys didn't want the relationship to become public. They decided murdering your friend and the manager was safer than paying the bribe."

A sob caught in Liria's throat and she scooted away from Arty, the sheets tangling around her wrists and ankles. "You're mixed up with the people who killed him!"

"No, Liria. *Please.*" She took her hand. Liria twitched, but didn't jerk away. "I had no idea it would turn out like this. If I had, I wouldn't have ever taken that shithead to that bar. I didn't want anyone to get hurt." She sighed, frowning. "I had no idea what sort of fucking idiot I worked for."

Liria stared at her, feeling nauseated. The hustle was opening its foul-smelling mouth, waiting to swallow her up again. Her job was gone, her best friend was dead, and who was this woman in front of her?

"Why am I here?" Liria said, her eyes smarting from unshed tears. "I should go."

Arty took her other hand. "Don't go," she said. "You're in danger. If the people that fuckhead is involved with find out you were friends with the dead guy, it'll be bad for you. I'm afraid that if you leave here, you'll be next." She held Liria's gaze, her thumb tracing tickling circles on her palm. "Did your friend send you any texts on Friday night after he left?"

Liria shook her head.

"Good. Maybe these people will just forget about it. But give it a couple days, okay? Stay here with me. Is that so bad?"

Liria looked up at her through her tears. Arty sat in her panties, her green-eyed gaze meeting Liria's. If she stayed, Arty would fuck her again, and they'd eat French toast and fall back asleep. Or she could go out penniless into the cruel world and dodge bullets.

"Why do you work for this guy, if he's involved with people like that?" Liria asked.

Arty's brow furrowed. "I don't know. I'm starting to think I should quit." She stared distantly out the window for a long time. When she seemed to come back to herself, she got up off the bed. "In fact, that's exactly what I'll do. I'll quit."

Liria watched after her as she walked into the other room, the round curves of her ass cheeks showing beneath her underwear. *I'll stay.*

***

They spent most of the day in bed, watching TV and dozing. Liria would wake up each time she drifted off, a shock of pleasure running through her to find herself in bed with a beautiful woman. She'd pull her closer and let her hands feel all that smooth, pale skin, let her lips find every spot on her that made her shiver. Her thighs had a few freckles, but not many.

Liria was almost able to forget the world outside. In idle moments, she kept wanting to get her phone, to gossip with Lee Harvey. Then she'd remember. It was confusing, like one of her legs had suddenly disappeared and she kept trying to step on it, but she kept falling.

In the afternoon, Arty's phone rang. She glanced at Liria, then took it into the other room to answer it.

Liria sat with her arms crossed, staring unseeingly at the television. She could hear the murmur of Arty's voice. She sounded tense and angry, but Liria couldn't make out the words. She dug her fingernails into her skin. *She can have a private phone conversation, but not me.* She took a deep breath, blew it out. *Who would I talk to, anyway?* Grief grappled with her anger, dismembering it.

Arty finished her conversation and came back in, settling back into the bed with a furrowed brow. Liria glanced at her, her arms still crossed, but before she could ask questions Arty spoke.

"I quit my job," she said.

Liria raised her eyebrows. "Just now?"

"Yep."

She shifted uncomfortably. "Do we...do you have to leave? Isn't your senator paying for this hotel room?" Liria's heart sank. She wasn't ready to crawl out of the warm blankets yet. She didn't want to think about what happened next. But Arty smiled slightly at her and reached out to brush her knee with her fingertips.

"We don't have to leave yet. Not for a couple more days. The room's already paid up and it's best not to rock the boat."

Liria relaxed a bit. *I don't have to worry about it yet. Maybe I can figure something else in a couple days.* She glanced sidelong at Arty, who broke into her cute, childish smile.

"Let's order a whole chocolate mousse cake from room service while it's still on my work tab."

Liria grinned back. "I'm down for that," she said.

***

Liria dreamt that night of wandering through a neighborhood of dilapidated warehouses with Lee Harvey, searching for their connection. "Guy said he'd meet us behind the dumpster," Lee said, but every time they thought they saw a dumpster, they'd get closer and see it was actually a recycling bin, or a strange-looking car, or a plywood box with a very bizarre puppet show going on inside.

She awoke feeling restless and sad, the desire for a shot burning in her. Outside, the horizon was just turning pink.

Arty turned over and opened her eyes, then smiled sleepily. "Good morning, beautiful," she murmured, her fingers curling around Liria's waist and pulling her closer.

Liria kissed her, pushing back her anxiety. *I don't have to figure out anything else today.*

They ordered another huge breakfast from room service, then stretched out in bed, eating and watching HBO. Liria put her bacon between slices of French toast and ate it with a fork, licking the syrup from her lips. Arty watched her in fascination while she picked at the plate of fresh fruit on her lap. "How do you eat like that and stay so skinny?"

Liria shrugged. "I don't usually get to eat like this." She glanced up to find Arty looking at her with pity in her eyes, and forced a smile. "Thanks for the food, and thanks for the place to stay." She stirred a sausage link around in a puddle of syrup; she held it there, watching the syrup drip off, and stirred it around again. She could feel Arty looking at her.

The older woman gently took the plate away and put it on the bedside table, taking Liria into her arms. She shut off the TV and held her, rocking slightly.

Liria lay quietly, listening to Arty's heartbeat. She enjoyed feeling her warmth, feeling her breathe.

Liria's phone started ringing in the next room, and Arty went stiff. "I'll get that," she said, and got up.

Liria hesitated a moment, then jumped up and

followed her. She started toward Arty, ready to snatch her phone away, but Arty leaned against the wall, staring at the screen, making no move to answer it. She shot Liria a look. "Who's Cyryl?"

Liria clenched her fists, her breakfast going sour in her belly. "He's my dad."

The ringing stopped. Arty frowned, scrolling down the screen. Her eyebrows shot up and she looked at Liria sharply. "These texts don't look like they're from your dad."

Liria sprang forward and grabbed her phone. "That's none of your fucking business." Arty regarded her with a creased brow, and Liria huffed. "He's not my real dad."

"Yeah, I hope not."

Liria's face grew hot. "Fuck off. You don't fucking understand. I had nowhere else to go. Cyryl has always been nice to me. And I have no one else. Lee Harvey was my one other friend, and he…I was living with him, but his boyfriend kicked me out." Liria's voice caught and she squeezed her eyes shut, her knuckles white as they grasped her phone.

"So you went and fucked this Cyryl guy for a place to stay?"

Liria opened her eyes again, but could barely see through the tears, could barely speak through her clenched teeth. *This fucking rich bitch has no idea.* "I didn't…I thought he was my dad. Or at least I thought that *he* thought that. I…I didn't want…"

Liria spun jerkily on her heel and went back into the bedroom. Hurt and hopelessness engulfed her. She pulled on her shorts and started looking around for her shoes. Arty came in and leaned against the doorframe.

"Liria…"

"No, *fuck you*. I don't know what your real game is, but this is bullshit." *She'd kick me out tomorrow anyway.* She found her shoes in the corner and slipped them on, pushing past Arty to the door.

Arty caught her arm. "Stop."

Liria tried to yank out of her grip, but Arty held tight.

"Get the fuck out of my way," Liria said. Arty's tits were pressed up against hers, warm and soft.

"No. I'm not going to let you go out there and get killed."

"Oh, what-the-fuck-ever."

"*Listen,* Liria. You can hate me all you want, but don't leave. Please. I feel bad enough that shit happened to your friend. I don't want it to happen to you too. I'm sorry I grabbed your phone. I'm sorry about what I said. Please."

Liria stood glaring at her, breathing hard. "Why the fuck are you holding me hostage here?" She didn't try to jerk her arm away again.

"I'm not holding you hostage. I just really don't want you to leave."

"Then why are you not letting me talk to anyone?"

"I don't think you should let anyone know where you are right now. People may have their phones bugged, especially your friends from the nightclub. And I don't trust this Cyryl guy, either."

Liria stared at her a few moments longer, battling her anguish and longing and indecision. She pulled her arm out of Arty's grasp and flung herself back on the bed, curling around a pillow.

After a few minutes, she felt the mattress sag as Arty laid down next to her, stretching out with her bare legs touching hers. She ran Liria's hair through her fingers, brushing it away from her cheeks and shoulders, stroking her back with her fingertips.

Arty took a deep breath. "Liria, I'm sorry, but…" She sighed. "This Cyryl guy?"

"What about him?" Liria hugged her pillow tighter.

"You thought he was your dad, but he's not?"

Liria huffed. "My mom said he was. But I never really believed it, and he said that he's not, he's sterile."

The older woman's fingers traced slowly along her spine. "Were you working for him?"

It took a few moments for this to register. Liria turned to look at her, scowling. "Huh?"

Arty watched her closely, her fingers going still, but then she smiled and shrugged. "I mean, I was just wondering."

Liria continued to scowl at her in bewilderment.

Arty looked at her searchingly for a few more moments. "I'm just wondering about this relationship, that's all. I'm just trying to understand. You went to him because you needed a place to stay, and you thought he was your dad?"

"Yeah," Liria said, still feeling like she was missing something.

"But then he wants you to fuck him? I'm sorry, but that's messed up."

Liria's gaze fell to the sheets. She twisted the pillow between her fingers. "He gave me a place to stay when no one else would."

"Still, I'd like to kick him in the nuts."

"He's not bad. It's not his fault I can't love him that way."

"But he was your father-figure." Liria didn't respond. Maybe she wasn't missing anything. Maybe Arty was just being protective in a weird way. She curled back around her pillow, but Arty pulled it from her arms and snuggled closer to her.

"I want you to stay here, but you can leave if you want," Arty said. She paused, running a lock of Liria's hair between her fingers. "Please stay."

Liria looked up into her green eyes, her brow still furrowed. Her vision blurred as tears welled up. Of course she would stay. Where else did she have to go? But tomorrow, when Arty left…

Desperately, Liria pressed her lips against Arty's. Arty kissed her back hungrily. Her body was warm and solid and lithe, and the way she touched her, the way she looked at her and how her breath came hot and fast when they fucked, made Liria feel alive and like she wasn't alone. Liria clung to her, and Arty slid her leg between hers and pulled her closer, her hands on her back. It was sweet being there; Liria could forget everything but her soft lips and warm skin, and her words, *Please stay.* She could forget about Lee Harvey, Cyryl, and the hustle waiting to swallow her back up tomorrow when Arty left again.

Arty broke away, laughing. She caught Liria's hand and brought it to her mouth, sucking on her fingers. "You're all covered in syrup." Her smile softened. She kissed her nose. "You're beautiful."

Liria's heart ached. "So are you."

Arty kissed her again. She slid out of bed and pulled her into the bathroom, turned on the spigot of the huge, jetted tub.

Arty stripped off Liria's shirt and panties, then took off her own. She was willow thin, her shell-pink ass reflected in the mirror. Liria couldn't keep herself from sighing a little, and grabbed her around the waist with her sticky fingers. She kissed her, feeling all that skin against hers. Arty's tits fit perfectly in her hands, and Liria cupped both of them, caressing her nipples with her thumbs.

Arty coaxed her into the tub, and it filled up around them as Liria ran her tongue down her belly to her fiery strip of pubic hair, finding her clit, making her moan, the warm water lapping against her chin. When the water got too high, Liria put her fingers inside her, moving her lips up her belly, licking and sucking her candy-pink nipples until Arty's hips shuddered, pressing hard against Liria's hand.

Arty turned on the jets and pushed Liria's pussy up against one of them, putting her fingers inside her from behind. She kissed her neck as Liria came.

They lay in the tub in each other's arms. Liria didn't want to say anything, afraid she might break her eggshell-thin contentment. Arty rubbed the spicy-smelling hotel soap all over her, and washed her hair, massaging her scalp gently, pulling her fingers through the tangles.

Finally the bathwater got tepid and they got out, wrapping themselves in thick towels. When they went back out into the bedroom, Liria's phone was buzzing again.

Liria clutched the towel to her chest. Arty looked at her uncertainly as she picked it up, her lips drawing tight as she looked at the screen. Liria's heart squeezed as she watched her hit the answer button.

"Hello," Arty said. Liria felt like she couldn't breathe, but she didn't grab the phone away. She could still feel Arty's fingers in her, her hands tickling her scalp. She could still feel her arms around her, hear her words, *Please stay.*

Arty listened to the voice on the line, her face expressionless. "This isn't Liria."

She listened again, her eyes flashing. "Never mind who I am. I don't want you to call her anymore."

Liria could hear Cyryl yelling, and Arty held the phone away from her ear slightly. "Don't fucking call her anymore, you asshole, do you hear me? She doesn't need to talk to you."

She hit the disconnect button, and her gaze found Liria, who stood there, the blood draining from her face.

Liria's knees gave out and she sat down stiffly on the bed. Arty came over and sat next to her.

"What did you do that for?" Liria asked.

"He sounds like a fuckwad. Why would you even want to talk to him?"

"He's all I have!" She clutched the towel at her breast, her hand shaking. "Lee Harvey's dead, and Cyryl is all I have left. You say I need to stay here with you, that you'll keep me safe from the scary gangsters, but you leave tomorrow, and then what?"

"Liria…"

Liria flipped her wet hair out of her face with a jittery hand, and her towel fell open. "Fuck this. Fuck this all to hell. Maybe you didn't know Lee Harvey was going to die, whatever, but all I know is my only friend is dead because of the people you work for. You drugged me and you say you don't want me to leave, supposedly trying to keep me safe from your own fucking people. I lost my job, my only source of money. You told my only ride out of town to fuck off, and then did the same thing to my only friend, the only person that might have taken me in after you boot me out of here. So what do I do now?"

She glared at Arty, tears spilling from her eyes. Arty stared back at her, and Liria's insides hollowed out. She'd overplayed her hand. She'd made a miscalculation.

Arty scooted over and squeezed her tight.

Liria closed her eyes and let herself be held, hope seeping in as she held her breath.

Arty pressed her lips to the top of her head. "You can stay with me," she said. "I'll make it work somehow. They won't find out who you are, and you can come with me when I leave."

Liria took a shuddering breath. "Really?"

Arty stroked her hair. She pulled away. Liria's heart jumped when Arty turned her arm over, examining the fading bruises with a humorless smile. She glanced up at her. "You haven't gotten high while you've been with me, and you aren't sick."

Liria's heart hammered. "I quit about a week

ago."

"You start doing drugs again, I'll kick you out. I can't be around that stuff."

"I won't," Liria said quickly. "I promise."

Arty looked into her eyes and smiled slightly. "I believe you."

Their lips met, and Liria kissed her passionately, pulling Arty's still-damp body tight against hers. The older woman would kick her out eventually, but it might be a while before that happened, because Liria didn't have to pretend this time.

Chapter 16

They spent the rest of the day in the room, eating room service, fucking, and watching TV. Arty didn't like cartoons or reality shows. She was more into the heavy, intellectual dramas. Liria found that these weren't so bad when she had Arty sitting next to her in her underwear, feeding her onion rings and explaining the backstory.

Cyryl kept calling, and Liria turned her phone off. Her guts squirmed when she did so. When her grief for Lee Harvey was in the back of her mind, Liria felt more content with Arty than she ever had in her life. But she'd only known her a few days, and she'd known Cyryl for years. He'd saved her life, and he'd promised to get her a job, and Arty...well, Liria couldn't help but have doubts.

Late in the afternoon, Arty's phone rang on the bedside table. She muted the TV, staring thoughtfully at Liria for a moment before answering it, crossing her bare ankles and leaning back on the pillows.

"Hello?"

Liria watched her as Arty sat there scratching her bare, freckled knees.

"No, fuck that," Arty said, her eyes darting briefly to Liria. "What do you want me to do? He's a grown man. You think you can do a better job, do it yourself. I'm done."

Liria could hear the murmur of a voice on the other end, speaking in a clipped, raised tone. Arty's jaw tightened and her nostrils flared as she took a deep breath. "No, you...listen, fucking *listen*, for once in your goddamn life. If you'd listened in the first place, we wouldn't even be involved with that fucking shit-for-brains. And then you step in and fuck it up even worse." She listened to the response, her face looking older than usual, her eyes dull, frown lines appearing beside her lips. "No, he's on his own. There's nothing you can say at this point. Yeah, yeah. Whatever. I'll see you. Yeah. Tomorrow night." She hung up and turned to look at Liria, like she didn't quite see her. She got up out of bed and went into the other room. "Bring me your ID, I have to book you a plane ticket."

Liria got up and fished her ID out of the pocket of her crumpled shorts, taking it in to her.

Arty's face was lit by the glow of her laptop. She grabbed the card from Liria's hand and looked at it. "Czetski, huh? That's, what, Polish?"

Liria picked at her cuticles. "Yeah, but I'm not...it's Cyryl's last name."

"Huh," Arty said. She set the card down next to her keyboard and started typing. "You ever been to New York?"

"No."

"Really? Because there's a family of Czetskis in New York." Arty looked over at her watchfully, and Liria's scalp prickled.

"I don't know anything about them," she said.

Arty looked back at the screen, and Liria stood, stiff. Arty flipped the laptop closed and stood up, handing the card back to Liria. She smiled as if nothing were wrong. "Well, you'll be going to New York now. It's a great city, you'll love it." She took Liria's hand and led her back to the bed. Liria settled down in the crook of her arm while Arty flipped through channels disinterestedly with the volume muted.

"What am I going to do in New York?"

"Hang out in my apartment for a while, until I figure a few things out."

She twisted the blankets harder. "What things?"

Arty gave up flipping through channels and tossed the remote aside. "What I'm going to do next." She was silent for a while, her finger tracing the curve of Liria's neck. "I'm not going to do this bullshit anymore. I'm tired of this game."

Arty gazed off into space, chewing on her lip, and Liria kept silent.

***

That night Liria lay in bed listening to Arty's quiet breathing and watching the patterns of light on the ceiling. Eventually, she dozed off and found herself sitting in the waiting room of a strange bus station.

A large family took up the entire row of chairs in front of her. Two of the brothers were struggling to keep their huge mound of mismatched suitcases from toppling over. A stolid grandmother sat on top near the ceiling, gripping the armrests of her fabric camp chair. She stared off into the distance with a dignified look as her grandchildren jostled and stacked the unsteady pile, inserting a bag there, catching another there, leaning against it so that it wouldn't crumble and send the old woman crashing to the ground.

Liria felt a vibration in her back pocket, and pulled out her phone.

Lee Harvey: Hey, Jet Ski.

Tears came to Liria's her eyes. She couldn't quite say why. Lee Harvey was dead, but that didn't matter. She could still talk to him, because he had his cell phone with him.

Liria: How are you?

Lee Harvey: I'm super awesome. How are you?

Liria wiped her eyes. In front of her, the grandmother's chair was tipping over. The old woman didn't move or change expressions as her grandsons hollered and rushed to catch her.

Liria: I don't know what to do, Lee Harvey.

Lee Harvey: It's a choice between two rich

195

people who want to use you for sex, so just choose the one you like fucking more.

Liria sniffed and wiped her eyes again. The grandmother flopped like a rolled carpet into the arms of her grandsons. They set her back on her feet and she straightened her dress, folded her camp chair, and began climbing back up the mountain of luggage with the chair under her arm.

Liria: Cyryl might be safer. Arty is mixed up in some sort of gangster shit.

Liria felt someone looking at her, and looked up. Standing against the wall to her left was Justin in his tiger hat, his hands tugging alternately at the earflaps. He grinned. Her phone buzzed again and she looked down.

Lee Harvey: Everyone is mixed up in shit, Liria. Besides, it's better to hold the monster's hand than hide from him in the closet, because then at least then you know where his hands are.

Liria stared at the text and snorted.

Liria: That doesn't make sense, Lee Harvey.

Lee Harvey: Sure it does, Jet Ski.

She looked over to Justin, who had flopped down to sit on the floor cross-legged. He took off his *shoes and emptied a huge pile of sand out of them, the grains sliding down and spreading out over the tile. He ran his palm over the pile, flattening it out, and started doodling in it with his fingers.*

Liria looked away, and a tear made its way down her face.

Liria: I miss you, Lee Harvey.

Lee Harvey: Don't miss me, Jet Ski, I'm right here.

Lee Harvey sat down next to her, grinning teasingly. He was wearing a sailor suit, like the ones mothers dress their baby sons in. "I brought you something," he said, and wagged a tiny baggy in front of her face. A nugget of black tar was smooshed into the bottom.

Sick joy bloomed in her stomach. Her shoulders tensed up, anticipating the rush she'd get. She longed for the bliss of being high. It would make everything better, if she could just get blasted. Everything would make sense again...Arty's weird behavior, Cyryl, Lee Harvey being dead. She reached up to take the baggie, but before she could, a hand snatched it away.

Justin stood looking at her with a little frown, and shoved the baggie in his pocket. "He's not really your friend," Justin said, jerking his chin toward Lee Harvey.

Liria looked over at him, and panic coursed through her. Justin was right: it wasn't Lee Harvey at all but an animated corpse, his face waxy, his eyes blank.

Liria sat up in bed with a strangled cry, her ears ringing. Arms came out of the darkness and pulled her close. Liria gasped and struggled for a moment until she heard Arty's voice and remembered where she was.

"It's okay, baby," Arty said. "It's all right."

Liria let out a breath and snuggled against Arty's warm body, cold sweat drying on the back of her neck.

"Bad dream?" Arty mumbled, kissing her lightly.

Liria cuddled closer, a warm feeling spreading through her. It felt so good to be next to her. It was better than dope.

"I was dreaming about Lee Harvey," she said.

Arty held her, stroking her back with her fingertips. "I'm so sorry, Liria. I'm so sorry."

Liria pressed her cheek against her chest, listening to her heartbeat. "Arty?"

"What is it?"

"What happened to Lee Harvey? To his body? Did the police do anything?"

Liria felt Arty's breast rise and fall. "They did an autopsy, ruled it death by overdose. His mom came and got him."

Liria winced as a hot wave of anger tore through her, imagining The Mare's face contorted with disgust as she gazed upon the body of the son she'd never loved, never understood.

"But it wasn't an overdose," Liria said.

Arty stroked her hair with stiff fingers. "It was," she finally said, "but it wasn't. Your friend was

198

given some shit so strong it would have been impossible for him not to go out."

Liria tensed up, her fists clenching. "What about Cameron?"

"Same thing with him. Overdose. The news is portraying it as a bad batch of dope."

Liria curled against her, not speaking, and Arty held her. After a while, Liria realized the lights from the Strip were being drowned out by the grey light of dawn. Arty stirred, kissing her on the forehead. "Come on. We have a plane to catch."

***

They took a cab early that morning to the airport. The crowds on the Strip were reduced to street cleaners, long-wearing drunks, and people on the way to work. The sun touched the tops of the buildings and bronzed the distant ridges.

Liria watched blearily, tugging nervously at her blouse. She had abandoned her backpack in the hotel room she'd shared with Nestor, too paranoid to retrieve it, so she was wearing some things of Arty's. They fit well enough, though the top was tight around the chest and the shoes were half a size too small.

Arty grabbed her hand and held it. "Don't pull off the buttons," she chided. "That blouse cost three hundred dollars."

Liria looked down at it, squirming in her seat.

***

199

Liria had only been on a plane once. She and her mom had been living with some guy in the depths of Oregon, and her mom had decided it was time for her to visit Cyryl. That had been over five years ago, and she barely remembered what it had been like to fly.

The airport was crowded and chaotic. Security made her nervous; all those people in uniform with their hard and suspicious cop faces. Liria folded her arms to hide the yellowing bruises.

When they were through, she slipped her shoes back on and followed Arty to the gate. She marveled at how the other woman walked, upright and businesslike, her heels clicking. She hadn't looked so proper that morning on the floor of the shower, where Liria had her pinned for ten glorious minutes.

Arty bought her a coffee and they waited at the gate, watching their plane taxi in. She took Liria's hand and Liria smiled, interlacing her fingers with hers.

When they called for passengers to board Liria discovered they were in first class. She glanced sideways at the other woman, wondering. Arty let her have the window seat, and Liria kicked her shoes off and curled up under the woolen blanket the flight attendant gave her.

Arty grinned childishly and pointed at a page of the in-flight magazine. "Look, an electric earring rack. Now I know what to get you for your birthday."

Liria broke into a smile and Arty kissed her briefly, drawing fascinated looks from the men across the aisle.

It was a long flight. Liria looked out the window and dozed while Arty read and answered emails on her phone. Liria's own phone had been off since Arty had yelled at Cyryl. She imagined that when she turned it on it would explode with his texts and voicemails, and spent some time mentally crafting her response. *Cyryl, my friend is dead and I'm scared...Cyryl, the people who owned the restaurant turned out to be gangsters and I'm hiding...*

She curled up around her knees, watching her future fade into uncertainty in the distance. She was used to that. Maybe she should just block Cyryl. Never answer his calls or messages. Give him no explanation at all.

She glanced at Arty, who was chewing on her cheek and staring at her phone, her red hair falling over the shoulders of her expensive suit jacket. *I'll just wait and see how this goes.*

***

They landed at JFK in the early afternoon. It was crowded and smelly, and everyone seemed pissed off. Arty collected her luggage and they went and got a cab.

Rain slammed against the windshield as they pulled out into traffic. Liria watched it dripping down the fogged windows. She couldn't remember the last time she'd seen rain like that. She cleared a spot of condensation away with her fist and gazed in awe at the mist hovering around the tops of the

Manhattan skyline. She hadn't known they made cities so big.

"You've really never been here?" Arty asked.

Liria shook her head. "Going to Vegas, it was only my second time being out of California."

Arty pointed out landmarks to Liria and argued with the driver about their route. The drive took a long time, but finally they pulled up in front of a three-story brick apartment building on a tree-lined street. Arty swiped her credit card in the cab and Liria glanced at the screen. The fare was seventy-six dollars. For someone supposedly out of a job, she sure didn't skimp.

Rain dripped from the branches and eaves, running cold down the back of Liria's neck, and she hugged herself against the chill. Arty unlocked the door to the building, and they tracked mud into a marble-floored vestibule. They took the elevator up to the top floor.

Arty's place had wood floors and window seats. A grey cat trotted in, belly swaying, to rub furiously against Arty's legs.

"Yes, Shirley, I'll feed you, you fatty," she said. She picked up the massive animal, who purred like a passing train, and went to tend to him while Liria walked up to the front windows.

She gazed out through the warped glass and misty rain to a small, sodden park across the street. A man sat on a bench, huddled in a raincoat, a bulging plastic bag taking up the spot next to him. The leaves of the trees were starting to turn orange, and flapped limply in the wind.

Liria felt damp and cold and like she didn't

belong. She wondered if she'd be out there soon with that man. She only had about two hundred and fifty dollars, and no clothes of her own.

Arty came up from behind her and put her arms around her waist, kissing her neck. "You like Chinese food?"

Liria leaned back against her. "Yes." She smiled and turned to kiss her. Arty kissed her back, sliding her hands up her shirt, inside her bra.

Liria was sure Arty's life included things besides sex and food and TV, but she tried not to wonder what those things were. *I can't fuck this up.*

Later, when they were eating Mongolian beef on the couch, Arty trying and failing to instruct Liria on the use of chopsticks, Arty got a call. Her face hardened as she looked at her phone, and she put down her plate and went into the bedroom, closing the door.

Liria muted the TV, and she could hear Arty talking through the wall.

"Yeah?"

"I put my resignation through the official channels. I'm gonna lay low now for a couple weeks."

"No, fuck you. It was pointless to spend…"

"Then pull your investment. It was a bad one to begin with. The guy's a fucking train wreck."

"What did you expect me to do? I didn't fucking know. And then you went and fucked it up a million times worse. It would have been cheaper to just pay them off."

There was a longer pause, and then she laughed, but there was no mirth in the sound. "Really? This is your punishment? Why not have me come over and clean your garage? It'd save you having to pay the maid at least."

"Okay, whatever. What-the-fuck-ever. Yeah. Of course I'll do it. It's better than babysitting that dipshit, and fuck it, it's your money."

"Yeah, just go ahead and try. What would you do without me? Huh? What do you think would happen? Yeah, I know. Yeah, yeah."

There was a ringing silence. "*What?*" When Arty spoke again, her voice was husky. "What the fuck…? Why are you snooping in my business? A friend. Yes. No, I…No. No fucking way. Are you joking? I don't want to risk chasing her off." She sighed long and heavily. "Yeah. *No*. Keep wishing, see where it gets you. No. I'll discuss this with you later. Later. Like, when you're fucking dead. Yeah. Bye, then, whatever."

"*Fuck,*" Arty spat. "That fucking cunt."

Liria quickly unmuted the television.

Arty came back into the living room, pale and livid. Liria looked down at her plate, drawing patterns in the sauce with her chopsticks. Arty looked at her, and Liria glanced up fleetingly, trying to smile. *Try harder. You can't fuck this up.*

Arty sat down. "I have to go to Chicago the day after tomorrow. Just for a couple days."

"Why?" She looked over and met Arty's searching gaze.

"New job."

Liria pressed her lips together, but couldn't stop herself asking. "What kind of job?"

Arty's gaze fell away from hers. She tapped her

foot on the floor.

Liria put her plate down. She wasn't hungry anymore. She dug her fingers into her arms and stared out the darkening windows.

Arty's face crumpled and she hid her face in her hands. She looked back at Liria and sighed. "Liria...I really like you."

Liria's heart accelerated, though the fact annoyed her a bit at the moment. "I really like you too."

"I'm not...I haven't been exactly truthful with you."

"Yeah, I get that feeling."

"You know I'd never hurt you, right? You know I'd never hurt anybody?"

Liria stared at her grimly. "You never really worked for that stupid senator. You work for these 'shady characters' he's supposedly connected with."

Arty nodded, rubbing the spot between her eyes. "But I didn't have anything to do with your friend getting killed, or the other guy. That was pure bullshit."

Liria clamped her chin to her chest, and Arty stomped her foot on the floor. "Please believe me!"

Lee Harvey's face flashed across Liria's vision, and she clutched her arms harder. She could imagine what he would advise her. *Sure, she's mixed up with the people who killed me, but she's a great fuck, and she's loaded. Plus she's hot and she's nice to you. Ride that bus to the end of the line, Jet Ski. Even if it ends up plunging over a cliff.*

"I believe you," Liria said.

They gazed at each other. "Come with me to Chicago," Arty said.

"What will we be doing?"

"Transport. Cocaine."

Liria chewed on her lip. It could be worse. She nodded. "Okay."

***

That night, after Arty was asleep, Liria got up to use the bathroom. When she came out, she saw her phone sitting on the hall tree and picked it up almost out of habit.

She muted it and turned it on. As she'd feared, there were sixteen voice mails from Cyryl, and twenty-four texts. She didn't read them, but stood staring at the notifications for several minutes, her head hanging.

Liria looked around at the dark apartment, the streetlights casting a dull glow over the long, blocky couch. The tidy bookshelves were topped with bronze Hindu statues, Russian dolls, and blown-glass sculptures. Rain pattered against the windows, and the fat cat twined between her ankles, purring. Liria felt a rush of warmth when she thought of the woman who lived here. *I really like you,* she'd said.

Liria read the string of texts below Cyryl's, the ones from Lee Harvey. Her stomach dropped.

She clicked on them, and sat down with her back to the wall reading them, tears flowing down her cheeks. It seemed so unbelievable. His living fingers had typed those only a few days ago. She wondered if there were some way to keep them forever.

She sat for a long time, reading. His teasing

jokes. His advice.

> **Lee Harvey: Play your cards right, this could turn out really good for you. And if you get married, you won't even have to change your last name.**

Liria stared off into space. She sniffed and wiped her eyes, and opened the string of texts from Cyryl.

> **Cyryl: What the fuck, Liria? I'm going to come find you if you don't call me,** the last one said.

That had been twelve hours before, and a chill tore down her spine. She wondered if he had any way of tracking her down. But he hadn't even known she'd gone to Vegas, much less New York, and she'd been working under a false name.

> **Liria: Cyryl, the woman you talked to turned my phone off. I'm sorry. I'm okay, but I can't talk. Things are fucked up. The people who owned the restaurant were involved in some bad shit.**

Her phone started buzzing immediately with a call from him. She jabbed the reject button.

> **Liria: I told you, I can't talk. I'm okay, but my friend that I was working with is dead and I had to leave town. I'm with someone safe now, and I'll come back when I can. I'll call when I can. Otherwise I have to keep my phone off or I'll**

get in trouble.

Cyryl: Fuck that. Where are you? I'll come get you, wherever it is.

Liria: No, Cyryl. It's too dangerous. I'll be fine here.

Cyryl: Liria, don't do this to me.

Liria: I'm just trying to be safe.

Cyryl: You'll be safe with me. How would they find you?

Liria: I don't know, but I worry they would, and then you'd be in danger too.

Cyryl: Fuck that. I don't care about those fucks.

Liria: I think you would if you met them.

There was a pause.

Cyryl: Your friend is dead? What happened?

Liria: He did some illegal things. I didn't know that was happening at that restaurant. I didn't do anything illegal, but I think they would have asked me to eventually. Lee messed with the wrong person and he got killed.

Her tears spattered on the screen, and she wiped them off.

I had to get out of there for a while in case they found out I knew something.

Cyryl: Oh my fucking God, Liria. That's bullshit.

Liria: I know.

Cyryl: Baby, come home. I'll keep you safe. I swear it. I won't let them touch you.

Liria hid her head in her knees. She pictured him in his living room, his face pale, his jaw twitching. Her heart squeezed. He really did love her.

Liria: Cyryl, I miss you.

Cyryl: Baby, please. I don't know who the fuck these people are, but you're safer with me. I'll call the police, and they'll find you if you don't tell me where you are.

Liria: No, Cyryl! They'll kill me if they find out the police are looking for me.

She started to regret talking to him.

Cyryl: There's no fucking way I'm going to let you be out God knows where with God knows who. I'll find you. I'm going to find you.

Liria: I told you, I'm fine.

Cyryl: You are not fine. Liria, I need to know what's happening. I need you back with me.

Liria: Cyryl, I have to go. Please, don't worry.

Her phone buzzed with another text, but she didn't read it and turned her phone off, sighing. She put her cell back on the hall tree and clutched her knees, staring out the windows at the raindrops glittering orange in the streetlights. Arty stirred in the bedroom. Liria heard the sound of her bare feet on the wood floors.

"What are you doing out here?" Arty asked sleepily, coming into the hall. "Come back to bed."

Liria looked up at the older woman, pale and naked and lovely. She stood up, and they crawled back under the warm covers together.

Chapter 17

Two days later, they flew to Chicago, in first class again. They rented a car at the airport and drove to a hotel on the outskirts, then ordered a pizza and ate it sitting on the bed.

Liria insisted on watching Adventure Time. She was tired of heavy drama. Arty stared at the cartoon with a furrowed brow, pulling at her pizza slice and slurping up the stretched cheese. Halfway through the first episode, she grinned. "This is just fucking crazy." She covered her mouth as she laughed so she wouldn't spew crumbs.

"Exactly," Liria said. She closed her eyes and lay with her head in Arty's lap.

She dozed off, and woke when Arty ruffled her hair. "Time to get up."

Liria sat up and stretched. The sky outside the rain-streaked windows was dark. Arty got out of bed, dug through her suitcase, and came up holding two handguns. She held one out to Liria, who backed away.

"I don't know how to use one of those."

211

Arty smiled, the skin around her eyes crinkling. "Really?" She came around and showed her. "This is the safety. This is off, and that's on. And this is the thingy you pull to make it go bang."

Liria wrinkled her nose. "Why do I need it, anyway?"

"You probably won't. But I'd feel better if you had it." She pressed it into Liria's hands, and Liria reluctantly took it. The metal felt strange against her skin, as if it were vibrating with energy.

"Just keep it by you," Arty said. "When Al comes, make sure the safety's on and stick it in your pants." Arty grinned and hooked the waistband of Liria's borrowed jeans with her finger, kissing her nose.

They watched more cartoons. Arty got on the carpet in front of the TV and did yoga, the gun beside her. Liria stretched out on the bed and watched her muscles moving under the Lycra of Arty's pants.

About twenty minutes later there was a knock on the door. Arty stood, shoving the pistol down her yoga pants and pulling her t-shirt over the bulge. Liria copied her, the gun seeming to bite at her waist, making her sweat. She stood awkwardly by the bed as Arty opened the door.

"Hey, Al," Arty said, grinning warmly. Al was tall and powerfully-built, but with a softness around his waist, his salt-and-pepper hair feathered back from his ears.

"Missy!" he said, laughing and pulling her into a one-armed hug. "What the hell? Why you back doing this shit, girl?" His sharp, brown eyes fell on

212

Liria and he tensed up slightly. "Who's your friend?"

"Al, this is Fiona," Arty said. It was a nickname they'd agreed on beforehand. "She's a friend of mine."

Liria smiled weakly as he stepped forward to shake her hand. His palm was slightly damp, and so was hers. "Nice to meet you, Fiona." He glanced at Arty. "She going to be taking over this route or something?"

Arty shut the door and heaved the two suitcases he'd brought up onto the bed "There's been some shit going on, so she and I might be handling it together for a while."

"Oh?" He glanced back and forth between the two of them.

Arty opened one of the suitcases and started pulling out rectangular packages, a red scorpion stamped on their white paper wrappings.

"There wasn't a problem with the other guy, was there?" Al asked, rubbing the back of his neck.

"No," Arty said, piling the packages up on the bed. "No, no way. Carson's fine. Shortround just gets capricious sometimes."

Al broke into a grin. "Capricious, huh?"

Arty zipped open and unloaded the other bag. She carefully tore the paper away from the corner of one of the bricks and stuck her thumb in. It came out covered in white powder, which she snorted. Liria's stomach clenched hard.

Arty stood there a moment, sniffing, then her posture shifted slightly and she grinned. "Woo. Good job, Al."

He chuckled, and Arty gave him a high five. She pulled out her phone and started typing, still sniffing and wiping her nose. Al pulled his phone out too.

"There's your money," Arty said, jabbing one last button and pocketing her phone.

Al stared at the screen. "I see it." He shoved his phone in his front pocket and wiped his palms on his jeans. Then he shook Arty's and Liria's hands. "Nice to meet you, Fiona."

He left, and Arty started carefully packing the bricks back in the suitcases. Liria took the gun out of her pants and put it on the bed, rubbing the skin it had rested against. "You do that shit often? Snort coke?"

Arty glanced up at her knowingly. "No fucking way. That shit bites."

Liria's shoulders relaxed a little. Arty zipped the suitcases back up and stared at her for a moment, tapping her bare foot against the floor. She went over to the window and spent a couple minutes peeking out at the gap between the curtains. "I think we should leave now."

Liria's lips twisted into a grin. "You're just high and can't sit still."

Arty smiled over her shoulder and shrugged. "Maybe a little. This is good shit. But I wouldn't be able to sleep with that much in the room, anyway, and we've got a fourteen hour drive ahead of us."

Liria nodded. She'd been looking forward to spending the night curled up next to her, but she started gathering her things.

They wheeled the suitcases out to the car. A

gusty, balmy wind blew, carrying tiny droplets of rain. Liria peered around in the darkness, on high alert. A car passed in front of them in the parking lot, and her heart pounded, but it kept going, the streetlight illuminating the profile of a bored-faced middle-aged woman.

They loaded the bags into the trunk of the rental. They jumped in, Arty in the driver's seat.

Arty scanned their surroundings as they pulled out of the parking lot and onto the freeway onramp. She heaved a sigh once they were in traffic. "Al's good, but you just never know," she muttered.

Liria stared out the window at the city skyline in the distance, the windows of the skyscrapers little points of light in the darkness. She kicked off her too-small shoes and propped her feet up on the glove box, tapping her toes.

Arty shot her a grin. "Nervous?"

"Of course."

Arty laughed. "Don't worry. I'm a pro."

"Why do you do this shit, anyway? Didn't you go to college?"

Arty blew a raspberry. "My bachelor's degree doesn't count for shit. Business Administration, and a stupid minor in political science. I was mostly dealing drugs in the dorms and running internet scams the whole time. I wouldn't be able to get a regular job anywhere, and this pays better than anything else, anyway." She glanced sideways at her. "You never ran drugs?"

"No."

Arty pulled at her lip, looking between Liria and the road, and Liria crossed her arms.

"Cyryl supported me, mostly. And I lived with other people. I was in foster care until a year ago. I never sold my ass."

"I didn't think you did," Arty said quickly. She was silent a moment, shooting her odd glances. "You're so young."

Liria raised an eyebrow. "How old are *you,* anyway?"

Arty avoided her eyes. "Thirty-one."

Liria's lips curved into a smile. "You don't look that old."

"Thirty-one isn't *old.*"

"Keep telling yourself that, Grandma."

Arty smacked her lightly on the shoulder, and Liria smacked her back. There was a short giggling tussle until the car swerved a bit and Arty suddenly got serious, gripping the wheel. Liria's scalp tingled, thinking of all those drugs in the back. Arty checked the mirrors, and relaxed, leaning back. She gazed distantly out the windshield, and signaled to pass a truck. The huge wheels kicked spray onto the windshield.

"So, anyway. This Cyryl guy…"

Liria picked at her cuticles. "What about him?"

"How did you even…I mean, what's up with that guy? You thought he was your dad but he's not?"

Liria looked away, wondering why Arty wouldn't just let the subject die. Droplets of misty rain arced over the glass, leaving trails. "He's not on my birth certificate. Never got a blood test. He looks nothing like me at all. When I went to his house a couple weeks ago, looking for someplace to stay, he told me he's not my dad, he's sterile. He was just paying child support because my mom was blackmailing him somehow." Liria risked a glance at her and cringed. "He's not a bad guy. He helped me kick dope. And he saved my life."

"He saved your life?"

"I overdosed and he gave me CPR."

"You overdosed? Is that why you quit?"

"I guess that's part of it. And it was just shitty, to be hooked. It feels good, but you just fucking *need* it, every goddamn day, or your life crashes in on you, and the hustle is hard."

"I know," Arty said.

Liria glanced up at her sharply. "You do?"

She smiled faintly. "When I was younger I dealt heroin. By the time I was your age, I was hooked on it. I eventually figured out that that wasn't a fun game to play. I was twenty-two before I kicked for good." Arty's lips twisted wryly. "I'm lucky I had my parents, someplace to go, someone to feed me and take care of me while I figured it out. It made it a lot easier to stay clean. You don't have anyone, but you're still doing better than I was at your age." She gave Liria a quick glance. "You're going to be all right."

Arty stared out the windshield, the reflected glow of the headlights showing the faint crease in her brow. The only sound in the cabin was the hiss of tires on wet pavement. Liria tried to imagine Arty on heroin. It was a stretch. She seemed so together.

"How did your mom die?" Arty asked.

Liria scooted back and pulled her knees to her chest. "Hepatitis. Her liver just gave up."

"Ah." She reached out and squeezed Liria's

knee. "Sorry for the questions. I was just curious. I know you don't like to talk about this stuff."

"No, it's okay."

Arty brushed an escaped tendril of strawberry-blonde hair from her face. "Families are fucked up."

Liria examined her. "What's your family like?"

Arty shifted in her seat and shrugged, grinning. "My dad's a fuckhead, my mom's another fuckhead. You know. Regular Brooklyn family."

"I guess I wouldn't know."

"Lucky you," Arty said, and turned on the radio.

***

They drove all night through the prairie and across the Appalachians, talking. Liria told her about Lee Harvey and The Mare. She even told her the story of how her mom had tried to sell Liria's virginity to her dealer for a few grams when she was fourteen. Arty talked about her brother and sister and a hilarious boyfriend she'd had in high school.

The cloudy horizon began to gleam silver in front of them, and Arty rubbed her eyes. They stopped for breakfast: bacon and egg sandwiches in greasy, crinkly, wrappers and cups of strong, bitter coffee.

They drove on. Arty told a story about a Christmas when she'd talked her brother into helping her steal her sister's candy, then had only given him a twenty-five percent cut.

Liria giggled. "That's pretty messed up."

Arty shrugged. She was paler than usual, her

crows' feet showing. "Yeah, but you gotta follow your muse, I guess. I am who I am—an asshole."

"You're not an asshole."

Arty smiled. "You're my first girlfriend to ever say that."

Warmth spread through Liria's chest, all the way to her limbs, and she reached out to take Arty's hand.

"I've always wanted to quit this hustle, though, even if it is what I'm good at," Arty said, her brow furrowing.

Liria gazed at her. "You should."

Arty sighed, and gave her a wan smile. "I will someday. Just gotta figure out how."

***

Soon the Manhattan skyline rose up amongst the broken clouds. They waded through traffic, returned the rental, and got a cab to Arty's apartment. By the time they got there, Liria felt like her head might melt from fatigue.

Arty dialed her phone as soon they closed the apartment door. "I'm back," she said. "Can you come pick it up now?" She scowled, stood up, and walked into her room as Liria watched her. "He said what?"

Arty let out a tortured sigh. "Okay, I'll call him. Yeah. Thanks, Lalie."

The older woman muttered some curses. Liria squatted down to pet the cat, who almost threw her off balance by head-butting her knees.

"It's me," Arty said from her room. "What the

fuck did you tell Lalie I had to call you for?"

She laughed in disbelief. "Oh, *no*, no, no, no. No fucking way. I'll bring it to you tonight."

There was a pause, then Arty exploded. "What the fuck! No!" There was a thud loud enough to make Liria jump and send the cat streak off with flattened ears. It sounded like Arty had pounded her fist against the wall. Liria stood and tiptoed over to the couch. Arty took a deep breath and let it out slowly. She spoke in a measured tone. "Listen. You don't need to involve her in this. She's not involved. Okay?"

She sighed again. "God," she moaned. "Jesus fuck. Okay. *Okay.* Whatever. Just…just give us a few hours to rest, all right? We drove all night. Oh. Shit, yes, well…*Jesus*, Dad, what did you expect me to do?"

Liria went cold. *Dad.*

"Well, okay then. Okay. Six thirty. See you then."

Arty made a strangled noise. "Fuck, fuck *fuck*."

Liria sat frozen. *Dad.* Arty didn't come out of her room for a while. The fat kitty hopped up into Liria's lap and purred insistently, kneading her thighs, and she petted him absentmindedly.

Eventually Arty came out and stood by the couch. Liria didn't look up, but she could hear her fidgeting.

"Liria…"

Liria's eyes snapped up. "Your dad. He's the one, right? He ordered Lee Harvey dead."

Arty pressed the heels of her hands into her eyes.

"I'm not fucking stupid," Liria said.

"I know." She sighed and took her hands away, fixing Liria with a desperate look. "Yeah, it was my fucking dad."

Tears came to Liria's eyes and her face crumpled. She pounded the couch cushions, and the cat jumped up and ran off. She felt ill. Here she was, in fucking New York. What was she going to do? And she didn't want to leave. She liked Arty.

She started to cry, and Arty sat down next to her, slid her hands around to her back and hugged her tight. Liria let her.

"I'm so sorry," Arty said. "I fucking hate that dick. I hate him. He just doesn't understand that he's hurting people, I think. And not only that, but it's completely pointless. Lee Harvey should still be alive. What he did was fucking stupid." Liria pressed her face into Arty's neck, every muscle in her body rigid. *I should go. I should leave. I should go.* But she didn't. She sat in Arty's arms, breathing steadily through her constricted throat and gulping back her sobs.

"You have to believe that I never wanted Lee Harvey or Cameron to die," Arty said, running her hands up and down her back. "That all happened completely off my watch, and I didn't find out about it until afterwards." Her voice broke. "I feel like a complete shithead. I know it's no comparison to how you feel, but still. I was sent to babysit that fucktard of a senator, and my dad tells me, 'Let him have his blow and his little boys; just make sure he's smart about it.' Well, I thought I was doing the best I could. But I fucked up. I didn't know. I didn't know."

221

Liria took a deep breath. "Why were you babysitting him in the first place?"

"My dad needs a contact in the Senate. He contributes to the guy's campaign, and in return the senator helps my dad out in a lot of ways. Usually it's a mutually-beneficial relationship, but lately the senator has been going a little off the deep end. Fuck him. I'm not dealing with him anymore."

Liria took another deep breath. *She didn't kill me*, Lee Harvey's voice said in her head. *It's okay for you to like her. In fact, I insist on it.* Liria wiped her nose.

"And that's not even the worst of it," Arty said, her voice dull.

Fear seared through Liria's nerves; what could be worse than Arty's dad killing Lee Harvey? But then she understood. "The worst of it is your dad's coming over, right? I have to meet him."

"Exactly. He knows I brought you back from Vegas because he saw the credit card charge for your flight. He's nervous you were mixed up in that deal somehow and wants to meet you." She huffed. "I fucking *hate* that dick."

Liria curled into a ball around her knees. Arty hugged her tighter. "Liria, I'm sorry. Please forgive me."

"Why do you have me here? Your dad will kill me if he finds out who I am. Am I some sort of game to you? Some sort of project?"

"No! Liria, *God*."

Liria struggled out of her arms and glared at her through her tears. "Seriously, Arty. This is crazy. You say you want to keep me safe but it ends up your fucking dad is the one who I need to be scared of. Now I have to actually *meet* the asshole. I don't understand what you want with me. I'm all the way in New York, with no money and no one because of you. Just cut the shit and tell me what you plan to do with me, because I don't believe you'd be stupid enough to risk your father's organization just because you wanted to screw some junkie slut you met at a bar in Vegas."

Arty's eyes narrowed, but there was a glint of embarrassment behind her anger. "You aren't a junkie slut, Liria. And why do you think I'm risking my dad's operation with you here? Are you working for someone else?"

Liria scowled. "What? No!"

Arty nodded slightly. "Well, then, are you going to go to the cops?"

"No fucking way."

"You're not a risk, then, right? And if I thought you were, I wouldn't have brought you here, no matter how hot you were. You're a sweet girl, and you fuck good. I just wanted you here, that's all. Plus, your life really *is* in danger, Liria, I wasn't lying about that. You're much better off with me than out wandering the streets."

Liria sniffed and wiped her nose, taking a shuddering breath. "I like being with you, Arty, but…" She winced.

Arty heaved a sigh. "But my fucking dad, right? Listen, I understand. And if you want to leave, it will fuck me up, but I won't stop you. But please, Liria. Don't hold what my dad does against me. If I could keep him from being a dick, believe me, I would. But I have no control over that ass."

Liria wiped her eyes and squinted at her. Every part of her hoped that Arty was telling the truth. "You really didn't have anything to do with...with Lee Harvey?"

"I really didn't." Arty leaned forward and kissed her lips, wet because of her tears. She pulled her closer, into her arms. "I've been selfish, and stupid," Arty murmured. "I'm sorry. But please stay. Please give me a chance. I care about you, Liria."

Liria let out a breath. She felt good in her arms, like everything was going to finally be okay. *She said she cares about me.* This beautiful woman with the goofy smile and the nice apartment and seemingly endless supply of money said she cared about her. *She wasn't involved in Lee Harvey's death. That was her dad, not her. She wouldn't do anything like that.* Liria screwed her eyes shut and repeated that mantra over and over in her head.

"Will you stay?" Arty murmured. "Will you forgive me and stay?"

Liria nodded. "I'll stay."

Chapter 18

They slept until late afternoon. Liria drifted slowly out of a beautiful dream of floating down a clear creek fringed by bright spun-glass orchids, and found herself warm in Arty's arms, the grey light of the rainy afternoon filtering through the plantation shades.

They took a shower, then sat close together on the couch as Arty flipped lazily through the on-demand selections. Liria bushed her wet hair, watching the broken clouds spit down rain and sunshine on the park across the street.

As evening began to gather, there was a knock at the door. Liria went rigid. Arty squeezed her thigh. "You okay?"

Liria nodded, her teeth aching from being clenched. "I'm fine."

"All right. One thing, though. Don't tell my dad your last name. The less he knows about you at this point, the better. Tell him your last name is Gonzalez if he asks."

Liria's brow furrowed, but she nodded again.

225

"Okay."

Arty got up, and Liria heard the door squeak open. "Hey, Dad."

"Hey, Fireball." Liria stood up as they came into the room, her stomach heavy. Arty's dad stopped when he saw her, looking her up and down. His ready-made scowl drained from his face and he held his hand out. "Hi, I'm Morton."

Liria shook his hand, forcing a smile to her lips. He had a firm, dry grip, like a man used to shaking hands. "I'm Liria. Nice to meet you."

He stood squinting at her, fingering his cleft chin, one corner of his mouth twitching up. Liria remained still, twisting her hands together in front of her. Arty stood next to her dad, looking back and forth between them. She was a couple inches taller than he was. After a moment, she rolled her eyes. "Sit down, unless you two are going to start circling each other like roosters."

Morton seemed to come back to himself. He flopped down in an armchair, sighing and running his hand across his sparse, brown hair. The other two sat on the couch.

"Parking's a fucking bitch in this neighborhood," he said. "I don't know why you insist on living here."

"What, it's better in Brooklyn?" Arty said.

"It's always better in Brooklyn." He fixed his keen blue eyes on Liria. "What part are you from?"

"I'm from L.A.," Liria said.

Morton raised his eyebrows. "L.A.? You an actress or something? Model?"

"She was working with Mister Mike," Arty said,

glancing quickly at Liria.

"Pssh," Morton said, wincing. "That fuck." He smiled slightly, his squint gone. "You're well shut of that guy. I should have him toasted." Liria kept herself from cringing. He tapped his palms on the armrests and looked at his daughter. "Let's go get some dinner or something. There's food around here, right?"

"No, they haven't discovered food yet in the Village," Arty said. "We just photosynthesize like plants."

"You live entirely on your own inflated sense of self-worth." He winked at Liria. "Bunch of fucking fatheads around here."

"You would know." Arty stood. "Come on. There's a good Japanese place down the block."

"I could go for some Japanese." Morton pushed himself to his feet. He was short and had a gut, but the way he moved gave the impression of fitness.

Liria followed them out the front. Arty put on a wool cardigan and passed Liria a quilted jacket, taking it from a hook on the hall tree. Morton buttoned up his wool overcoat. "You didn't bring your own jacket?"

"I'm from L.A.," Liria said. "I don't own a jacket." She caught Arty's smirk.

"That's right, you don't have weather in L.A.," Morton said. "Lucky you."

They took the elevator down. Morton rocked back on his heels. It wasn't raining when they got outside, but a breeze shook droplets onto their heads from the leaves. Arty took Liria's hand.

"Your stinking brother-in-law got some job in

New Hampshire, so he and Marta are moving at the beginning of the year," Morton said, his eyes darting to their clasped hands.

"What?" Arty exclaimed. "Are you serious? They just moved to Yonkers like a year and a half ago."

"Yeah, but he got some promotion."

Arty held open the door of the restaurant for them, and the smell of food reached out into the damp air to drag Liria in, making her stomach growl despite the how nauseated Morton made her. The waitress seated them by the window and poured them hot tea as they hung their jackets on the backs of their chairs. Arty drew circles on Liria's palm under the table while she and her father stared each other down like sparring cats.

"How's Mom? She still have that thing with her foot?"

"Oh yeah, she's still wobbling around like a chair with a leg missing. Doctor says it's the cartilage between her toe joints."

Arty frowned, pursing her lips in an overblown expression of sympathy. "Aw. That's too bad."

"Might need an operation."

"An operation. Mom will hate that. She'll be flat on her back in bed. Get her a walkie talkie so she can still yell at the maid."

Liria sipped her tea silently, casting veiled glances at the man who had ordered Lee Harvey's murder. He didn't look like the type, exactly. He had eyes the color of his daughter's, and an open, straightforward expression.

The waitress came. Liria ordered the pork katsu.

228

Arty and her dad squabbled over sushi choices for three minutes while the waitress sat tapping her pen, looking a bit frightened. Finally, they ordered about thirty things and the poor woman scampered off.

Morton leaned back in his chair folding his hands over his gut, and looked at Liria. His face split into a stained-toothed grin. "So you're gonna work for me now, I take it."

Arty's hand clenched hers. "Did she say that? No one said that, Dad." The older woman looked quickly around the room. "Let's not talk about this shit here."

"Whatever you say, Princess. I just find it interesting, is all."

Arty's lips were so tight that Liria worried they'd snap as she forced them into a smile. "Do you?"

He flopped his palms open briefly on his belly and shrugged. "Sure. You come back from Vegas with some arm candy and all of a sudden you've got her working with you." He smiled at Liria. "She doesn't usually do stuff like that. You must be a special gal."

Liria slumped lower in her chair. Arty sat rigidly, her nostrils flaring, her brittle smile hanging precariously on her face. "She is a special gal, Dad. She's going to move in with me."

His eyebrows shot up, and his mouth fell open slightly. He reached out to fiddle distractedly with his teacup. "Isn't that something?" He gazed at Liria with a faraway look, some of the tension draining from his face. "Hey, is gay marriage legal in this state yet? Maybe you two could get a stud and make some grandbabies."

Liria twitched and rubbed her nose, glancing longingly at the street outside, now shrouded in bitter rain and growing darkness. Arty took a moment to get herself under control, then gave her an apologetic look. "I don't think you're making joining the family look very attractive, Dad."

He sat up a bit and rolled his eyes. "Ahh. I'm sorry. I don't mean to be that way. It's a hard business, is all. I worry, and you know I have concerns. You come back from that fiasco in Vegas with some chick I don't know. You gotta figure I'm going to worry."

"Well, let's worry about it later," Arty said.

Morton let the subject drop, so conversation during the rest of the meal was somewhat less strained, but Liria still felt the tension as they walked home. She shared an umbrella with Arty, raindrops snapping against it. Arty kept her arm around her, but they didn't speak until after they shook off their umbrellas and entered the elevator.

"Not looking forward to driving back in this weather," Morton said.

"You'll survive," Arty said, as if the notion disappointed her.

They went into the apartment and took off their damp coats. Morton settled back into the armchair in the sitting room. Arty and Liria sat on the couch side-by-side, Liria picking at her cuticles. Her dinner churned in her stomach as she avoided looking at Arty's dad.

"Okay, let's just get this over with," Arty said. "Liria worked for Mister Mike for two years. She's not a security risk. But I'm not bringing her here to work for you. She's here because she's my girlfriend, pure and simple."

"Fair enough. But you took her on a run already."

"What choice did I have? You sprung that shit on me the day I got back from Vegas. I'm supposed to leave her here?"

"Why not? What, she's going to chew on the furniture like a bored puppy while you're gone?"

Arty sighed, pinching the bridge of her nose. "How did you ever end up married, Dad?"

"Who, me? You're the one talking like a coke transport makes for a great first date." His eyes glittered as he looked at Liria. "And why did you come back with her from Vegas, if you're from L.A.? How were you involved in that bullshit?" Arty opened her mouth, but Morton held up a hand. "Let her talk. I want to hear what she has to say."

A pang of fear struck the pit of Liria's stomach, but hot anger rolled over it. "I wasn't involved in whatever happened there. I met Arty in Vegas because I wanted to see her."

"How'd you like the senator?"

"I didn't meet him. I did other things while Arty was working."

"Ah. It's only later she decided bringing you to work was a good idea."

Arty sighed in exasperation. "Dad, it would have been really fucking inappropriate for me to bring her with that fuckface while he followed his prick around like a divining rod. And about that…"

"Oh, here we go."

"Yeah, here we fucking go. Why did you sink

money into that hole, anyway? And then, when he shows what a fucking idiot he is by leaving those goddamn texts and emails on his cellphone and letting himself get blackmailed, you just dig yourself deeper instead of cutting your losses." Arty clutched Liria's hand tight enough to hurt as she stared her father down, her chest heaving. Morton met her gaze with a grim smile.

"The senator is invaluable to the operation. I wouldn't expect you to understand."

"No, *you* don't understand," Arty said. Liria finally had to take her hand away before her fingers got crushed. Arty didn't even seem to notice. "You're so far up on your little pedestal, your tinfoil throne, that you have no idea what's really going on out there. If you had actually *seen* what a fuck-all moron that senator is, you wouldn't have wasted time and resources on him. You wouldn't have…" She clamped her lips shut and closed her eyes, taking a deep breath.

"Listen, Fireball," Morton said calmly, leaning forward with his elbows on his knees, "that *fuck-all moron* has saved my ass, *our* ass, more times than I care to count. He's tipped us off about investigations and kept the feds out of our business. He's helped us with legislation. And all he wants in return is some modest contributions and a trip to Vegas now and again. But if you're gonna judge the guy because he likes gay sex and getting high once in a while, well, I don't know what to tell you."

Liria watched Arty warily, surprised when she actually seemed to grow calmer. "If he keeps on like that," she said, "he's going to lose his seat, and we'll go down with him. At the very least all the money will go down the shitter, and you'll face a shitton of heat from further up."

"That's why I put you in charge, because it was very important that not happen. But I know now that was a mistake."

Arty grew calmer still, and Liria was reminded of a tiger preparing to pounce. "Dad," she said, but Morton cut in.

"Your problem, Arty, is that this is a much bigger game than you're playing. I know this stuff isn't always pretty, but that's the way it is. It's our game, and we've gotta play to win."

Liria fought back her fury. Arty smiled coldly. "I guess I have a different definition of what it is to win." Her smile faded, her face blank as she stared at her father. He held her gaze with a slight smile. After a moment, he tapped the armrests with his palms, then stood up.

"I should get going. Where's the damn suitcases?"

Arty rose from the couch and wheeled them out of her bedroom, passing the handles to him with raised eyebrows.

Morton smiled down at Liria before he headed for the door. "It was very nice to meet you, Liria. I hope to see you again soon. You're bringing her to Marta's thing, right?"

"Yeah, Dad," Arty said tiredly.

"Good." He stared at Liria thoughtfully, fiddling with the button on one of the suitcase handles. "If you're ever looking for a stud for your babies, think about keeping it in our family, you know? It's more real that way, like real grandkids."

He grinned as every muscle in Liria's body went taut. She fought the urge to scream or run or punch something. He turned and went out, and Arty practically slammed the door after him. "That fucking *ass,*" she bellowed as she flopped back down on the sofa. She hid her face in her hands for a moment then looked at Liria, her expression pale and strained. "I'm so sorry," she said.

Liria sat at the other end of the couch, curled into a ball. She didn't see what was in front of her; she saw Lee Harvey, collapsed awkwardly on the hotel room carpet like a discarded doll.

Arty scooted over and put her hand on her shoulder gently. Liria flinched, but relaxed as Arty stroked her skin with her slender fingers. "I'm sorry, Liria," she murmured.

The flyaway hairs of Arty's bright red ponytail were haloed by the light from the floor lamp, and something in Liria softened. She crawled over and put her head in Arty's lap, breathing steadily.

"I fucking *hate* that guy," Arty said.

Liria cuddled closer to her. "I don't think much of him either," she said, and Arty's silent chuckle burst into a full-blown laugh.

Chapter 19

Liria woke up the next morning alone in bed. The smell of coffee drew her out of the covers and into the kitchen.

She poured herself a cup, and mixed in cream with three spoons of sugar. She went out into the living room where she found Arty on the couch in a t-shirt and underwear, her laptop open on her bare knees.

Arty glanced over and smiled, but her attention was immediately drawn back to the screen. Liria sat down next to her cross-legged, resting her warm mug on her bare heel and peeking at the computer. It looked like Arty was scrolling through bank account transactions. Her lips moved silently as she worked.

"My dad never learned how to hack," Arty said after a moment. "He always lets me handle that sort of thing." A childish grin spread over her face, then faded again. Her eyes remained focused on the screen, alight with concentration.

Liria studied the screen. "You're fucking with

235

his money?"

"Yeah. I'm gonna bleed him dry before I bring him down."

Liria clutched her coffee cup. "You're going to…what?"

"I've had enough of his bullshit. I'm going to destroy the motherfucker."

Liria pursed her lips in disbelief, feeling something between happiness and fear. Her nerves felt like they were tangled up in knots. "What are you going to do to him?"

Arty stopped typing, stretched her arms above her head. "I don't know. I'll see what I can work out with some of his rivals. Just dismantle his business."

Liria smiled. "Good," she said. "That's awesome."

Arty grinned back. "I thought you'd like it." She settled back typing again, and Liria gazed unseeingly at her coffee cup. She imagined Morton huddled on a park bench in the rain, all his remaining worldly possessions in a plastic bag next to him. She imagined him dying of pneumonia or something even more painful like syphilis or AIDS, because he'd had to sell his ass for booze money. Her guts burned as she saw in her mind the desperate look in his eyes as he took his last, labored breath, saw the realization dawn on him, *I shouldn't have killed Lee Harvey. I'm a fucking bastard who doesn't deserve to live, and I'm going to spend eternity in Hell.*

Arty was watching her from the corner of her eye. "Are you okay?"

Liria blinked. The vision faded, and she let her shoulders relax. "Yeah, I'm okay." She glanced over at the screen. "What are you doing?"

Arty chewed on her lip. "Changing the passwords and setting up alternate accounts to funnel money into."

Liria's heart beat a little faster. "Won't he notice?"

Arty scowled. "Not if I do it right. He's an idiot."

Liria sipped her coffee, pulling at the ends of her hair, watching Arty type and scroll through columns of transactions. She didn't understand what she was looking at, and fell into a reverie again. This time she imagined Arty being hauled off in handcuffs, then face-down on her bedroom floor in a pool of blood.

Liria winced and squirmed, taking a deep breath. *Arty knows what she's doing.*

"Arty?" she said hesitantly

"Mmm?"

"What are you going to do if…if this works out?"

Arty blinked, then grinned. She leaned over and kissed her. "Take the money and run."

Liria twirled her coffee cup in her hands as Arty resumed typing. "Will you take me with you?"

Arty looked over at her, obviously startled. "Of course."

Liria scooted over so that her thigh rested against Arty's. She sunk into a pleasant mental haze. Arty cared about her. She wanted to keep her around. And now she was going to hustle enough money so that they never had to hustle again.

Arty jerked her out of her rose-colored musings.

"I need you to call your friend Nestor," she said.

Liria blinked at her. "What?"

"I want you to tell him you have info to pass on to Cameron's boss."

That sank in. "You fucking act all scary bitch to him on the phone, and then want me to call him?"

"Tell him you got away from the scary woman, and now you want revenge on the people who killed Lee Harvey."

Liria studied her. "You're going to have these people kill your father?"

"No. I'm just going to pass them some select info to fuck with his operations and get him in a corner. That way I have negotiating power."

Liria chewed on her lip, then nodded. "Okay. What do you want me to tell him?"

"Say you want to send Cameron's boss a text or email or instant message, or talk to him on the phone, whichever he'd prefer. You just need to know how to contact him."

Liria sighed and rubbed the spot between her eyes. The thought of talking to Nestor hurt. He'd told her there was no catch about that job. She'd liked him, but he'd lied. It was a small price to pay to kick Arty's dad in the dangles and to start a new life, but still, she didn't want to do it.

"I'll do it," she said.

Arty kissed her. "Thank you."

Liria scowled. She got up and poured herself another cup of coffee, grabbed her phone, and came back to the couch. When she turned it on, a slew of texts and voicemails poured in from Cyryl. She saw Arty trying to peek, so closed the window without reading them. She looked Nestor's number up in her contacts. Her heart pounded as she punched the call button.

He answered on the third ring, sounding frantic. "Liria? Is that you?"

"Nestor, you're okay. Thank God."

"I'm fine. Are you okay? Where are you?"

"New York."

There was a short silence. "*New York?*"

"It's a long story. I ended up with a woman who worked for a senator…" She let it sit there.

"Oh shit," Nestor said. "Oh, fuck, Liria. Are you all right? Can you talk?"

"Yeah, I can talk. I'm okay. I got out of there. I'm not with that bitch anymore." She shot Arty a look. The older woman smirked.

"Liria," he said, "I'm really fucking sorry I put you in this position. When Cameron asked me to bring him girls from Cassie's club, I just thought he wanted hot slutty girls. I mean, no offense…"

"It's okay, Nestor."

"I had no idea it would turn into this."

"It's okay," she repeated. She met Arty's gaze with her own. She wanted him to be telling the truth, but if he were, he may not be able to help them. "Listen," she said. "I have some information I want to pass to Cameron's boss. I know who…I know who killed Lee Harvey and Cameron."

"Jesus," he muttered. "Fuck, Liria, you don't want to tell him that. Don't get involved in that shit."

She winced. "Lee Harvey was my best friend. I want to get back at those people. Please, Nestor. If you know how to get a hold of him…"

"How did you even become associated with those people?" Liria heard the note of suspicion in his voice, and had to fight back a wave of anger and nausea.

"I didn't know them before," she said. "This woman, the one that worked for the senator…she came in when I'd just found Lee Harvey…dead. She told me my life was in danger and hid me." Her brows knitted. "How do *you* know about them, though, if you supposedly didn't know anything about what was going on at the club?"

"I don't know much about them really," he said quickly, but Liria could hear the sincerity in his voice. "I only figured out what was going on after, when I was talking to people."

Liria didn't respond, but waited, wiggling her foot nervously. Finally, he let out a long sigh. "It just so happens I might know who you want to talk to, but I'm not sure. There was a guy that came into the club the night you didn't show up. He told me Cameron was dead, and he was asking all sorts of questions. That and the fact that you weren't there freaked me the fuck out, so I took off. But he did give me his number. Let me call him and sound him out."

Liria let out a breath. "Thank you, Nestor. That's really cool of you. Tell him I can send him some info by text or email or whatever he wants."

"Yeah, all right." He didn't sound happy. "Are you really okay? Do you need someplace to go?"

"No, I found a place."

"In New *York*?"

Liria giggled. "You talk like it's the middle of bumfuck and there's no places to stay here."

"It's just weird, is all."

"And what about you?" she asked. "Are you okay? You got out of there, right?"

"Yeah, I got the hell out of there. I'm in San Francisco now."

"San *Francisco*?" Liria said, giggling. "Where's that? Have they discovered fire there yet? Did you find a cave to live in?"

He laughed. "Oh, stop it."

"But you found work? You're doing okay?"

"Yeah, I'm doing all right. I got some shit going on here."

Liria didn't want to ask what it was, but she hoped it was a good situation. "I'm glad you got out of Vegas okay."

"Me too." He sighed. "Be careful, all right? I'll get a hold of this dude and I'll call you back."

"Thanks."

Liria hung up and leaned back on the couch, glancing at Arty. "If something happens to him…he's a good dude."

"Nothing's going to happen to him. Why would anything happen to him? He's just helping you pass a message."

Liria didn't respond. She brought her knees to her chest, and Arty watched her for a few moments. "I'll make you a breakfast sandwich. That will make you feel better."

Liria broke into a grin. "Thanks, Arty."

***

Liria was eating a toasted English muffin with egg, Canadian bacon, and grilled pineapple when her phone rang. She put her sandwich down and snatched it up with sticky fingers.

"Hello?"

"Hey, Liria."

Nestor's voice sounded flat, and her guts went hollow. "What's wrong?"

"I got a hold of the guy. His name's Thomas."

Liria waited a breathless moment, but he didn't continue. "And?"

He heaved a sigh. "He wants the information in person. He tried to tell me it'd be safer for you."

The breakfast sandwich crept back into her throat. "What? But I'm all the way across the flippin' country!"

"He says he'll pay your flight and your room."

Liria exchanged a look with Arty. "I...this is weird. Does he just not trust me?"

"He's paranoid about something, I guess."

"Can I call you back? I gotta think about this."

"I don't blame you. Yeah, call me back."

Liria punched the disconnect button and exchanged a terrified look with Arty.

"He wants an in-person?" Arty asked.

"Yeah. He even says he'll pay for the flight and the room. What do I do?"

"Say okay. But say you'll book your own flight and hotel and he can pay you back. You don't want to give him your real name, and he'd need it."

Liria's brow furrowed. "No fucking way. I'm not

meeting with him."

"Liria, please…"

"You grabbed my phone away and told Nestor to eat shit, and drugged me, and kept me in that hotel room. Now you want me to…" She pounded her thighs and squeezed her eyes shut, feeling dizzy. "I thought you wanted to keep me safe? I thought you wanted it to look like I'm not involved in this? Well, I'm *not*. Now you want me to *become* involved in it."

Liria could feel Arty looking at her. She gazed out the window at the glare of the morning sun. Her emotions punched her guts. She really liked Arty, and she needed her. But this request made her feel like she was freefalling into a dark abyss. She crossed her arms.

"I'd make sure you'd be in no danger," Arty said quietly.

"Fucking around in gangster bullshit, there's no way to make sure of that. Lee Harvey is proof. All he wanted is to make a few bucks having fun and getting high, and now he's dead. The same could happen to me."

"I cut my teeth on gangster bullshit, and I know what I'm doing. You'd have a very small part to play, and they'd never know your real name."

"You talk to him. You meet with the guy. I'm out of it."

Arty laughed derisively. "He'll know I'm not you. He might've even seen me with the senator. He'll see me coming a mile away, and investigate and find out who I am. Then, if he talks to me at all, he's going to try to cut some deal, and may turn it around on me and go to my father." She and Liria glared at each other. "But you're some girl who's just trying to get revenge on the people who killed her friend and basically kidnapped her. That will float. Your motivation is clear. He won't think three times about it."

"Why is he doing this? Why does he want to meet me in person?"

"I don't fucking know. Probably he's paranoid about technology, though he's too small-potatoes to have to worry about that shit. Or he just wants to get a look at you, make sure you are who you say you are."

"I've never met him."

"Yeah, but I'll bet he's seen you. You just didn't know it."

Liria looked down at her lap for a long time. The image of Arty's dad was burned into her brain. *What a fucking shithead.* And he'd killed Lee Harvey. *That guy* had killed, funny, kind Lee Harvey. She clutched her middle. What other choice did she have? If she didn't do this, Arty would get mad. She'd resent her for making her do all the work to support them.

Finally she swallowed the bile that had risen into her throat. "Okay, whatever. I'll call Nestor back in a minute, set it up."

Arty broke into a grin, then leaned over and kissed her. "Thank you."

Liria nodded listlessly, avoiding Arty's gaze. She sucked at her teeth. She had pineapple strings stuck between them. "Do you have any floss?"

"In the medicine cabinet." She picked up her

laptop and started working on the accounts again.

Liria got up and slouched into the bathroom, closing the door. She stood looking at herself in the mirror. *Everybody always wants something out of you.* Her reflection blurred as tears came to her eyes, and she hugged herself.

Just because she wants something out of you doesn't mean she doesn't care about you. You want something out of her too.

She got some toilet paper, wiped her eyes, and blew her nose. She missed Lee Harvey. He hadn't wanted anything out of her, just her companionship. *Why did you have to kill him, you fucking cocksucker?* She clamped her chin to her chest, fighting back a fresh wave of grief.

She took a couple deep breaths and dabbed at her eyes again. Her reflection looked back at her red-eyed, and she wrinkled her nose at it.

She opened the medicine cabinet and found the floss. She was about to close it again but something caught her eye. A prescription pill bottle bearing the name of a familiar medication.

She grabbed it, her stomach swooping as it rattled. Oxycontin. And it was full. She turned it around and around in her hands. *She says she can't be around this stuff, but she has this shit in here.* It was dated almost a year ago. No true addict would have been able to keep it more than a few days.

Her stomach clenched, and she felt cold sweat prickling on the back of her neck. Arty had told her she'd kick her out if she did heroin…would she kick her out for a couple pills? Would she even notice?

She won't kick me out, she needs me. She needs me, but not in the way I want her to need me. She swallowed the lump in her throat.

It wasn't heroin; it was just pills. And it would feel so good to be high right now. It would make her feel better, help her think straight, without all the emotional bullshit getting in the way.

She took the cap off and shook some out into her palm. Three, four. She paused, considering. It was a full bottle, and one of the big ones like they give cancer patients. How many would she notice gone, if she even looked? She shook out a round dozen. She closed the bottle and put it back.

Liria swallowed four with water from the sink, and put the others in her pocket. She flushed the toilet for effect then wandered back out into the living room, flossing the pineapple out of her teeth.

Arty barely looked up from the computer screen as she came back in. *She'll never know.* Liria sat back and turned the TV on, flipping through the on-demand selections until she found Adventure Time, waiting for the bliss of the dope to hit her in the back of the skull.

***

Arty got someone to take care of the cat and they flew back to Vegas the next day. They purchased the tickets separately, from separate accounts— Liria's from her own, which Arty set up for her with her dad's money. Liria watched her do it, not quite understanding and feeling nervous about it. "Now you have ten thousand dollars of your own," Arty

246

said.

"Someone's going to notice that."

"Not the way I did it. Chill out. I'll set you up a better one later."

Liria chewed her cheek. "Why are you giving me money?"

Arty kissed her. "Because you're hot, and I like you." Liria tried to smile. "And also because it's better to spread it out to different accounts."

Liria picked at her fingernail polish and looked away.

***

The flight was coach this time, and they sat separately. Arty flew under a fake name just in case. They also had separate rooms in separate hotels, but they got dinner together after they checked in, in a restaurant off-strip.

Liria sat in the booth across from Arty and listlessly poked her onion rings into the ketchup. It wasn't just the prospect of meeting with the Thomas guy that was bugging her. It was that she could feel Lee Harvey here. She wondered if his mother had buried him yet, if he'd had a funeral, a gravestone. She hadn't had the guts to look up the news about his death.

Arty nudged her foot with hers. "You okay?"

"Yeah."

"We'll be back home this time tomorrow. You'll feel better."

Liria folded an onion ring between her fingers, getting crumbs and grease on her hands. "This is mega fucking stupid."

Arty smirked and took her greasy hand. "Liria, I…just, thank you."

Liria nodded, not looking at her.

***

She met the guy in a dark corner of a little bar on the second floor of the Cosmopolitan. It was quiet; there was a middle-aged man with ruddy sideburns at the bar, staring at the football game on the TV, his hand wrapped around his beer. The only other person there was the guy she was meeting.

Liria spotted him as she came in, right where Nestor had said he'd be, leaned back in a blue velvet sofa amongst the draping curtains of crystals hanging from the ceiling. He was familiar somehow; she must have seen him at the nightclub at some point, but couldn't remember when. He was a young-looking guy, with short black hair, a thin build, and he wore jeans and a short-sleeved button down shirt. He sipped his drink with raised eyebrows as she came up, then set it down and stood up to shake her hand.

"You're Thomas?" Liria asked, trying to keep her voice steady. She'd taken a few more pills before she came, which helped.

He smiled. "You must be Andrea."

Liria nodded. "Nice to meet you." Andrea Laird was the name she'd worked under in the nightclub, and he must have known that. They sat down, and the waitress came over to take her order. Liria had a tense moment, thinking she'd ask for her ID even though she only ordered a Coke, but she didn't. When she left, Liria and Thomas gazed at each other.

"Thank you for coming," he said. "I understand you had to fly all the way from New York."

"Yeah. But I felt like I had to, for my friend, you know?" She looked down at her hands clenched in her lap. They were sweating.

"His name was Lee Harvey?"

Liria nodded and made herself look back up at him. He squinted at her thoughtfully. A couple walked into the bar, young and smiling, dressed up in a suit and evening gown. Thomas watched them for a moment before looking back at her.

"I'm sorry about your friend. It was total bullshit, what happened to him."

Liria nodded and wiped her eyes.

"How did you end up in New York?"

She shifted in her seat. Her heart pounded so hard she was sure it was making the front of her shirt throb. "There was a woman…it was fucked up. I met her in the bar the night I started working, and I liked her, you know? She was beautiful, and funny, and nice. She seemed interested in me."

A smile flitted across his face. "You like women?"

It was hard to tell what he was thinking in the dim light. "Yeah."

He shrugged. "Just curious. Cameron told me he thought you did. Please, go on. Sorry to interrupt."

She picked her cuticles. "Anyway…so…I found Lee Harvey's body in the hotel room." She paused, closing her eyes. The waitress came, bringing her

Coke. Liria thanked her, then sat stirring it with the straw. She glanced up to see Thomas watching her closely, his chin resting on his hand.

"That really sucks."

Liria swallowed. "It did. It fucking sucked. And then that woman from the bar that I liked showed up right when I found him. She said she'd heard the maid screaming." Liria clutched her soda, the ice cubes rattling gently as she trembled. *You've got to get through this shit, for Lee Harvey.* She took an unsteady breath and steadied her hand. "She took me back to her room. I didn't really know what was going on for a while. All I knew was some hot chick was taking care of me for some reason. But then she wouldn't let me talk to anyone. And she was asking all these questions. I felt weird about it, but I just kept my mouth shut, because why wouldn't I? What else was I going to do?"

"You did the right thing," he said.

Liria sipped her Coke. "Eventually I figured out she worked for a senator named Melvin Capella, and I heard other shit when she was talking to people. I suspected something weird was going on, but I tried to tell myself it was nothing. She got me to go with her to New York." She paused, and Thomas uncrossed his legs, crossing them the other way.

"How the hell did she get you to do that?" he asked.

Liria felt heat crawl into her face. "I liked her. I thought she liked me." She shrugged her tense shoulders, looking away. "And she had money, you know? I mean, I knew something was fucked up, but I wanted to believe…I wanted to think she just liked me." Liria closed her eyes briefly. For a dizzying moment she actually believed her story. Her vision blurred again with tears and she wiped them away, taking a deep breath. She'd rehearsed this line in her head a billion times, but hearing herself say it out loud was different. "Really, I think she just wanted to keep me around, to make sure I didn't know more than I was letting on. I guess I should be grateful she didn't just have me killed, like her dad did to Lee Harvey."

Thomas went still. "Her dad?"

Liria nodded. Tears streamed down her face, and she let them, dabbing at her cheeks and wiping her nose with a napkin. "I met him, and I heard them talking. They weren't really that careful—I think they just thought I was an idiot or something. Her dad is a guy named Morton Kopanis."

Thomas pursed his lips. "You were involved with Morton Kopanis' *daughter?* You *are* lucky to be alive."

Liria grimaced. "I don't know much about him except he's a fucking dick, and he ordered Lee Harvey's murder."

Thomas gazed at her thoughtfully. "He's a dick, that's true. He comes out of the old school, I guess you'd say, but now he's connected with one of the big players of the new school. Got himself set up pretty nice." He sipped his drink. "And yeah, he's the one that had your friend and Cameron killed."

Liria let her grief and anger course through her. But she also set part of herself aside, watching her feelings as an impartial observer. She was playing her part. "I fucking hate that guy. Him and…and his fucking daughter."

Thomas brushed her arm with his fingertips. "I'm really sorry, Andrea." He looked quickly around the room, and Liria glanced around too. The lone guy at the bar sipped his drink and looked at his phone. The well-dressed couple sat down close together on a couch in the opposite corner. None of them seemed to be paying attention to them.

"Sorry, I'm too loud," she said, sniffing.

"It's okay," he said. "It's an emotional issue for you." He took her hand and squeezed it, then kept holding it, and she let him, her heart pounding. "How did you get away from them? The Kopanises?"

Liria shrugged. "I think eventually Arty just got tired of me. She figured out pretty quick I hadn't known jack shit about them being involved in Lee Harvey's death. Or at least I didn't, until I figured it out from them." Liria scowled. "They thought I was so stupid, but they're the fucking dipshits."

Thomas laughed. "True, that."

"She gave me some money and kicked me out. But not before I heard some shit you might be interested in."

He watched her closely. "What shit?"

Liria made herself stay very still. She didn't want to shake or bite her lip or fidget. She wished he weren't holding her hand, but didn't want to take it away. *You already got through most of this conversation. The rest should be easy.* "I heard them talking about how they'd given Senator Capella a house in the Bahamas somewhere, a couple of classic cars, and some time with a male prostitute in exchange for him supporting legislation that gave the Kopanises an effective monopoly on online gaming in New York State."

Thomas' eyebrows shot up. "Ah."

"Also, I heard them talking about a big shipment of heroin coming in from Chicago in three weeks." Liria took her sweaty hand from his and dug in the pocket of her shorts, taking out a folded half-sheet of notebook paper. "I wrote the details down." She held out the paper to him.

He took it, gazing at her distantly with his mouth slightly open. He tore his eyes away from her and unfolded the note, reading it. "Good stuff," he mumbled. He shot her a faint half-smile. "Thank you."

She nodded. "Just bring him down, okay? Make sure he fucking rots in jail for what he did to Lee Harvey."

"I will." He considered her a moment. "You're not going back to New York, are you?"

"I don't know."

"You should stay here, work for me. It's not safe for you anymore in New York."

Her heart thundered. "You're not going to fucking tell them I came to you, right? That would be pretty fucking dick."

"I'm not going to tell them," he said quickly, and laughed. "Get real. Why would I do that? But they may figure it out anyway. Why take the chance? I could use a smart girl like you too."

Liria tapped her foot against the floor. "I don't know. I don't want to get mixed up in this shit, really. I just wanted that douche to pay for what he did to Lee, that's all."

He nodded. "I understand." He reached into the pocket of his jeans and pulled out an envelope, then pulled a second one out of the other pocket. He handed both of them to her. "This is for your expenses, and your trouble. But please consider staying here. I can protect you, and you can make a good living."

She took the envelopes, running them through her fingers. "I'll think about it."

"Good. Your friend Nestor knows how to contact me."

He stood up and so did she. They shook hands. "Thank you," he said. "I'll make sure that bastard gets what's coming to him."

"Thanks," she said.

He smiled. "I hope to talk to you again soon."

Chapter 20

Liria walked through the balmy twilight on the Strip, watching the lights twinkling against the pink and grey sky. *I did a pretty good job at that shit.* She felt weak and trembly. She took a deep breath. *It's finally over with.*

She wondered if her efforts would bear fruit. What would happen to Morton Kopanis, and to his daughter? Liria let the thoughts roll around in her head, but she didn't know the situation well enough to figure it out. *And what happens to me, if something happens to her?* The thought of something happening to Arty made a sort of blackness rise up in her. She didn't want to think about that possibility.

She took a deep breath and let her worries evaporate. Her whole body buzzed with warmth from the pills and the aftereffects of her adrenaline rush, so it wasn't hard. Everything was going to work out perfectly. As she skipped between crowds of tourists and street performers, she got wrapped up in daydreams of lounging in a secluded villa

255

with Arty, secure in the knowledge that their fat bank account would never be depleted, since Morton had bled to death after having his dick cut off in prison.

As she opened the door to her hotel, she happened to glance back down the sidewalk. Her insides froze. Strolling through the crowd was a middle-aged guy with ruddy sideburns. He looked a lot like the guy that had been sitting at the bar at the Cosmo.

Liria ducked inside the hotel, her heart hammering. She made her shoulders relax as she walked through the slot machines to the elevator. *Don't look back.* She kept her eyes on the patterned carpet, sure he was following her, feeling his gaze boring into the back of her head.

Only after she'd punched the button for the elevator did she risk a glance back the way she came. There was no sign of the man with the sideburns. She let out a breath. Maybe it had just been a coincidence. Maybe he hadn't been following her at all.

She remembered the envelopes Thomas had given her, and opened them on the way up to her floor. The first one had five hundred in it. The second one was much fatter, and when she opened it, her jaw dropped. "Holy shit," she whispered. It was a huge pile of hundreds. She was a little more than halfway through the pile and had counted up to three thousand when the elevator doors opened again, and she shoved the cash back into the envelope, stuffed the envelopes back in her pocket.

She sauntered down the hall, her head in a fog,

and slid her key into the slot. When she walked into her room, she gasped. A figure was just inside the door, silhouetted against the light from the bedside lamp. The person grabbed her around the waist.

Liria let out a terrified squeak before she smelled strawberries and coconut, felt familiar lips against her neck, and her heart crawled back down out of her esophagus.

"Jesus fuck, Arty! What the fuck are you doing here?"

"I was worried." She kissed her and then clasped her tight in her arms, running her hands up her shirt, against her bare back. "Liria, I was so worried." She kissed her again, and Liria kissed her back, a slow joy blooming in her chest. She slid her hands over Arty's hips and pulled her gently closer.

"I should have gone with you," Arty murmured.

"You couldn't have gone with me. He would have figured out who you were in a second. He seemed to know who you were."

"I could have at least followed you and kept watch. It was hell waiting, worrying."

Liria tensed, and Arty pulled her lips from hers, looking at her quizzically. "What's wrong?"

"You really didn't have me followed, right? Because there was a guy in the bar, and I think I just saw him outside the hotel as I came in."

Arty's face hardened. Her voice dropped to just above a whisper. "Fuck." She went over and latched the door, then pulled the curtains, even though they were fifteen floors up. "What did he look like?"

"Mid-forties, maybe, normal height, stocky. Thinning reddish hair and sideburns. Kinda pasty and ugly."

Arty's eyes glittered. "Doesn't sound familiar."

"Maybe it was nothing. Maybe it wasn't even the same guy. There's plenty of ugly-looking white guys in Vegas."

Arty broke into a slow grin. "That's true." She took her by the hand and led her to the bed. "Come sit and tell me how the meeting went."

They stretched out on the bed and Liria told her while Arty stroked her hair. "So he wanted to offer you a job," Arty said. "I guess that's why he wanted you to come in person."

"He could have offered me a job over the phone, or whatever."

Arty's lips curled in a half-smile. "Not as effective that way. I'll bet he wanted to see what you looked like, if you were actually the girl from the nightclub, and gauge whether you were telling the truth. And I'm assuming he gave you money, to make the offer more attractive."

Liria squirmed slightly, and Arty grinned and tickled her on her ribs. "How much did he give you?"

Liria convulsed in giggles, squirming. "Fifty dollars!"

"Fifty dollars, right. How much?"

"Okay, seventy five. Stop it! Stop tickling me!" Liria smacked her hip, and Arty finally stopped. She twined her legs through Liria's and put her arm around her.

"I'm not going to steal your money," Arty said, smirking. "I just want to know."

"I know you're not going to steal it." Liria gazed

into her beautiful eyes and sighed. She rummaged in her pocket and brought out the envelopes. "I didn't count it all yet, but I think it's about fifty five hundred."

Arty took the envelopes, raising her eyebrows. "Fifty five hundred?"

"Yeah, it seemed a little much."

Arty shrugged and sat up against the headboard, opening the envelopes. "Those guys throw around money like confetti, especially when there's a hot girl around." She took the cash out and counted it. "Yep, fifty-five. When you put this in your suitcase, distribute the cash through the pages of some magazines, so that the airport scanners don't pick it up. Five thousand isn't technically enough to land you in trouble, but better safe than sorry." She handed the cash back to Liria, who set it aside on the table, staring at it. She looked back at Arty, who still smirked.

"You going to work for him?"

Liria wrinkled her nose. "No."

Arty smiled, then pulled her closer, putting her lips close to her ear. "Liria, I love you," she said.

A happiness stronger than dope bloomed in Liria's breast, and she melted into it. "I love you too."

***

Liria woke up the next morning to find the spot beside her empty and cold. Arty was sitting in the alcove above the air conditioner, hugging her bare knees and looking out at the sunrise. She looked much younger than she actually was, in her tank top and boy shorts, her hair curling loose down her back, her freckled face lit by the pink dawn.

"What are you doing?" Liria said, sitting up and rubbing her eyes.

"Just looking," Arty said. "Seeing if I can see anything weird going on from here. I think we should leave for the airport separately. I shouldn't have even stayed here last night. I'm worried Thomas is onto us."

Liria's scalp prickled. "Why? Did you see people watching the doors or something?"

"No, nothing like that. It's just a feeling."

Liria attempted a smile. "You're just being paranoid."

"Maybe. I hope so. But I think he did have you followed last night. I would have. If he's watching, it'll be a dead giveaway if we leave together."

"I'm glad you did stay with me, even if he is watching."

Arty smiled. "Me too." Her smile faded and she ran her fingers through her hair. "But it was stupid."

Liria picked at a lingering scab on her arm. The bruises were almost completely gone now. "What will he do if he figures it out?"

Arty frowned. "I don't know. There are a few things he could do." She slid out of the window nook. "So, we'll just be careful. I'll go first, then you leave fifteen minutes later. Okay?"

"Okay," Liria said.

They took a shower. Arty left after giving her a quick kiss. Liria stared at the closed door for a minute after she was gone, then walked over to the window and looked out. The morning sunlight spread out over the Las Vegas valley, cutting through the haze of dust and smog, gilding the mess of the Strip with light like a cheerful mother visiting her son the night after a horrible party. Was Thomas out there, waiting? She clutched her elbows and turned away from the window, pacing the room. She pulled the last two oxycodone pills out of her pocket and stared at them. *She said she loved me,* she thought with a rush of warmth. *I could lose that, if I take these and she finds out.*

Guilt and fear bubbled up inside her, but then receded. *You already stole them, just take them, and then they'll be gone and won't be able to tempt you any longer. You won't need them anymore, anyway, once this gangster shit is over and you're off with Arty somewhere where no one can find you.*

Liria stared at the pills a moment longer, then swallowed them with tap water.

She grabbed the envelope of money from the bedside table, taking the promotional magazine from the table and spreading it through the pages before stuffing it in her suitcase. She headed out, wheeling the bag, her stomach clenched around the pills.

The hallway was deserted except for one man in cargo shorts and a t-shirt, who walked unsteadily toward her, still wearing his sunglasses. Liria didn't think much of him, just another young dude drunk in Vegas, until she passed by and felt his hand close around her arm.

She gasped and let out a little yelp. She felt the pressure of a gun barrel in her belly and went very still.

"Stay quiet," he murmured.

Liria broke out in a sweat, her breath coming fast. The man's face was very close to hers; she could see herself reflected in each lens of his sunglasses as she nodded, the shadow of his long-lashed eyes behind the lenses. He smiled faintly, pushing slight wrinkles into his stubbly cheeks.

"Good girl, Andrea. We have your girlfriend. We just want to have a little chat with both of you. You cooperate, then you can go and do whatever you want. You try to get away or try any other bullshit and things are going to get complicated. Got it?"

Liria nodded again.

"I'm going to put the gun away now, but it's still right in my pocket if I need it."

The pressure of the pistol barrel disappeared, and Liria took a deep breath. The man put his arm around her shoulders. "Let's go."

He guided her toward the elevators. Liria rolled the suitcase behind her, her hand shaking so bad that it kept rolling off its wheels onto its side. Sweat ran down her spine, and she stumbled on the carpet. The man steadied her with his arm.

"It's okay, Andrea. Don't be nervous. You're going to be fine, as long as you do what you're told."

"And my girlfriend?"

"That's up to her."

A cold wave of anguish rolled over her as the man pushed the down button for the elevator. "Do I get to see her?" she asked. The signal dinged, and a pair of doors opened down at the other end of the lobby. Liria jumped when they got in and she saw her terrified expression reflected in the elevator's mirrored back wall.

"You get to see her, yes." The doors slid closed. His arm was still around her; she perspired heavily under his grasp.

They were silent as the elevator descended. Liria felt the pills take effect, warmth creeping into her belly, then up her back into her limbs and skull. She took a deep breath, her shoulders relaxing. *It's going to be okay*. The dope let her believe it.

The doors opened on the ground floor. A skinny middle-aged guy in glasses stood waiting for the elevator, a cup of coffee in each hand. He smiled at them as he whisked past into the elevator, not noticing Liria's distress.

They went out onto the casino floor. Early morning gamblers sat hunched and glassy-eyed at the slots and tables, clutching mugs of coffee or tumblers of booze, depending on where they were with their circadian rhythm. Liria barely glanced at them. They couldn't help her, even if they'd known she needed help. Her heart pounded hard, and she fought back her dizziness, letting the pills flood her nerves. *It's going to be okay.*

He led her past the cashier's desk and down a quiet hallway, the noise of the casino fading behind them. He knocked on an unmarked door. "It's me, Jason," he said.

The door cracked open, then swung wide to reveal a bony, nervous-looking guy in a grey suit. He stood aside to let them in.

It was a windowless office with blue-grey

carpets. Behind a cheap desk sat Thomas, also in a suit, watching them with raised eyebrows. Arty sat across from him, gripping the metal arms of her chair. A look of relief passed over her pale face when she saw Liria.

Liria sat down in the chair next to her, and Arty took her hand, squeezing it. "I'm so fucking sorry," she murmured. Liria rolled her eyes and smiled faintly, a fresh sheen of sweat breaking out on her forehead and upper lip.

The skinny guy who let them in sat down on a couch behind them, along with Liria's captor. Thomas sat gazing at Liria with his chin resting on his knuckles. His eyes flicked to Arty. "I knew you'd never dump a girl like her. It was a ridiculous story."

Liria felt a stab of guilt. She'd been too nervous the day before. She'd landed them here.

Arty twitched. "Now that we're all present and accounted for, what do you want, Thomas?"

"We both apparently want the same thing: your dear father's assets. I don't think it's fair that you try to trick me into doing your dirty work for you. If I'm going to help bring him down, I deserve a cut."

Arty snorted. "I thought I was being pretty fucking generous. You have a shot at a whole shipment of heroin, and all you need is a few armed men and to make a couple phone calls."

Thomas raised his chin and smiled. "But it could be so much more lucrative for both of us if we worked together."

"More lucrative for you," Arty said.

"And for you. You can't take it with you when

you go. Dead women are rarely rich."

Arty dropped Liria's hand, crossed her arms, and rolled her eyes. "How do you think that would work out for you? Whatever my father and I think of each other, he'll still murder the fuck out of you and everyone you hold dear if I turn up dead or missing. He'll figure out I went to Vegas and he'll know right away what happened."

Thomas leaned back in his chair and tapped his fingers against his knees. He looked young in his suit, like a boy fresh out of high school at his first job. Liria could hear the two men on the couch shifting in their seats.

"I don't want to kill you, but I'll risk it if I have to," Thomas said. "However, I think we can work something out. I can be of more use to you than just as a pawn to put your father in an awkward position."

"How?" Arty squinted at him, looking angry, not scared.

"I have manpower. You don't."

Arty scowled. "You wish."

"Come on, Kopanis. You're here alone with your girlfriend. I'm not fucking stupid. Your dad still controls his network. I'm sure you could be successful in taking it over, if you worked with me."

"I would even if I didn't work with you," she said.

He shrugged. "Maybe so, if I let you out of here. But it'd take you a lot longer, and you wouldn't be in as strong a position."

Arty stared at him, and Liria watched her, her

heart thumping. Then Arty smiled grimly. "Okay, you help me, then you become part of my network. Anything passes through here, goes through you."

Thomas grinned. "That's a start."

They began negotiating distribution routes, percentages, and investment capital. Liria listened closely. It was complex stuff. Her stomach knotted. Arty wasn't planning on retiring. She was planning on taking over for her dad. How long, then, before she was the one ordering people's murders?

After a bit, the two seemed satisfied with their deal and shook hands across the desk. Arty stood up, And Liria got to her feet, rubbing her nose.

"We've missed our plane," Arty said.

"I'm sure there's another flight," Thomas said. He exchanged a look with the men on the couch, and they stood, as well. "Efrain and Harris will give you a ride to the airport."

Arty gazed at the three men for a long moment, and nodded. "Okay."

She and Thomas shook hands one last time, then Efrain and Harris escorted them out. Arty and Liria followed them across the casino floor, rolling their suitcases behind them. Arty was tight-lipped and silent, ignoring Liria's glances.

They got in a while Cadillac SUV parked in a reserved spot in the garage. Arty and Liria sat in the back. No one spoke during the ride to the airport. Arty gripped Liria's hand and stared out the side window.

The two men dropped them off and helped them unload their luggage, as if they were friends or cab drivers. The man who had stuck the gun in Liria's belly smiled at both of them before getting back in the SUV. "Have a good flight," he said. "Hope to see you ladies again soon."

As they walked into the terminal, Arty let out a sigh through puffed cheeks and looked at Liria. "I'm fucking sorry."

"It's my fault," Liria said.

They waded through the crowd to a ticket counter. A corner of Arty's mouth quirked up. "How is it your fault?"

"I must have done a bad job yesterday telling my story."

Arty shot her a veiled look. "I doubt that's it."

They got tickets for the next direct flight and went through security. Arty chewed on her lip the whole time, keeping silent, and Liria didn't intrude on her thoughts. She was worried about the pile of cash in her carry-on, but they made it through without problems.

They found seats at their gate, which was mostly empty. There was still an hour remaining to boarding time. Arty sighed and put her arm around her. Liria rested her head on Arty's shoulder, closing her eyes.

"It's not your fault," Arty said. "It's my fault for underestimating that douche."

"What are you going to do now?"

"Play the game, same as always. And Thomas has a point, though don't tell him I said so. An alliance with him strengthens my position."

"Arty…" Liria ran her finger along the seam in the other woman's jeans. "I thought you were going to take the money and run?"

Arty sighed. She kissed the top of Liria's head. "I still want to do that. But it's gotten more complicated now. I'll have to figure something out."

Liria curled up against her, her stomach souring, her rose-colored daydreams slipping away, the hustle settling back around her with bleak certainty. *But at least I have her.*

Chapter 21

Liria wasn't exactly sure what to expect when they arrived back in New York. She figured Morton's goons would be waiting for them outside Arty's apartment, with their beefy arms crossed over their chests, the butts of their guns showing under their suit jackets. Either that, or the cops, with their black boots and square jaws, there to haul them to federal prison. But the only one waiting for them was Shirley the cat, with her prim meow and insistent demands for affection.

Arty sighed and made tea, then got into her yoga pants and watched one of her HBO dramas while she did her exercise routine on a mat. After a while she got back on her computer and went to work on the accounts.

Liria curled up next to her on the couch and fell asleep.

She dreamt she was walking through a forest of tall, twisting oaks. Men in suits crawled around up in the branches, watching her with round and gleaming eyes. Some of them were talking on phones; she couldn't hear what they were saying, but she knew they were talking about her.

She ignored them, keeping her eyes on the ground. Flowers grew, wilting and sad, their faded orange petals dragging in the dirt. Liria gathered them up. They would get her high if she cooked them up a special way. If she got high enough the people watching her from the branches would go away.

She realized Justin, the boy from the park, was walking beside her. He grabbed her wrist as she went to pick another bunch of the dope-flowers, and took the bouquet from her hand. She scowled at him and tried to grab them back, but he held them up over his head, gazing at her with a patient expression.

"These are an illusion, see?" He rubbed the flowers between his fingers. They dissolved into black ashes which floated away on the breeze, twisting in sinuous patterns.

"I needed that!" Liria said, huffing. She started looking around for more, and spotted some by a rusty rotary mower under one of the oaks. But when she bent down to pluck them, she realized they weren't the dope flowers, they were really just a pile of discarded candy wrappers. She picked one of them up; it read "Yum Nuggets".

"That's not the way," Justin said, putting his hand on her shoulder. "Come on, I'll show you the way."

Liria stared at him. Above her head, a group of men in suits had crawled down out of the top of the *tree to watch her from a low branch, perched like goofy birds. She could hear them murmuring.*

"Come on," Justin repeated.

Liria followed him behind the huge trunk of the oak. There was a large hole at its base. Liria could see the metal steps of a spiral staircase descending into it.

"Down here," he said. "Wait until you see." He smiled, tugging excitedly at the earflaps of his tiger hat. Liria smiled back. He started down into the hole, and Liria went after him, carefully placing her foot on the first rung of the staircase.

She awoke with a start as Arty kissed her lips. She was still on the couch, her legs cramped and cold.

"Come to bed, beautiful," Arty said.

***

The next day was windy and rainy, but Arty made her put on a raincoat, pull on the boots she'd gotten her at a boutique down the street, and follow her out into the weather.

"Where are we going?" Liria asked.

"To meet a friend at a coffee shop. I have a present for you."

"What sort of present?"

Arty just grinned mysteriously. "You'll see."

Liria pulled the hood of her coat up and huddled against her as they went down the sidewalk. Her hands were freezing and her face was damp by the time they stepped into the warm café, puffing and shaking the rain from their hoods.

They wrapped their hands around hot mugs of coffee and sat by the window, listening to the cooing of a girl folksinger over the sound system. Liria kept glancing quizzically at Arty, but got nothing but a faint smirk in response.

"What do you think the weather is like in L.A. right now?" Arty asked.

Liria gave her a dry look. "Sunny with a hundred percent chance of douche. Seriously? We're going to talk about the weather?"

Arty snickered, sipping her coffee. She sat up, her gaze falling on a man walking into the café. "This is him," she murmured.

Liria examined him over the mug of her coffee cup. He was an older guy, short and thin with heavy frown lines, grey hair peeking out from under his stocking cap. He got a coffee, then came over to join them, his emotionless grey-green eyes lingering on Liria as he sat down.

Arty scooted over and embraced him, and he smiled, some warmth seeping into his eyes. "Nice to see you, sweetheart," he said, ruffing her hair up a bit. His gaze fell back on Liria. "Who's your beautiful friend?"

"Frances, this is Liria."

He shook her hand. "Liria, huh? That's a pretty name. Nice to meet you."

Liria smiled. "Nice to meet you too."

Frances reached under his puffy, quilted jacket and brought out a small, rectangular box wrapped in polka-dotted paper and tied with a blue ribbon. "Happy birthday," he said, grinning at Arty.

Arty laughed and took it. "Oh, Frankie, you shouldn't have." She clasped his hand, and Liria saw her deposit a wad of bills there, which he slipped into his pocket.

Liria twisted her damp hair between her fingers, focusing on the package.

They sat talking about books and movies for a while as they finished their coffee. When they all got up to leave, Arty shoved the present into an inside pocket of her jacket.

Frances embraced Arty one last time under the awning of the café, and shook Liria's hand. "Nice to meet you. Hope to see you around." He walked off down the sidewalk, and she and Arty headed in the opposite direction, pulling up their hoods.

"What's in the box?" Liria murmured.

Arty shot her another sly grin. "Not until we get home."

They walked back holding hands, their shoes squelching on piles of sodden, dead leaves. Arty didn't speak. Liria tried to guess what was in the package, but couldn't.

Finally they got back to the apartment, and hung up their damp coats. Arty took the box out of the inside pocket and took it into the bedroom. "What's in it?" Liria asked following her, and Arty laughed.

"Come change out of those wet clothes."

Liria huffed in annoyance and stripped out of her damp jeans and sweater while Arty did the same. Before Liria could pull on her lounge pants, however, Arty caught her around the waist. "Did I ever tell you you're gorgeous?" She kissed her, running her hands along the curves of her waist, sliding down and around to find her clit.

Liria let out a little gasp, but pried herself away, stomping her foot. "Stop teasing me and being a jerk. What's in the package?"

Arty giggled. "Okay, okay." She knelt down to get the present from the bed, but then seemed to get distracted. She turned to kiss Liria's pussy, her warm tongue and soft lips caressing her clit.

Liria pressed her hips against Arty's mouth, her body aching sweetly. "You are such a bitch," she muttered. Arty let out a muffled laugh and pulled her down onto the bed, letting the mystery box fall to the ground and thrusting her fingers deep inside her. "You want me to stop?" she asked.

Liria's annoyance ebbed, no matter how hard she tried to sustain it. "Don't stop," she breathed.

Arty took her fingers partway out. Her tongue darted lightly over her clit. "Are you sure? We could open the box now."

"Goddammit, don't stop," Liria said, and pressed her hips against Arty's hand and mouth. Arty put her fingers deep inside, and Liria moaned, the irresistible heat of pleasure overtaking her. It was good, so good, and she wanted her warm, firm tongue, Arty pounding her fingers deep inside her, harder and harder, deeper and deeper until her pussy burned hot. "Oh, Arty, I love you," Liria said as she came, arching her back. "I love you."

Arty sat up, smiling and wiping her mouth. "I love you too, Liria." She kissed her, her naked body warm against hers. Liria slid her hand down to press one finger lightly against her hard, hot clit. "I'm not going to fuck you until you tell me what's in the box," she said.

Arty laughed softly, still kissing her. "Please," she murmured, pressing her pussy against Liria's hand. "Please, baby."

Liria rubbed slowly, softly, with two fingers. "Do you want it harder?"

"I need you. I love you, Liria." She moved her hips. "Oh, God. Rub me harder, please. I need it."

Liria pressed her clit harder. "Oh, please fuck me," Arty moaned. Liria slid her fingers inside her. "Oh, baby, fuck me, fuck me. I want you." Liria moved her fingers, stroking her deep inside, and Arty shuddered and cried out, pressing rhythmically against her hand as her pussy tightened around Liria's fingers. "Oh, baby, that's so good," she said. "I love you so much, so much."

She lay back, gasping, and wrapped her arms around Liria, pulling her close and kissing her. She gazed at her with her lips twitching.

"You bitch," Liria said, pinching her on the hip. "What's in the fucking box?"

Arty shook with giggles and rolled over, leaning over the edge of the bed to pick up the package. She started to slip, and squealed as she slid off the mattress and hit the ground with a thump. She laughed.

"You okay?" Liria asked, peering down at her.

"I'm fine."

"Give me my damn present, then."

Arty snorted, then crawled back into bed beside her. She handed her the box, smirking and raising her eyebrows.

Liria tore the paper off greedily, tossing it aside.

She took off the lid.

She stared, her brow furrowing. On top was a U.S. passport, and Liria flipped open the cover. It had her photo, along with the name Christina Guzman.

Beneath the passport was Christina Guzman's Michigan driver's license, a Social Security card, and a birth certificate saying she was born in High Point Michigan in 1995 to Morgan Hanson and Luis Guzman. Liria looked at Arty, who watched her with a strange look.

"A fake identity," Liria said.

Arty nodded. "I thought it'd be a good idea."

Liria ran her fingers over the smooth face of the passport photo. "These are really good forgeries."

"The best."

"Thank you. They couldn't have been cheap."

Arty wrinkled her nose and kissed her. "Nothing's too good for my girl."

Liria smiled, then set the box of documents on the bedside table and settled into Arty's arms. "Why do I need those?"

"To keep you safe." She smiled, but a crease formed between her eyebrows. "When we take the money and run, we don't want anyone tracking us down, right?"

Liria studied her, smiling tentatively. "No." She cuddled against her, smiling wider, her hands exploring Arty's little, firm breasts. "Where will we go, when we run away?"

"Cypress? St. Lucia? Switzerland? I don't know. Where do you want to go?"

"Anywhere, as long as you're with me," Liria

said.

Arty kissed her softly. "I love you," she murmured.

"I love you too."

Arty's lips tickled against the soft skin behind her ear. "And that's not your only present," she whispered.

"It's not?"

"Nope."

She got up out of bed, prancing stark naked into the living room, where the curtains were wide open, and Liria laughed to herself.

Arty came back carrying her laptop and an unfamiliar cell phone. She crawled back under the blankets and handed Liria the phone. "This is yours."

Liria stared at it. It was a brand new iPhone. "Thank you," she said, giving her a perplexed look.

"I don't want you to give that number to anyone, okay? It's just for me to call you in case of an emergency. That will make it harder to trace your calls."

"All right." Liria frowned. "But why would you need to call me? I mean…"

Arty sighed and ran her fingers through her hair. "It's just in case. Hopefully, everything will go as planned, my dad will go to jail and…arrangements with Thomas will work out perfectly. But you just never know." She fixed Liria with a serious stare. "And keep your fake documents on you at all times, okay?"

"Okay," Liria said, chewing on her cheek. "Have you heard anything from Thomas yet? What's going on with him?"

"These things take time. Be patient." She squeezed Liria's knee. "And one more thing." She opened the laptop and turned it on. Liria tugged at her hair and scooted closer to look at the screen. Arty went online to a banking website, pulling up an account. She pointed at the screen to the name on it. It was Christina Guzman. "I gave you some more money under your fake name."

Liria's eyes scrolled down the screen to the total, and her heart stumbled over itself. "Holy fuck," she whispered. She pulled the laptop closer to her to make sure her eyes weren't playing tricks. They weren't, and Liria looked up at Arty, her mouth hanging open, her skin prickling. "There's two and a half million fucking dollars in there."

Arty's lips twitched. "Don't spend it all in one place." She opened the drawer of her bedside table and took out a debit card, handing it to her.

Liria looked down at it, running her fingers along the raised lettering of her fake name. She looked back at Arty, shocked into silence. She swallowed. "Your dad's going to notice…"

"In a few days it won't matter."

Tears sprang to Liria's eyes, and she sniffed.

"Don't cry," Arty said, setting the laptop on the table and taking her into her arms. "Why are you crying?"

Her throat closed up with emotion. She wasn't even sure which emotions they were. It seemed like pretty much all of them. "Why are you doing this?"

Arty hugged her tighter. "Because I love you. And because I want to be with you."

Liria pressed her lips against Arty's neck. "Thank you."

"That money's yours, Liria. If you want, you can leave here right now and go off and do whatever. I don't want you to do that. I want you to stay with me. But the choice is yours."

Liria twisted in her arms and crawled on top of her. "Are you fucking kidding? Of course I'm staying with you."

Arty smiled, and Liria kissed her. *I'm never doing dope again. No more pills. And I'm throwing my other phone out the window. Cyryl can go to hell.*

Chapter 22

Later that afternoon, Arty sat on her mat doing yoga in front of the TV. Liria stood staring out at the pouring rain, tugging at the strings of her lounge pants. Inside the apartment it seemed warm and lazy, but she had the unsettling feeling that things were going on all around her that she couldn't grasp or understand.

Arty had said Thomas had taken steps toward starting an investigation of Senator Capella's involvement with Morton Kopanis. "But don't expect constant, gossipy phone calls, Liria. That sort of thing wouldn't go unnoticed."

"Why can't we just take off *now* to Greece or wherever?" Liria asked.

"It would put my dad on guard." Arty bent over her straight legs to touch her toes. "We have to go back to Chicago in two days, like nothing's the matter." Liria scowled, and Arty looked at her knowingly. "You can go to Greece, if you want. My dad wouldn't like it, but I'd cover for you. I'd meet you there in a couple weeks."

"No way," Liria said. "I don't want to go anywhere without you."

But she paced in front of the windows, unable to keep her teeth from clenching. She felt the walls tightening around her like a fist. "I want to go out," she said.

Arty glanced out the foggy, rain-streaked windows and raised her eyebrows. "You've got to be kidding." She looked at Liria, whose mouth was screwed up in a knot as she chewed on her cheek. She had tugged her lounge pant straps into noodles.

Arty stood up and took her into her arms, kissing her on the forehead. "Why don't you go spend some of your money? Get some clothes or something. Maybe a nice bikini for lounging on the beach."

Liria clasped her hands over the small of Arty's back, leaning into her. "I can spend the money? Shouldn't we wait until your dad's in jail?"

"No way. That money's yours. It'll take him a while to notice because of the way I funneled it around, and because of the, shall we say, complicated nature of his finances. By the time he figures it out it'll be too late, so don't worry." She kissed her. "Go. It'll keep your mind off things."

Liria pulled on a sweater and some real pants, and tugged on her boots. She sat examining her fake ID for a moment, then shoved it in her pocket along with her real one and her debit card. She took her new phone too, to play with in some café, maybe, while she had a cup of coffee.

She gave Arty a lingering kiss before she headed out the door. "Thank you."

Arty tenderly brushed a lock of hair from Liria's

forehead. "Have fun."

Liria took the elevator down and went out the front doors, huddling under her umbrella as she strolled out into the grey afternoon. It felt weird to be out in Arty's neighborhood alone. It looked different when she wasn't around.

She looked in shop windows at dresses and handbags and shoes. It took her forty-five minutes before she realized that she could actually afford to buy something. She went into one of the stores.

She tried on a few things, some jeans and sweaters and skirts, a dress with an interesting geometric pattern and asymmetrical hemline. She made herself buy them, squirming as she handed the clerk the debit card.

It rang up at well over fifteen hundred dollars. Liria's stomach clenched, expecting the clerk to frown, to give her a suspicious look. *"I'm sorry, Miss...Guzman, or whoever you are,"* she would say, *"but there's a problem with your card. I'm going to have to call the police."*

But she didn't say that. The lady handed her the card back along with her receipt and the bag, a smile on her face. Liria felt giddy.

She skipped back outside. The sun shone through a gap in the clouds, turning the raindrops to golden glitter, and Liria let it run over her face for a moment before she put up her umbrella. *I'm a fucking millionaire.* A laugh rose up inside her as she stomped in the puddles, drawing brief glances from passersby.

She stopped at another boutique with interesting jewelry in the window. There was a necklace of gracefully draped opal and amber teardrops she thought Arty would like, so she bought it for her even though it cost almost eight hundred dollars. In her mind, Lee Harvey teased her about it being almost a month's worth of dope money, but she'd never need dope money again.

She left the store, feeling warm thinking about giving Arty her present. Maybe it was petty compensation for taking in a homeless junkie and making her a multimillionaire, but it was a start.

The holes in the clouds had closed up and the sun had set, the grey day fading into darkness. It was raining harder than ever. Other people on the sidewalk looked like shadows in the mist. Liria walked quickly back toward the apartment, wanting dry clothes and the warmth of her girlfriend's embrace.

There was a man leaning against the wall on the steps up to the apartment building's entrance. Liria slowed when she saw him, but he barely seemed to notice her. He had his hands in his pockets and the air of a man waiting for his ride. He nodded at Liria in acknowledgment as she fumbled in her pocket for the door key.

She was just about to fit the key into the lock when something jabbed roughly into her back and she jumped and gasped, dropping the key and her shopping bags. The man next to her grabbed her arm. She was about to scream when he placed his fingertips lightly over her lips.

"Shhhh, Miss Czetski," he said, smiling at her thinly, his eyes darting around. "George here has a .357 Magnum in your back, and none of us want any more noise than necessary."

Liria made a small, strangled sound, and the man patted her arm. He took his fingers from her mouth, and she stared up at him, her ears ringing. The orange streetlight gleamed off his sharp green eyes. "It's okay," he said. "Get your bags. We've gotta get going."

Her heart raced painfully, sweat mixing with the dampness from the rain on her skin. The man raised his tangled, greying eyebrows expectantly, and the barrel of the gun pressed harder into her back. She bent down and grabbed the handle of her shopping bags with rubbery fingers.

"There we go," the man said, patting her arm again. The pressure of the gun disappeared, and the man steered her around with a firm grip.

The man behind her—George—still had the gun in a leather-gloved hand, hidden partially in the folds of a wool overcoat. He was thin and somewhat stooped, with a weak chin. He nodded in greeting, looking her over.

A car pulled up to the curb, a beige Subaru, and the men led her toward it. George got into the front passenger seat, and the other man opened the back door and climbed in after her. It was warm and humid in the car, and smelled like cheap coffee. The man driving gave her a brief glance over his shoulder, his hazel eyes alight with curiosity. His thick, stubby fingers gripped the steering wheel.

They pulled away from the curb, and Liria watched Arty's doorway receding behind them, tears springing to her eyes.

"Where are you taking me?" she asked.

"You'll see soon enough," the man beside her said. He buckled his seatbelt over his leather bomber jacket and settled back into his seat. He jerked his chin at Liria, then at the driver. "Buckle up. This cocksucker drives like a moron."

"Fuck off," the driver responded jovially.

"No, but seriously," Bomber Jacket said when Liria made no move toward her seatbelt.

Liria hesitated a moment, then pulled the seatbelt over her chest. She fumbled with the clasp, her hands trembling too badly to get it latched. Finally, Bomber Jacket helped her, taking the buckle from her hands and securing it. "There you go," he said when it clicked. "All safe." He looked around out the windows and scowled. "Hey, take a left here. You wanna get on the freeway."

"Freeway's all clogged up," the driver said. "We'll be stuck there for hours."

"It's still better," Bomber Jacket said.

"I swear to Christ, if you guys don't fuck off with the arguing about which way to take, I'll fucking kill the both of you," George, the man with the gun, said in a quiet voice from the passenger seat.

Bomber Jacket rolled his eyes and leaned his elbow against the side door. The noise of the windshield wipers and rain on the roof filled the silence. Liria clutched her knees, trying to stop shaking.

They came to a stoplight and Liria tensed up, wanting to unbuckle her seatbelt and dive out of the car.

"Don't try it, Miss Czetski," Bomber Jacket said

tiredly. "We don't want to shoot you, and the child locks are on anyway."

Tears dripped down Liria's chin, and she leaned back against the seat.

"Hey, there's that gyro place," Bomber Jacket said when the light turned green and they pulled across the intersection. He glanced over at Liria. "You ever been there? It's great."

Liria shot him a look from the corner of her eye. The driver glanced at her in the rearview mirror, and Liria caught sight of him, the streetlights shining through the rain streaking the windows and leaving blotchy shadows on his face. "Aw, stop hitting on her, Kenneth. She's got enough to worry about."

"I'm not hitting on her. Hell, I've got a daughter her age." Liria wiped her eyes on her sleeve, and Bomber Jacket—Kenneth—patted her on the arm. "Don't cry. You're going to be fine as long as you keep calm."

"Please," she said. "Please don't do this. Please let me go."

"Wish we could, sweetheart," Kenneth said. "But we've got a job to do."

"What do you want with me?"

Kenneth and George stared at her with a sort of fascination. The driver glanced at her reflection in the rearview.

"Taking you to a guy we know," George said.

"Who?"

George shook his head grinning slightly, and Kenneth smirked, but none of them answered.

Liria's heart sank. These must be Morton

Kopanis' men. He must have figured out what Arty was up to. What would Morton do with her? Torture her to get information? Take back the money Arty had given her, then kill her and dump her body?

Briefly, Liria considered offering them money, but decided that would be a bad idea and would probably backfire. She was sure anything she offered them wouldn't be enough, and they'd just take it and hand her over anyway. She pictured Arty back in her apartment, waiting for her. When she didn't come back, what would she think? *She'll think I ran off with the money. She'll think I took the two and a half million dollars and ditched her.*

And what would Morton do to his daughter, to punish her for trying to double-cross him? Liria leaned against the cold window, overcome by anguish.

The men talked about basketball. Liria ignored them, her thoughts racing, engulfed by wave after wave of adrenaline. Cold sweat soaked the grey sweater of Arty's she was wearing. It still smelled like her, and longing overpowered her until she broke into tears again. Kenneth gave her a pitying glance, but didn't say anything.

They drove for a long time. By the time the pulled up to a curb again, Liria felt like it must be three in the morning, or the next week, or years since they'd grabbed her from the sidewalk. She raised her head and looked around. They were on a residential street lined with huge trees and old, three- and four-story houses.

Kenneth got out, then came around to her side and opened her door. "Come on," he said. "Get your bags."

Liria unbuckled her seatbelt and slid out, grasping her shopping bags. She felt unsteady on her feet, her legs weak. Kenneth put his arm around her shoulders and led her toward one of the houses. Behind them, Liria heard the car pull away, and hunched under her captor's arm.

They passed beneath a dripping rose arbor and followed a brick walkway lined with low hedges. They stopped in front of the front door, which was painted royal blue and had a beveled glass window. Before he could knock, Liria looked up at Kenneth through her eyelashes.

"Please," she whispered, raindrops skirting her cheeks along with the tears. "*Please,* I'll give you anything."

In the porch light she could see pity and longing in his eyes, maybe even a hint of amusement. He squeezed her shoulder. "I'm sorry, sweetheart," he murmured. "But you're gonna be okay. He's not gonna hurt a girl like you if he can help it. Just do what he says, and you'll be fine."

He knocked. Liria stared at the door wide-eyed, her hands gathered into fists, her eyes darting around, looking for some means of escape, but she didn't know what she expected to see.

Maybe Arty wouldn't believe she'd run off, and she'd figure out what had happened, and come save her. Liria gulped the damp night air.

The door was opened by a short woman with dyed-black hair in a ponytail, thin lips, penciled-in eyebrows. She appraised Liria, her hazel eyes keen. She smiled at Kenneth in a way that made Liria's overwrought brain think of a frog. "Come on in," she said.

"How's it going, Mary?" Kenneth said.

"Not bad, not bad. Traffic okay?"

"Pish. It's always fucked."

She shut the door behind them and led them through the entry. Mary's long, narrow, bare feet padded noiselessly on the hardwood floors as they passed through a sitting room with a fire going in a grate. Liria smelled something cooking and heard a television somewhere. She closed her eyes against a new wave of grief. If this hadn't happened, she'd be curled up on the couch with Arty, eating dinner and watching some trashy TV show.

"He's in his office," Mary said. "He'll be glad to know you're here."

"Thanks, hon," Kenneth said.

Mary smiled and went through a doorway to their right, while Liria and the man turned the opposite direction, down a blue-walled corridor hung with wooden masks and framed landscapes. He knocked on a door. "It's me."

The door opened, and there was Morton Kopanis. He grinned and slapped Kenneth on the back. "Thanks, Kenneth," he said. "Why don't you have Mary make you some coffee? This weather's the pits."

"Thanks, Mr. Kopanis."

Kenneth shot Liria one last pitying glance before going back off down the hall, leaving her alone with Morton.

"Liria Czetski, is it?" he said, then shook his head. "My fucking daughter, I tell you." He laid a hand on her shoulder, and she flinched. "Aw, don't worry, honey, I'm not going to hurt you. Come in and sit down."

They entered an office with wide, shuttered windows. A laptop was open on the leather-topped desk. Morton closed the door and gestured to a chair. "Sit." He settled behind the desk, not taking his eyes off her.

Liria sat, trembling, trying not to cry. She realized she was still clutching her shopping bags in a sweaty hand. Arty's present was in one of them. "Please, Mr. Kopanis, what did I do? Why are you doing this to me?"

He regarded her a long moment. "What's your angle here?" he asked sharply. "You spying on us? Trying to cut us out of it?"

Liria's eyebrows drew sharply together. "What do you mean?"

"Cut the shit, Czetski," he said tiredly.

Liria just stared at him, a fresh wave of tears washing over her cheeks, and she wiped them away with her sleeve, sniffing. "I don't know what the fuck you mean." Her heart felt like it was trying to run in six directions at once, and her brain was churning frantically.

Slowly, the sharpness left his eyes. A grin bloomed on his face and he chuckled. "Holy shit, she was right, wasn't she?" He leaned his elbows on the desk, propped his chin on his clasped hands, smirking at her. "Never mind, then, Liria. What happened is I figured it out, that little deal you guys had going with the guy in Vegas." He sneered. "Thought you were being real smart I'll bet."

Liria sat very still, tears streaming down her face. "I don't know—"

"Oh, stop it. You made a deal with him to have me thrown over. Then, to have him come to me pretending to double-cross, but all the while having that be a setup too, thinking you can fake your deaths, pretend to have his people kill you, and everyone gets away with a chunk of my fucking money. Then you can come back later to finish the job on me right when I'm not expecting it. Real fucking smart, Miss Czetski. Unfortunately for you, I'm a lot smarter."

Liria's brow furrowed. She opened her mouth and shut it again as he watched her closely.

"I don't know what you mean," she said carefully, and he broke into a grin.

"Didn't tell you that part, huh? Yeah, that's my fucking daughter for you. Maybe she planned on getting what she could out of you and taking off, also. Maybe we're in the same boat, Liria." He leaned back with his hands behind his head, his smile fading.

Her heart raced. *She wouldn't. He's lying.* She clutched the handle of her shopping bag, her sweat soaking into the hemp twine. Where was Arty now? Was she being held in another room in this house? How were they going to get out of here?

"What are you going to do to us?" she asked.

He sighed and folded his hands in his lap, looking at her for a long time. "I don't think you're guilty of anything but getting taken for a ride by that good-for-nothing daughter of mine. Hard to believe, but true."

"She's not good-for-nothing!" She began to shake. "Please, just let me see her. I'll do anything you want, just let us go. This is all just a misunderstanding."

His expression softened as he watched her. He looked surprised. "You cared about her, right? You don't want to believe that she was a fucking cunt."

Liria felt heat rise to her face. She stared at him across the desk, her blood pounding in her temples. *Just keep quiet and let him talk. Somehow, we'll get out of this. He's her dad, and he won't hurt us.*

Morton sighed. "Listen, you don't owe me loyalty, and I don't need it from you. Except for this: you need to keep your mouth shut about all the shit that's gone on during the last few days, since you started working at that place in Vegas, got it? As long as you keep your mouth shut, you stay alive."

Liria nodded, wiping her eyes. "Of course. I would never say anything. Please, just please let me go back to Arty, please…"

"No, Liria, there's no going back to her."

"*Please!* I don't believe she fucked me over, please…whatever punishment you have for her, I'll take it too. Take all her money away or whatever, just let me go see her…" She hated herself for begging, but she couldn't help it.

He shook his head, giving her an odd look. "I'm sorry, I really am. She fucked up, and if she wants to play that game with me, she's going to lose. It's just business. I did what I had to do."

Liria went very cold, the air draining from her lungs. "What…what do you mean?"

His eyes locked on her, watching her closely. "I'm really sorry, Liria. I am. But you're better off without her. The whole world is better off without her."

Liria froze. Darkness closed in on her mind as his meaning sank in. She couldn't believe it. She *wouldn't* believe it. Then it was as if she burst wide open. "*No,*" she screeched. "You're lying! You wouldn't! She's your daughter!"

He scowled. "And I'm her father, and it didn't stop her. She knew what the odds were, and what the consequences would be. You're just lucky I'm a nice guy, or you would have gone the same way she did, no matter what your fucking last name is."

Liria hardly heard him. She stood up and lunged across the desk, knocking the laptop aside and pounding him with her fists. "Fuck you! How could you? Fuck you!" She hoped he'd shoot her, that he'd pull a gun out and blast her point-blank, and it would be over. He should blast the brains out of her head so she couldn't feel the pain any longer.

But he didn't. He caught her wrists as she struggled, laying across the desk, knocking the laptop off as she thrashed around.

"Take it easy, Liria. Jesus. Calm the fuck down."

"*Fuck you.*"

The door opened behind her, and hands grasped her under the arms, pulling her away.

"It's okay, sweetheart," Kenneth said soothingly. "It's okay."

Liria struggled. "Kill me too, then! Just fucking shoot me, you fuckhead! You think you're so fucking smart, so tough, then shoot me!" She felt like her brains would explode out her ears even if he didn't shoot her. There wasn't room in her body for all the things she felt.

Morton gazed at her in fascination. "There's truly no need for that, Miss Czetski." His eyes flicked to Kenneth. "Take her to the back guestroom and get her under control, eh?"

"Will do, Mr. Kopanis," he said, sounding a little out of breath. "Now, come on, Miss Czetski, calm down and give me a break, will you?"

Liria thrashed as he dragged her out, bile burning her throat, blinded by tears of rage and disbelief. "No," she said. "No."

Kenneth hushed her when they were out of the room. "Come on, please," he muttered. "I didn't do anything to you, please don't kick my ass, okay?"

Liria gasped and sobbed. "I'm going to fucking kill him."

"Ssssssh! Don't say that. You're young, and you're gonna want to live when this is all over. I promise."

"No."

"I promise," he repeated. "Now come on, just put your feet on the ground and let's walk, okay? There you go."

He led her, stumbling, down the hall to a bedroom. It had a queen bed with a blue quilt, but that was all. There was no window, no other furniture. He put his arm around her and sat her on the bed. She did so numbly. She started to shake, her rage and grief tugging and tearing her. "I'm going to fucking kill him," she murmured again, and this time Kenneth chuckled.

"I'm not saying we all haven't felt the same way at some point." He pulled her head onto his shoulder. "I'm really sorry, Miss. I know you don't know me, but I am sorry. I've lost a brother and several friends to this stupid fucking business and I know how it is. But when you sign on, you know what the stakes are."

Liria's teeth clenched. "She wanted out. She just wanted out." Her mind struggled to understand. She flashed between a desperate belief that Morton was lying and that Arty was still alive, and rage, and unendurable pain.

He hugged her. "Shhhh, I know. I know. It isn't fair."

She didn't know how long he sat with her. Liria watched a spider crawl along the base of the wainscoting, his little jointed legs tickling the ground. Had Arty really lied to her? Had she planned on taking off and leaving her behind? Liria didn't believe it. It didn't fit. Morton was lying, just trying to fuck with her. A fireball of rage rose up in her again, and she started to cry once more.

"Shhhh, it's okay," Kenneth said. "I'm sorry, but I have to go. I have to leave you here. Can I bring you some water or, you know…"

"No," she choked, and he sighed.

"I'm going to have to take your phone too."

Liria ripped it out of her pocket, her new phone that Arty had given her, a million years ago that morning, and threw it into his lap. "Take it. I don't have anyone to call. They're all fucking dead, thanks to that fucking asshole."

Kenneth squeezed her shoulder one last time, but

she hardly felt it. Then he left, shutting the door behind him. Liria heard a lock click. She sat there, hugging herself.

After a while, she curled up, clutching a pillow to smother the vacancy in her chest. The strangeness of the situation suddenly dawned on her. Why was she still alive? Why was she here? Her thoughts started to churn, trying to fit everything she knew together, but none of it clicked. Morton had found out about their deal with Thomas. Supposedly it was some sort of triple-cross that Liria hadn't known about. Then Morton had killed Arty, but not her?

She squeezed her eyes closed. She couldn't think straight. She needed some dope. She pressed her face into the pillow, sobbing. *I need Arty.* Her grief overwhelmed her. *Arty, I need you. I finally found someone to love. You can't be gone. It's not right. He's lying.*

She lay sleepless on her bed, staring at the wall, until a dull doze took her over.

Her dreams were hazy, made up of images of Arty hiding under her bed, waiting for Liria to find her; and others where Arty and Morton were out shopping for furniture together, and had locked her in a room because they didn't want her to come. "Sorry," Arty said, as she and her dad hauled in an elaborately-carved gothic armoire. "We just didn't trust your taste in decorating."

The haze abated and Liria opened her eyes, which felt dry as sand. The weight of her pain settled over her again. The ceiling lamp was still on, but there was no window, and no clock. She had no idea what time it was, whether it was night or day.

Liria got up and began to pace. Quietly, she tried the door handle, but of course it was locked. She pressed her ear to the door and heard voices, two men speaking somewhere else in the house. One of them sounded like Morton, but she couldn't hear what they were saying.

She laid back down on the bed, biting her cheek until she tasted blood. She thought about screaming until someone came and told her what was going on, but she didn't have the energy.

She heard footsteps approaching, and sat up.

The lock clicked, and the door opened. A man stood there, and her brow furrowed. It took her a moment to believe what she was seeing. "Cyryl?"

His lips twitched into a little relieved grin, and he let out a breath. "Baby," he muttered hoarsely, coming into the room.

Morton came in behind him, and Liria stiffened, looking back and forth between them. Cyryl grasped her shoulder, but she jerked it away. "Cyryl…what the fuck…are you in on this? Is this…did you…you're just trying to take me away from her!"

Cyryl was in on it. She didn't know how, but of course he was. He'd gotten Arty killed. She stood up, lunging toward Morton. "How could you?" Cyryl caught her, pinning her arms to her sides. "Let me go!" she yelled. "Let me fucking go, and tell me what's going on! Tell me what you did with Arty!"

"You know what I did with Arty," Morton said tiredly.

Rage rose up in Liria again and she thrashed in Cyryl's arms. "Let me go! You killed her! Fuck you, Cyryl! You're in on this bullshit too!"

Morton gave her a strange grin as Cyryl's strong arms tightened around her. "He had nothing to do with it," Morton said. "She brought it on herself. Mr. Czetski here just stepped in to prevent you from suffering the same fate. You should thank your lucky fucking stars he loves you so much."

Liria gradually quit struggling, her mind grappling with this new information, pieces finally clunking into place. Arty really was dead. It wasn't a joke. Hatred tore through her. If it weren't for Cyryl, she'd be with Arty. She'd be dead too, and wouldn't have to deal with this. She sobbed, and Cyryl clasped her tighter to his chest. "It's okay, baby," he murmured. "It's okay now."

"No it's not," she said. "It's not. It's not."

Cyryl put his mouth close to her ear. "Calm the fuck down, sweetheart, or we'll never get out of here, okay?"

"I don't care!" she said.

"I do," he said. "I do, baby. So stop it. Fucking stop it."

Morton stared at her wide-eyed, one corner of his lips curled in a smile of disbelief. "Listen to him," Morton said. "He's a smart man, and he saved your ass, Liria." He gave Cyryl a tight smile. "She'll get over it," he muttered.

But Liria knew she wouldn't. The first chance she got, she'd take enough dope to make the darkness close around her for good. Maybe she'd find Arty there, in the darkness. She wouldn't rule it out. But even if all she found was nothingness, it was still better than being alive without her. She took a deep breath. The thought calmed her. It would be over soon.

Chapter 23

Somehow, Cyryl got her into the front seat of his car. She huddled there staring blindly out the windshield, as he pulled out of the garage.

The horizon was sickly green with smog and pink with the coming dawn. Her eyeballs itched and she felt heavy and numb. *I'll get back to Avery's somehow. I'll talk him out of a couple of grams. That's all it will take.* She could feel Cyryl glancing at her, but didn't look at him.

"What did they do to you?" he asked. "What the fuck did those assholes do?"

Liria curled up tighter and didn't answer.

"You have that, what is it they call it, Stockholm Syndrome. Good fucking Christ, Liria, that woman took you hostage and now you're all fucked up over her."

Her face screwed up as the pain took her over again. "No," she moaned.

He cursed under his breath as she cried. They pulled onto the freeway, where traffic was jammed up. Liria stared unseeingly at the slow-moving river of cars, the jagged peaks of the Manhattan skyline in the distance.

After a while, Cyryl put an arm around her shoulders. "It's not your fault, baby," he finally said. "I'm sorry you went through that. We're going home, but we just have to make one stop. We've got to talk to my brother. Can you handle that?"

Liria looked over at him sharply. He looked pale and tired, a deep crease in his forehead. "Your brother?"

He grinned humorlessly. "Just so happens he's that stupid Kopanis asshole's boss. I was looking everywhere for you, then I get a call from him, asking if I knew you. That Kopanis called him saying he had some girl that was a Czetski." He squeezed her shoulder. "So fucking glad he called me. I don't want to know what would have happened otherwise."

She squinted at him, her lips twisting. "Your brother is Morton Kopanis' boss?"

"Yeah. That dick."

Liria blinked, her eyebrows pulling together. "That's why she was so fixated on my last name." She dissolved into tears again, more pieces clunking into place: being drugged, the questions Arty had asked. Had this all been some sort of game? Had Arty been using her as a pawn all along? She shook her head, clutching her knees. She didn't believe it. Arty may not have trusted her at first, but she had at the end. She had loved her. It had been real.

Liria buried her face in her knees, sobbing. "Why'd he have to kill her? It's not fair. It's not right."

301

Cyryl was silent for a moment, and she felt him tense up. Then he relaxed, sighing, and pulled her closer against his shoulder. "Because that's how mob bullshit goes," he muttered. "And, Jesus, Liria, she kidnapped you."

Liria made a strangled sound, and he sighed again, long and hard, hugging her tight against him.

"Never mind," he said. "You're safe now, baby."

They drove through traffic and pulled off at an exit not far away. This neighborhood was even richer than Morton Kopanis', with old, perfectly-maintained houses on sprawling grounds. Liria dully watched them slide by, with their horse pastures and tennis courts, their long driveways lined by huge old trees.

They came up to a wrought iron gate and Cyryl punched a button on an intercom. A voice hissed over it, and Cyryl responded, "I'm his goddamn brother, Cyryl Czetski." The gate slid back on automatic rails.

Liria watched the house approach as they headed up the long, paved drive. The building was four stories of weathered stone, and the brilliant autumn sun glinted off the windows. They parked in front of it on a circular drive, and Cyryl turned to her, brushing her tangled hair back from her shoulders.

"I'm sorry to have to do this to you, Liria, but my brother insisted. You just have to tell him what happened, and then we can go home and forget about all this, eh?"

Liria didn't look at him. He leaned over and kissed her temple, then got out of the car. She hesitated a moment, but got out also. What did it matter? Just one last thing to do before going home, catching the bus back to Paso, and finding Avery.

A blustery breeze ruffled her hair and misted her face with droplets from a fountain that played in front of the house. Cyryl put his arm around her shoulders as they walked to the front entrance, and some part of her was glad for it.

The door opened before they could knock, and a tall, blonde woman with an angular face ushered them in unsmilingly. "Hello, Cyryl. Peter is in the library." She had an accent heavier than Cyryl's, and her thin lips barely moved as she spoke.

"Thanks, Halina," Cyryl grunted.

He led Liria through the entry and a parlor, then down a hallway with floors of dark, polished wood. Even in her grief, Liria couldn't keep herself from glancing around in awe at the tall ceilings, the leaded glass windows, and the real crystal chandeliers. She'd seen houses like this in movies, but had never stopped to think that there were real people who were actually that rich.

They turned through a doorway into a large room, its walls covered with built in shelves lined with books. Thin, arched windows looked out on the parkland behind the house.

A man sat in a leather armchair, working on a laptop. He looked up and stood as they walked in.

He smiled and grasped Cyryl's shoulder. He looked a lot like Cyryl, but older and less stocky, with thinner hair and glasses. He said something in Polish, and Cyryl responded, patting his brother on the back.

"Liria, this is my brother, Peter Czetski," Cyryl

303

said.

"Nice to meet you," Liria muttered reflexively.

Peter studied her, then gestured to the chairs by his. "Please, sit down."

They did, Liria sinking into the soft leather. Cyryl reached over and took her hand, and she let him. Her head felt dull and dry, her body wrung clean of emotion.

Peter looked her over some more, then gave his brother a thin smile. He said something, again in Polish, and Cyryl responded. The words sounded angry to Liria, but Cyryl seemed relaxed enough, and Peter laughed. He turned to Liria. "I understand you've been through quite an ordeal." When he spoke English, his accent was lighter than Cyryl's.

Liria didn't know what to say, so she just nodded. Peter smiled slightly and bowed his head to her.

"I'm sorry, but I'm going to have to ask you to tell me about it."

Liria blinked at him. "What do you want to know?"

"Why don't you start with how you met Artemis Kopanis?"

A lump rose up in Liria's throat and she swallowed hard, squeezing her eyes shut. Cyryl squeezed her hand. "It's all right, baby," he muttered.

Liria thought of Morton Kopanis' warning, telling her to keep her mouth shut about what had happened, or he'd kill her. But she didn't care. She just wanted to get out of here as soon as possible and get to Avery's. Besides, this was that dick's boss.

So she told him. She started with how she'd worked at the Vegas nightclub, and related the whole tale in a dull voice. Her throat tightened when she talked about Lee Harvey, but she kept going. She told how Arty had brought her to New York, while Cyryl twitched and cursed softly in Polish beside her. She even told about how Arty had been trying to destroy her own father by taking his money and making a deal with Thomas. Peter listened to it all, his sharp, grey eyes watching her closely with great interest.

But when she got to the events of the previous day, her conversation with Morton Kopanis about what he'd done to Arty, she couldn't go on. Sobs tore up out of her belly and she took her hand from Cyryl's, wrapping her arms around herself.

Cyryl put his hand on her knee, and Liria sat trying to get a hold of herself. She could feel Peter watching her.

"I'm sorry to put you through this narrative, Liria," he said. "But I need to know. Did Morton Kopanis have his daughter killed?"

Liria squeezed herself tighter. She nodded as her body shook with grief.

"Okay," Peter said softly. "Okay, that's all I needed to know." She felt his fingers brush her shoulder lightly, and looked up, blinking at him through her tears. His eyes were full of pity and a sort of grim satisfaction. "You've been very helpful, and I won't forget it. I'm sorry the Kopanises dragged you into this mess. Just go home and forget about it, okay?"

305

Liria didn't say anything. It was a ridiculous request.

The brothers said a few more things to each other in Polish, then they stood up and embraced. Cyryl took her hand and gently pulled her up out of her chair.

"Come on, baby, all done now." He guided her back out to the car.

***

Cyryl fed her some Ativan before they turned in the rental car. "I got you some more of these, just in case. Take them. They'll make you feel better."

Dully, she picked up the little pills, and swallowed them dry.

They hit her as they went through airport security, and she slept most of the flight back to L.A. When they got back to Cyryl's condo, she crawled into bed in the spare bedroom and huddled under the blankets.

Cyryl tried to get her to eat. He even tried to coax her into his own bed. He was gentler with her than she would have expected, even though she could tell he was getting pissed off. Part of her wished she could just love him. He'd saved her life more than once, gone through a lot of trouble to find her and bring her back here. Now that Arty was dead and she had no one else, she should be happy to have him. But the thought of letting him fuck her made her squirm with disgust. She'd never fuck anybody ever again, now that Arty was gone.

Finally, as the light of day faded, he kicked off

his shoes and threw the blanket over the both of them, put his arms around her, and fell asleep. She fell asleep too, and didn't dream.

She snapped awake when Cyryl stirred, and opened her eyes to find him gazing at her. Dawn light glowed through the shutters. He smiled faintly, stroking her hair. "Good morning, baby," he said. "Ah, I'm so glad you're back."

Her senses pounded the memories and pain back into place, sleep's forgetfulness fading. Tears welled up, and Cyryl pulled her against him.

"Don't cry, baby."

She shook uncontrollably, bitterness twisting her guts. "You don't understand."

He tensed and heaved a sigh. "This is bullshit, Liria. You need to knock this crap off. That woman…she doesn't deserve for you to feel this way about her."

Liria didn't say anything, her jaw clenching. She struggled out of his arms and escaped to the bathroom, where she let the shower run over her for half an hour, just so she didn't have to look at him.

When she came back out into the bedroom, he wasn't there. With a heartfelt pang she saw that her shopping bags were in a corner, that he'd brought them all the way from New York. She fell to her knees beside them, pulling out the contents. With a trembling hand, she pulled out the felt covered box containing the necklace she'd gotten for Arty and opened it, tears blurring her vision as she stroked the amber and opals with her fingertips. She snapped the box closed again, tossing it back in the bag angrily.

She grabbed a pair of jeans and a shirt she'd bought instead. Something clunked into the bottom of the bag as she tugged them out. Her brow furrowed as she peered in.

It was the phone Arty had given her. Her heart pounding, she grabbed it, turned it on.

She stared at the screen as it powered up. No missed calls, no messages, no texts. Reality seeped in again, and she began to cry.

***

Cyryl didn't go into work that day, but dragged her off to see a counselor: a middle-aged woman with too much makeup, not like Rose at all. She frowned and asked all sorts of questions. She wanted to know what had happened with Arty. She wanted to know how Liria felt, but Liria felt nothing but hollowness and frustration.

"I don't want to talk to you," she said. "This is stupid. I don't want to talk about it."

At the end of the session, Cyryl and the woman had a murmured conversation in the next room, and Cyryl drove her home in silence.

When they arrived she headed for her room again, but he grabbed her arm and stopped her.

"Liria, fucking cut this shit out, all right? Look at me!"

She turned and stared up at him listlessly. His jaw was tight, his eyes flashing. "I risk my ass to go fucking get you in New York, to save you from those assholes, and this is what I get?" His grip tightened on her arm so that it hurt. "You never

308

fucking loved me at all. You've been fucking playing me the whole time. I love you, but you're hung up on some fucking cunt who almost got you killed. Fuck you, Liria." His voice was hoarse, and his fingers dug into her arm. "Fuck you."

Liria's sadness was like a bubble in her chest that kept her limp body afloat. "I do love you, Cyryl," she said. "I always have. Just not the way you want. I'm sorry. I tried."

He cursed and let go of her arm roughly, hiding his face in his hands. Liria's scalp tingled, wondering if he was about to beat the shit out of her. But instead he turned and stomped off to his room.

Liria went into her own room and curled up under the blankets. Cyryl left her alone for the rest of the day, though she could hear him moving around in the house.

That night, after she heard Cyryl go to bed, she put on the necklace she'd bought Arty. It hadn't ever really been Arty's, but it reminded her of her, anyway. She fingered the little droplets of opal and amber, tears running down her face, dripping down between her breasts. After she was sure Cyryl was asleep, she took her new phone, all her identification and her debit card, and snuck out of the condo.

She was sure the debit card wouldn't work. Morton would have figured it out and emptied the account, or at least frozen it somehow. But when she went to the ATM, it spit bills out at her, and her skin prickled in disbelief as she stared at the total on the receipt: still over two and a half million dollars.

She'd leave Cyryl instructions on how to access it after she was gone. He deserved that much, at least. He'd saved her twice, for what it was worth. He wasn't a bad man. She hoped he'd find someone to love him the way he deserved, someday.

She downloaded the app and called an Uber on the phone Arty had gotten her. It was the first time she'd used it. She gazed at the screen as she waited for the car to arrive, wishing it would ring, that Arty would call. She still wished that it had all been a mistake, or a joke, and that Arty was waiting for her at the airport with tickets to Athens.

The car came, and she climbed in, telling the driver to take her to the Greyhound station.

She spent the rest of the night sitting in a hard chair in the waiting room, staring at her knees. A young guy sat next to her at one point and tried to engage her in conversation, but she completely ignored him, and eventually he left, muttering insults.

Finally, as dawn began to brighten the horizon, they called her bus, and she climbed on, her eyes dry, every part of her aching.

She fell asleep with her head against the bus window and dreamt that she was in a strange room with walls and a floor of earth, sitting on a red leather couch. She watched a little group of mice playing with a tiny beach ball, rolling it back and forth to each other on the floor.

She was so tired. Fat tears leaked from her eyes, and fell sparkling onto her knees. The mice paused in their game and looked up at her, their whiskers twitching.

Someone laid a hand on her arm, and she turned to see Justin's sympathetic face. He was sitting next to her, wearing his tiger hat.

He smiled sadly. "She's not here."

Liria frowned. "Who isn't here?"

He gestured around the room, and Liria saw that it was crowded with people. Lee Harvey was in the corner, chatting animatedly with a guy in sequined overalls. Lee saw her looking and winked. Lying on the floor next to him was a very fat woman in a red dress. A small boy in a toga was jumping on her stomach like a trampoline, making her burp loudly every time his feet hit. Two more people were sitting at a table in the middle of the floor, playing a strange game of cards that apparently involved setting your opponent's hand on fire. One of the players was a bony woman with a full head of black hair. There was something familiar about her posture as she hunched over her flaming hand of cards. When she turned to glance in Liria's direction, Liria recognized her mother. Her mom smiled, the skin around her big, brown eyes crinkling slightly.

Liria turned back to Justin, her brow furrowing.

"See?" he said. "She's not here. You don't want to come to this party."

Liria woke up with a start, her heart hammering. Outside the bus's windows, the morning sun poured over the golden desert.

She's not here.

Liria wiped the drool off her cheek, then pressed

311

the heels of her hands to her eyes, fighting back her tears. *It was just a stupid dream. Arty's dead.*

***

It was midafternoon when she finally got to Paso. She didn't have her old phone, didn't have Avery's number, but she knew he wouldn't mind if she just showed up at his house.

If she slammed two grams at once, there's no way she'd survive it. She'd do it in a restaurant or gas station, and leave a note for Cyryl in her pocket with his address. That way he'd know she didn't just run off on him for no reason.

He'd be better off when she was dead. He really loved her, and when she was dead she wouldn't be able to hurt him anymore with her indifference.

But, as she left the bus station, her feet didn't take her to Avery's house. The sun was warm on her face, and people were laughing with each other on the sidewalks. She saw a couple holding hands, and her eyes smarted. The smell of food wafted out of the restaurants. It all soaked into her, as if she'd never noticed any of it before. She'd been blind to the world ever since she could remember, never realizing how beautiful the sun was reflecting on the shop windows and the bumpers of the cars. She'd never seen the happiness in peoples' faces before. She'd never sat to admire the graceful way the leaves twirled in the breeze.

She wandered into the park, lost in her thoughts, then sat on a bench underneath one of the huge oaks, the same one she'd sat in when she'd met

Justin. She gazed at the sunlight slanting across the grass and listened to the woodpeckers. *She's not here. You don't want to come to this party.* Tears welled up in her eyes, and she didn't bother to hide them, though people gave her odd glances and quickened their steps as they walked by.

After a while, she got up and crossed the street.

Justin's house looked even more dingy in the broad daylight. A planter next to the stoop held a jumble of faded fabric pansies, dead weeds growing around them. Liria's pulse pounded in her ears as she opened the squeaky screen and knocked at the door.

A woman with a weathered face answered the door, her dyed-blonde hair pulled back in a wiry ponytail. She squinted suspiciously at Liria, her crows' feet deepening. "Yes?"

Liria shuffled her feet. "Hey, uh…is Justin here?"

The woman frowned. "He doesn't live here anymore. He's back with his mom."

Liria's heart sank. "Oh. Where's that?"

"I don't know where they are. Who the hell knows? I think they were taking off to Idaho, last I heard." She looked Liria up and down. "Who are you?"

She squeezed her fingers in her fist. "Just a friend."

Justin's grandmother considered her a moment. "Well, I don't know what to tell you. If I hear from them, I'll tell him you stopped by. What's your name?"

"Liria."

"Okay, Liria, I'll tell him if I hear from him."

Liria bit her lip and nodded. She heard the door shut behind her as she walked back to the park. *It was just a dream.* Darkness closed over her again, banishing what hope she'd had left.

She sat on a bench and called an Uber. When it came, she climbed in the back and gave the guy directions to Avery's house.

Just as the guy pulled out into traffic, she felt her phone buzz in her back pocket. She stiffened, adrenaline spiking through her. She pulled it out.

Her heart leapt, beating rapidly. It was a number with a New York area code. Pain clutched her chest, making it hard for her to breathe. It was probably just a wrong number, or a friend of the person who'd had the number before. There was no point in answering it. *Maybe it's even Morton. Maybe he got this number somehow, and he's calling to threaten me because I told Cyryl's brother the whole story.*

Her hand trembled.

She punched the answer button. "Hello?"

There was a pause, as if someone were taking a breath. "Liria?"

Liria's breath stopped. It couldn't be. "Ar-Arty?"

Arty laughed her incredible laugh. "It's me, back from the dead."

Liria tried to breathe. "You're...oh my God, no fucking way!" Something that was half a sob and half a laugh rose up in her. "Oh my God, Arty, is it really fucking you?" Tears ran fast out of her eyes. She saw the driver glancing at her in the rearview, but barely noticed.

"Yes, I swear, it's really me. It's a long story, baby."

"Oh my God, Arty."

Arty laughed again. "I'm in Vegas," she said. "Can you meet me here?"

Liria dried her eyes and spoke to the driver, tapping her feet against the floor in excitement. "Change of plans," she said. "Take me to the Santa Barbara airport."

The driver gave her a weird look over his shoulder. "That's a long way," she said.

Liria laughed. "I can afford it."

***

It was the longest trip of Liria's life, but finally the plane landed. She couldn't keep herself from running up the walkway, pushing past the other passengers.

Liria noticed Arty right away, waiting outside the gate, even though her hair was dyed black and she was wearing huge, mirrored sunglasses. The tall woman stood with a little smile on her face, ignoring the men who craned their necks to check out her ass in her tight jeans.

Liria ran into her arms, and Arty hugged her tight. By her feet, Shirley the cat meowed in a carrier.

"Oh my God, Arty, it's really you."

"It's okay," Arty said softly, pushing back her sunglasses and pressing her lips to the top of her head. "It's okay."

Liria took a few deep breaths, then looked up at

her, into those blue-green eyes she thought she'd never see again. Arty smiled, brushing the hair from Liria's forehead.

"What the fuck?" Liria demanded. "What the fuck happened?"

Arty glanced around shiftily. "Let's go to our gate. I'll explain on the way."

"Our gate?"

"I've got your ticket here. We're going to Barbados for a while, then we'll decide where next."

Arty took her hand and they headed through the hurrying crowds. "I'm sorry that I had to put you through that, Liria," she murmured.

"Yeah, you should be fucking sorry. That was a fucking load of—"

"I know," Arty said, cutting her off. "But it had to be done. If I wanted out of that shit, I had to find some way of convincing Peter Czetski I was truly out of it, because I'm in too deep. He never trusted me to begin with."

Liria's stomach went hollow as this sank in. "So…you were just using me," she whispered hoarsely. "You were just using me to convince him. You wanted me to believe you were dead so that I'd tell him that." She stopped, staring Arty down with her fists clenched as the other travelers veered around them, glaring in annoyance. Arty stopped too, Shirley yowled, her carrier dangling from Arty's hand.

"Calm down, baby. This isn't the time or place to get all pissed off."

"Fuck that, Arty—"

"Shhh, not here." She grabbed Liria's arm gently. "I knew you'd be pissed off, but what did you expect me to do?"

"You could have told me!" Liria hissed. "I could have still lied to him. You didn't have to keep me in the dark."

Arty shot her a look, rubbing her nose. "You wear your heart on your sleeve, Liria. He would have seen straight through you."

Liria's guts writhed, but she held her burning tongue. Arty grasped her hand again. "Come on."

They got to the gate and sat down to wait; their flight left in forty-five minutes. They had no luggage at all besides the cat, and Liria wondered what they were going to do when they got there, but pushed the thought out of her mind. They had money.

She took a deep breath, and some of her anger evaporated. *Arty's alive, and we have millions of dollars.* She let that sink into her like soothing balm, taking the place of the grief that had so recently crushed her.

She turned back to Arty, who was sending her little darting glances, and crossed her arms. "So? You had this whole thing set up from the beginning? The whole thing with your dad and Thomas was just a ruse to convince me you were dead?"

Arty winced. "No. I really was trying to bring that fucker down. It just didn't turn out the way I wanted, and I had to think on my feet. After we talked to Thomas, I got to thinking. Things were getting too complicated, and I really just wanted to get out of this bullshit. So I came up with the plan to work with Thomas and Dad to pull the wool over Czetski's eyes. Both my dad and Thomas want to bring Czetski down, and I had some leverage with my dad because I had Thomas on my side, so I got him to agree. That was the only part I didn't tell you about, Liria. I wasn't lying to you the whole time."

Liria gazed at her, chewing on her lip. "But both you and your dad did have your doubts about me. Because of my last name."

Arty gazed at her seriously, and nodded. "When I first found out who you really were, right after your friend was killed and I did some snooping, I was sure that you were working for Peter. I thought you'd been sent to spy on us or bring us down. He's never liked us, never trusted us. So I kept you there, trying to figure out what your game was. But when I got to know you, it didn't fit. You were too sweet and honest, and didn't seem to know anything about any of that shit, and no one's that good an actor."

Liria pressed her lips together. "So you didn't care about me at all! It was just some game you were playing. You were holding me hostage because you thought I was some gang spy."

Arty grabbed her hand. "Shh, baby, no. I always liked you. You can't blame me for having my doubts and for being cautious, but I got over it." She leaned over and kissed her. Liria was still angry, but the feeling of her soft, warm lips against hers made her breath come fast and her heart race. "I'm sorry, Liria," Arty murmured. "Please forgive me."

Liria sighed and reluctantly turned her face away. "Your dad didn't believe you that I didn't know anything. When he talked to me, he asked me who I worked for."

Arty nodded. "Of course he didn't believe me. That fuckface thinks I'm still a child, that I don't have my own two eyes and a brain. But how you acted convinced him. It's another reason I kept you in the dark, because things would have gotten complicated if you'd acted sketchy and he didn't believe you." She ran her fingers over her black hair and sighed. "Scared the shit out of me that he'd still be a dick about it. But I knew you'd keep it together and convince him, and all's well that ends well." Arty smiled teasingly at her. "My dad really likes you, for what it's worth."

Liria felt a pang of nausea. "I'm touched, I really am."

Arty grimaced and leaned over to kiss her neck. "Come on, baby, don't be mad. I know I've been a bitch, but I just did what I had to do to get us out of there. I just wanted to keep us safe."

Liria sighed, pressing the heels of her hands into her eyes. She put her head Arty's shoulder. "You get to keep the money and everything?"

"*We* do. Yeah. It's not much of a price to pay to be rid of me, I guess. Besides, Dad owes me for all I've done for him."

Liria looked over at her, a reluctant smile creeping up to her lips.

Arty broke into a grin. "You are so beautiful, Liria."

Their lips met, warmth coursing through Liria, tears seeping out of her eyes. She wrapped her arms around Arty's neck, scooting closer. Finally, she pulled her lips away, breathless, and pressed her forehead into Arty's shoulder. "You're a bitch sometimes, but I'm so glad you're not dead."

Arty laughed softly. "My dad told me how you acted when he told you he'd killed me." She made her voice raspy, imitating him. "'Stick with that girl, Fireball, She's better than you deserve. Or send her back to me, I'll take her.'"

Liria wrinkled her nose. "No thanks."

Arty's smile faded, and she brushed her lips with hers softly. "I love you, Liria."

"I love you too, Arty."

She may not be perfect, but I love her and she loves me.

Acknowledgments

I'd like to thank Laura Kemmerer, my lovely editor, who has been so wonderful and helpful in getting this book and *Love or Money* into shape. I don't agree with you that "alright" isn't a word, but you're still technically correct, and I love working with you.

I'd also like to thank Limitless Publishing, for taking an even bigger risk than before on these characters, whose viewpoints are not particularly sexy, trendy or well-understood, but valuable, I think, all the same.

Thank you to all the usual suspects—my beta readers Faith, Aleena, Naomi…I think my mom actually read this one…and anyone else I'm forgetting. I'd also like to thank the people in my critique groups, especially the ones who told me Liria was unlikable and there was no way anyone would read a book about her. It brought home the fact that I'm a sort of version of Liria, except years later, and that I needed to work harder to bring people into her world and show them her potential, just like I had to work hard to get people to see mine.

Also thank you to Mark and Ben, who helped me muddle through learning how to write sex scenes. (Mark, friend, I hope you will read this somehow. I miss you, and I'm sorry.)

I'd like to express my thanks to all those who have stuck by me while I learned a new hustle, a new way of life. I'd like to thank the judge who looked me in the face and told me I was a good person who had lost her way, and not the pile of refuse I saw myself to be. I'd like to thank Eric, who took me in knowing—at least intellectually—where I'd been in life, and taught me it was possible for me to pass as a middle-class person. I'm sorry you changed your mind about that, but thank you for the ten years you gave me.

And thank you to Phoenix for reminding me who I actually am, but showing me that it's okay to be that person. Thank you for walking up to me in the park that day, with your cute smile and your white tiger hat, and telling me about your workout routine and how to make muffin pancakes. Things would have turned out a lot differently if it weren't for you.

Thank you to all of you who read this book, and who believe in Liria and care what happens to her. All those girls on the streets have their stories. Maybe if we care about them, they'll live to tell them too.

About the Author

Elizabeth Roderick grew up as a barefoot ruffian on a fruit orchard near Yakima, in the eastern part of Washington State. After weathering the grunge revolution and devolution in Olympia, Washington, Portland, Oregon and Seattle, she recently moved to the (very, very) small town of Shandon, California: a small cluster of houses amidst the vineyards of the Central Coast.

She earned a bachelor's degree in Spanish from The Evergreen State College in Olympia, Washington, and worked for many years as a paralegal and translator. She went on to study chemistry, physics, and higher mathematics, with the goal of becoming a research chemist, but was eventually forced to concede that graduate school would require too much time away from her husband and daughter, and that–despite her good-enough grades –she was perhaps the wrong kind of nerd for such pursuits, being more the type that likes to dress in cloaks and hauberks rather than lab coats and goggles.

She is a musician and songwriter, and has played in many bands. She's rocked pretty much every instrument, including some she doesn't even know the real names for, but mostly guitar, bass and keyboards. She has two albums of her own, which you can listen to at pimentointhehole.com. She writes fiction novels for young adults and adults, as well as short stories, and keeps an active blog at pimentointhehole.com/blog

Facebook:
https://www.facebook.com/elizabethroderickauthor

Twitter:
https://twitter.com/LidsRodney

Website:
http://talesfrompurgatory.com/

www.ingramcontent.com/pod-product-compliance
Lightning Source LLC
Chambersburg PA
CBHW031542240626
47153CB00002B/353